THE DEATH OF AN OWL

Andrew Landford is driving home one night along a dark country lane, when a barn owl flies into his windscreen. It is an accident, nothing more. However, Andrew is in line to be the next prime minister — and he has recently been appointed to a parliamentary committee concerned with the Wildlife and Countryside Act. Barn owls are a protected species, and it is a crime to kill one. With Andrew in the car is his old Oxford friend and political adviser, Charles Fryerne, who has spent many years quietly building up a successful career and is masterminding Andrew's rise to power. The death of the owl threatens to destroy everything both men have worked for. Should they come clean, or hide the story and hope it goes away?

PAUL TORDAY
with PIERS TORDAY

◆

THE DEATH
OF AN OWL

Complete and Unabridged

CHARNWOOD
Leicester

First published in Great Britain in 2016 by
Weidenfeld & Nicolson
an imprint of the Orion Publishing Group Ltd
London

First Charnwood Edition
published 2017
by arrangement with
The Orion Publishing Group Ltd
An Hachette UK Company
London

A catalogue record for this book is available
from the British Library.

ISBN 978–1–4448–3179–5

Published by
F. A. Thorpe (Publishing)
Anstey, Leicestershire

Set by Words & Graphics Ltd.
Anstey, Leicestershire
Printed and bound in Great Britain by
T. J. International Ltd., Padstow, Cornwall

This book is printed on acid-free paper

One Author's Note

I grew up thinking my father ran an engineering business. Naturally, I rebelled by harbouring dreams of becoming an actor or writer. This modified into becoming a producer, first in theatre then in television. I made other people's stories. But after about a decade, I'd had enough. I wanted something else. Which was when Dad dropped the bombshell . . . He had been writing a book all along. Not just any book either, but the publishing and film sensation that was *Salmon Fishing in the Yemen*.

I was immensely proud, and this gave me the confidence to undertake a creative writing course. It took a while, but four years later, I had published a book too — *The Last Wild* — the first in a trilogy about a boy trying to keep the last animals in the world alive.

Sadly, during that time, Dad had more dramatic but less cheering news — a diagnosis of stage-three kidney cancer. Miraculous drugs gave him another six years, and eight more wonderful books.

In the last year of his life — not that he knew that — he began writing his ninth book, called *The Death of an Owl*. It was, he told me, about a man who couldn't help but tell the truth, and how that played out when he gets involved in a scandal involving a politician who runs over an owl by mistake . . .

He really wanted to finish the novel. I know it was a lifeline for him when things got bad. But by the final weeks, it became clear he was not going to. Even so, he was still making notes until a few days before he died. We never talked much about what would happen to the book. There were more important things to discuss.

A few months after Dad's death, I began the process of going through his papers. I found the manuscript. Everyone — family, his agent, his editor — of course wanted to know what it was like. I knew he had been anxious that the painkilling drugs had addled his mind and that this would be evident in the story. I was relieved and delighted to find the opposite — a book that combined the political wit and perception of *Salmon Fishing* with the unsettling gothic tone he had made his own in *Girl on the Landing*.

I was gripped.

But it wasn't finished. It stopped mid-sentence at a key point.

I dearly wanted to find out what was going to happen next. But Dad was no longer around to tell me. There was only one thing for it. I was going to have to make it up myself . . .

Piers Torday
London, 2016

I

OXFORD AND AFTER

1

Autumn, 1981

As we bent our heads in prayer I glanced down and saw that beads of dew, left by the wet grass at the side of the churchyard path, where I had strayed for a moment to look at an old tombstone, glistened on my polished black shoes. The shoes were new; as was the dark grey suit I now wore, purchased in anticipation of my going up to Oxford in a few months' time. The decision to buy the suit had been brought forward a little due to the importance of the occasion: the memorial service for my Uncle Roland.

Roland Fryerne was my father's older brother. From this day on, my father would become head of our rather eccentric and dispersed family. If he chose to, he would be entitled to call himself 'Charles Fryerne of Fryerne Court': a feudal title dating back to the fifteenth century to which the family — if nobody else — attached great importance. Roland, genealogist and historian, had been cremated earlier in the day. The urn containing his ashes, no doubt still warm, nestled on a table garlanded with lilies, whose heavy scent filled the church. I felt no particular grief at my uncle's death. I had hardly known him, as we had lived abroad for many years. My uncle had visited us once in New York, when I was all

3

too young to remember, and half a dozen times in Lausanne, where we had lived for most of my life so far. He had not been at ease with children; or perhaps I had not been at ease with uncles.

Now my father's employers had transferred him to a position in Head Office in west London. 'Putting me out to grass,' my father told my mother. At the time I had no idea what the phrase meant, but I was captivated by the idea of my father standing in a paddock and kneeling down now and then to munch the fresh pasture. I could see his grey head and his broad pinstriped back directly in front of me now. My elderly mother stood beside him, wearing a formal high-necked dress of midnight blue. If you met my parents for the first time you would judge them as elegant if somewhat chilly, and I am not sure that further acquaintance would have modified this impression. They were very private. They had none of the bonhomie that some expatriates displayed on returning home to England — a form of insecurity as the newcomers struggled to rediscover their place in the social order, unconscious of the fact that 'society' was changing so fast they might as well have just stepped out of a time machine.

My father always took a perverse pride in describing his line as late developers, of which I was a prime example, not having been born until both my parents were well into their forties. They had been slow to marry, late to parenthood and now it seemed doubtful whether they would make anything of their retirement. But they were Fryernes and therefore had long ago chosen obscurity over insecurity as their distinguishing feature.

In Lausanne we had lived quietly, but all my parents' friends were comfortably off and so, I assumed, were we. Their social circle consisted of bankers, diplomats, or senior employees of organisations such as the United Nations and the Red Cross. Not merely a late child but an only one, the much older children of these professionals were my few friends; their mothers were my mother's friends. Cocktail parties and dinners were infrequent and discreet. Dances were occasionally arranged for the younger generation — evenings of extreme dullness and great propriety.

Amongst the three of us, though, we had fun whenever my father had some time off. Long walks in the hills above Evian in the early summer, amongst the alpine flowers and the remainder of that year's snow; sailing on Lake Geneva where we kept a small boat in one of the marinas; weeks spent in a rented villa in Menton, on the Côte d'Azur; and of course, skiing once the snow came.

I was already missing the shores of Lake Geneva. What I had seen of England so far did not encourage me to think life in west London would be much of a substitute for the life I had left behind. The prospect of going to university and mingling with a host of people who had all been at school together did not appeal either. I could speak three languages already, and the International Lycée I had attended had given me as good an education as you could wish for, but nobody I knew was going to Oxford. Those of my friends and contemporaries who had felt the need for further education had obtained places at Harvard, Princeton, the Sorbonne, Padua, Tübingen — even Cambridge. Already they resembled embryos of the successful Eurocrats or bankers they would no doubt one day become. If I was an embryo of anything, I didn't have any idea what it might be. I didn't really know what I believed in and I faced the future with a certain sense of dread.

The memorial service drew to a close. We shuffled out of our pews and processed behind the vicar out into the fresh air. I was standing beside my mother and, unaccountably, took her hand. 'Don't cling,' she said, but not unkindly. I let go. The congregation had broken up into small groups who were chatting and enjoying the autumn sunshine after the chilly gloom of the church interior. I turned and studied the view around me. A suburban road separated two very different worlds. Behind me was the ancient church of St Mary's-Without, a building of Norman origin, set in its own island of green and bounded by a copse of trees. A different landscape lay on the opposite side. I had seen the sign on our arrival: the road was called Fryerne Way. Behind me I heard my father say, 'And that is Fryerne Court Estate.'

I turned and recognised Bradford Fryerne, a distant American cousin who appeared able to drop everything and cross the Atlantic at a moment's notice in order to attend family gatherings of this kind. He had been a near neighbour in New York.

'Wow,' he said.

I gazed at the rows of detached houses, each with its own pocket-handkerchief-size front garden, off-road parking and garage. The few cars that were parked there at this time of day all seemed new or nearly new: Rovers, Jaguars and the occasional sports car. I could see nothing that warranted a 'wow'.

'No trace of the old family home, then?' asked Bradford.

'No,' said my father with relish. 'Not a brick. Not a chimney pot. There was no nonsense about listed buildings in those days. They got a wrecking ball in and flattened the lot.'

For a while longer we studied the housing estate. I had always imagined that the original Fryerne Court might at least have survived in the curve of an ivy-covered archway, or perhaps the remains of a kitchen garden or hothouse; a weed-shrouded knot garden. I had no excuse for such fantasies; my father had always assured me that nothing remained of the old house. It seemed as if Bradford had cherished a similar dream, for he stared at the row of houses as if at any moment he expected a veil to be pulled aside and the ghost of Fryerne Court to emerge like Camelot from the shining mist.

Once the memorial service was over the plan was for us all to make our way to the Fryerne Arms a mile or so away. We had passed this pub, draped in banners advertising 'All You Can Eat Carvery!', on our way to the church. It had been selected for the sentimental associations of its name rather than for any practical consideration. The fake-Tudor, half-timbered exterior and the fibreglass reproduction of our family crest attached to a pole in front of the pub were not inviting. The noise of car doors slamming stirred my father from his thoughts: reminiscences of Uncle Roland for his after-lunch speech; worries about his new job, or his new house.

'Lunch,' he said with a shudder. We moved off to join my mother.

★ ★ ★

My Uncle Roland's work as an historian had produced various short essays, published in architectural journals, of interest mainly to specialists in the design of church roofs. Later in life he took it upon himself to write *A History of the Fryernes of Fryerne Court*, which began with the events of Bosworth Field in 1485. The Charles Fryerne of the day had distinguished himself during the course of the battle — it was not clear how — and had earned the gratitude of Henry Tudor. In an untypical and unhistorical way, Roland had allowed himself to speculate as to what those services might have been. Rescuing the colours? Diverting an axeman from attacking the future king? No firm conclusion was reached, but it was a fact that the services had led to a grant of land on the edge of the South Downs. A few decades later the accumulated rents were sufficient to finance the building of a house, which became known as Fryerne Court. At first it was a simple, graceful structure with leaded roofs and mullioned windows and high chimney stacks. As the original Tudor building was added to by successive generations of Fryernes, it lost its purity of conception and form, and its domestic scale, and became a large and uncomfortable-looking house with a surfeit of tack rooms, stable yards and grooms' cottages. It also became too expensive to run on the income from farm rents, which had supported it quite comfortably for the first two hundred years of its existence.

Twenty-five years before he embarked on the project, someone had tipped off Uncle Roland that an oil painting of the original Tudor house was coming up for auction at Christie's. He bought it. A colour plate of this picture was reproduced on the dust jacket of his book. He also possessed a black and white photograph taken in 1920 of the much-enlarged building that was pulled down soon afterwards. This was reproduced as the frontispiece. My father believed that it was the oil painting that had originally inspired Roland to undertake his final, and greatest, project. The resulting self-published tome was the crowning achievement of my uncle's life.

The history of my ancestors, as related by Uncle Roland, was one of many small deeds and no great ones. The narrative sections of the work were brief, but undoubtedly dull out of all proportion to their length. The book was garnished with numerous genealogical tables, with headings such as 'The Fryernes of New South Wales'. Bibliographies, indices and extensive footnotes filled the rest of its pages.

Indeed the Fryernes had achieved a kind of obscurity so comprehensive as to be rather unusual in its way: not a single politician nor bishop nor general nor nabob graced our ranks. For the most part we lived out our lives quietly, most of us within our means, troubling nobody. The last Fryerne to live in the house itself was another Roland, my uncle's grandfather. This Roland was less dull and more ambitious than his forebears and it struck him that the family had played too modest a role in the country's affairs. He wanted a seat in Parliament and a larger house. The seat eluded him, but he went ahead with his designs to build a residence suitable for a county magnate and a man of standing. In order to finance the ambitious extensions to the original building he decided to invest in South American railway stocks, which promised spectacular results. The results were indeed spectacular, but not in the way investors had hoped. That earlier Roland clung on as long as he could in the financial wreckage that followed the South American Railway Crash, which also brought down the great banking house of Overend & Gurney and a host of other speculators, but a few years later, Fryerne Court had to be sold. My ancestor went off to die in a boarding house in Hove, ending his life racked with guilt for losing the house on his watch.

Fryerne Court was not long enjoyed by the new owners. It did duty during the First World War as a temporary nursing home and by the time it was handed back by the Army the house was in a bit of a state. There was talk about trying to convert it for use as a school, but in the end the least risky solution was simply to pull it down. After all, the new owners had hardly lived there. They had performed no heroics at Bosworth Field. The site had development potential, but it was not until the 1950s that some developers obtained planning permission for residential housing. Then the ruins, parks, and stands of trees, so carefully landscaped over the last four hundred years, were felled, flattened, ploughed up and built over to bring into existence the desirable executive housing that was the Fryerne Court Residential Estate.

I thought about this as I sat at a narrow and overcrowded trestle table in the dining room of the Fryerne Arms, squeezed in between my mother on my left and a very large lady who said she was my cousin on my right. It was difficult to move my elbows. My father had foregone the option of the carvery and had chosen the menu for all of us. The starter was a prawn cocktail, which required only a spoon and wasn't that tricky to eat. The second course was accompanied by bowls of steamed vegetables and mounds of mashed potato, placed at random around the table. On our plates were rubbery-looking chicken breasts. I managed to get the point of my knife into mine, and a thin stream of hot, garlicky butter shot across the table and splashed on to the plate of a girl sitting opposite me. I had noticed her in church: one of the few people close to my own age, although she was probably four or five years older than me.

'Hey!'

'Sorry. I didn't expect it to do that,' I said.

'That's the trouble with chicken Kiev. Don't worry, it didn't quite make my dress.' She dabbed some of the butter from the table with her napkin.

'Is that what this is? Chicken Kiev?'

'That's what it says on the menu. Now, which one are you?'

'I'm Charles Fryerne. Uncle Roland was my father's older brother.' I gestured to where my father sat by waving rather inelegantly with my fork.

'So now your father is the Fryerne of Fryerne Court?'

I had been listening to her voice. It was rather deep and melodious and had a familiar twang.

'He is now, I suppose. You're from New York, aren't you?'

'That's smart of you. Yes, I am.'

'We lived in New York when I was little. A block away from Brad Fryerne on the Upper East Side.'

'Oh, but Brad's my uncle! I'm Caroline Woodchester.'

I looked along the table at Brad. I could see no likeness. He was tall, pear-shaped, with thinning brown hair and a big moon-like face that had once been square-jawed but whose outlines were now beginning to blur. Caroline was about my height and solidly built, with dark hair and a lively, attractive face: not by any means beautiful, but a face you looked at and didn't forget. She watched me making comparisons and added:

'His niece by marriage, of course.'

As Brad had worked his way through several

wives, this connection was difficult to challenge, but I found myself wondering whether she wasn't really his mistress. My expression must have been easy to read, because a look of annoyance crossed her face.

'So what do you think of all this nonsense?' she said, somewhat abruptly.

'Nonsense?'

'The gathering of the clans. Talking about a house that was pulled down sixty years ago. Inheriting a title that doesn't entitle you to anything. Except maybe being teased?'

I didn't like the idea that anyone should mock my father. Still less did I believe that anyone would dare. I bent my head over my plate and struggled for a moment with my chicken Kiev. Brad's niece was nettled by my silence.

'I certainly won't be tricked into coming to one of these shows again. I'm only over here to see about getting on a course for a year or two and to escape from home for a while.'

'Your uncle seems to like coming to family gatherings,' I replied.

'Too much money and not enough to do.'

Looking up the table I saw my father hunting through his pockets, probably trying to find the notes for his speech. I turned back to Caroline.

'Well, to each his own, I suppose,' I said rather grandly, hoping to bring our prickly conversation to an end.

After a few moment's silence she said, 'Boy, was that a pompous remark.'

'I didn't mean to be pompous,' I apologised. Nor had I. I didn't want to quarrel with anyone, least of all this girl who would probably have been good fun if I had met her on a less trying occasion.

A look came into her eyes, an expression of pure mischief. She leaned forward a little so that only I could hear her words.

'Let's find a room upstairs before the speeches begin. There will be speeches, won't there? There always are when you English get together.'

'A room? What do we need a room for?'

I was mystified, but only for a moment. She mouthed, rather than spoke, the next words, but her meaning was unmistakable.

'Sex, of course.'

'What?'

I could feel the blood rising in my cheeks and my mouth fell open. I saw that Caroline was trying not to laugh, delighted with the effect her words had produced.

'It might be fun,' she added. 'God knows anything would be better than sitting here a moment longer.'

She rose from her chair and, not knowing what else to do, I began to struggle upright as well. This caught the attention of my mother who, until then, had been deep in conversation with her neighbour on her left.

'Where are you going?' she asked me, tugging at my sleeve.

'We thought we'd go and get some fresh air, Mrs Fryerne, and maybe Charles could keep me company while I smoke a cigarette. I'm dying for one but I don't want to light up while people are still eating.'

'Well, Charles can't go,' said my mother. 'It would be most inconsiderate of him to leave just as his father is about to make a speech. His father is head of the family now, you know.' These last few words were spoken with emphasis, as if she expected to exert her influence over Caroline as well as me.

'Thanks, Mrs F,' replied Caroline in a breezy manner. 'All the same, I think I'll sit this one out.' She turned and headed for the door, threading her way between the tables.

At the precise moment she left, someone tinged a glass with a knife and my father stood up. Clutching a sheaf of notes, he studied them intently for a few long moments until his audience began to fidget and worry that he had the wrong piece of paper in his hands: a laundry list, for example. Then he began, his speech slow and measured.

'I cannot say how much comfort it gives me to see how many of you have made the effort to come here on this day. Some of you have travelled great distances to be here: from New York, from Aberdeen, from the Solomon Islands . . . '

'What a very ill-mannered young lady,' my mother hissed in my ear. I did not react.

'From Santiago in Chile, from Saint Helier in Jersey, from Loughborough in the Midlands . . . ' said my father, continuing his eclectic selection from the points of origin of the guests.

But I was further away than the Solomon Islands. In my imagination I was outside the dining room. I was walking up the narrow flight of stairs to the first floor of the pub, a few moments behind Caroline so that we would not be seen ascending the steps together. Then we arrived on a landing. I took hold of her hand. In my imagination it was cool and firm and not trembling as mine was. Together we tried the door-handles of several rooms until we found one that was unlocked. We peered cautiously in. There was nobody inside. The single bed was neatly made and had an eiderdown on top. Caroline pulled off the eiderdown and sat down, pulling me beside her on to the edge of the bed.

'Now then, Charles, here's what we do.'

At the head of the table, my father was just beginning to get into his stride.

2

A few weeks before I went up to university, my father handed me the Chapman & Hall edition of *Brideshead Revisited* by Evelyn Waugh.

'It's all very well you choosing to study Politics and Philosophy or whatever it is, but don't neglect your inner life,' he warned me, without apparent irony. 'Now, this is mostly sentimental rubbish, but there are some passages about being an undergraduate in the twenties that might amuse you.'

His words, and the book, were forgotten in the flurry of activity required to send a young man away from home for about eight weeks. My mother supervised the packing of my trunk.

'You'll need a cricket bat, of course, and a tennis racquet.'

'But, Mummy, we didn't play cricket in Switzerland. I really would have no idea what to do.'

After much argument the bat came out and the racquet stayed in. Similar discussions arose over clothing. My mother's view was that I needed armfuls of tweed. I managed to sneak in a pair of jeans as well.

Then there were the books. Most of the volumes of history or philosophical tracts on my reading list could be purchased second-hand at Blackwell's, but like my father, my mother insisted on a few novels being packed, so that 'people can see you are not entirely illiterate'. I didn't rediscover and, finally, read the Evelyn Waugh until well into my second term.

I think they had both hoped that, like my father, I would read English, and perhaps develop a sense of belonging in our new home through an understanding of its literature. To be more precise, I think they hoped I would develop an affection for a particular type of novel that affectionately portrayed a certain class at a certain time. They so longed for me to discover the Britain they had once understood, but which, as far as I could tell, no longer existed in any meaningful way.

I had grown up in the long shadow of the UN, and mixed with the children of diplomats, lobbyists and politicians at international schools. Half awake as I was then, even I could see that the world was changing. Margaret Thatcher and now Ronald Reagan, both in power. Not only the Cold War but the whole post-war consensus, on everything from workers' rights to free trade, was beginning to disintegrate before our eyes. As the great powers began to shift and realign, a large part of me was curious to understand why. Studying novels and poems had only led my father to a dead-end desk job for a pharmaceutical company, and I felt no desire to follow in his footsteps. In the UK and America, a chorus of voices proclaimed a brand-new world. My sheltered upbringing with my parents had put me on the fringes of all this excitement. Now, on the cusp of adulthood, I had a craving to be — for the first time in decades — a Fryerne on the inside looking out, rather than the other way round.

I find it hard, however, to recall the Oxford I actually experienced. The university in the early 1980s felt very far from the world of Brideshead. Also my recollections are overlaid by images from TV programmes and films. A conflation of these produces a town forever bathed in afternoon sunlight gleaming on the domes of the Sheldonian and the Radcliffe Camera, and on the spires of St. Mary the Virgin and Tom Tower. In my memory the mediaeval city still dominates amongst the office blocks and some of the newer and more experimental college buildings. The reality in my own day was that one didn't look at the skyline too often because one's gaze was lowered to avoid the lash of incessant rain. You needed to keep your eyes focused and your wits sharp in order to avoid being mown down by marching columns of tourists following their guides, poking out the eyes of the unwary with the spokes of their umbrellas.

What it is like today, I don't know. Maldwyn Christie sometimes goes back to alumni dinners and will doubtless end his days as Master of some grand institution there.

I never go back.

My college was one of the smaller ones. It was — in those days — relatively undeveloped, with only one new dormitory block at the end of a row of converted houses where most of the first year had rooms. There were two quadrangles where we sometimes sat and picnicked on mossy, slightly damp green lawns. The dining hall was an imposing Victorian addition, no doubt a trade-off for the college when Fellows of the day accepted some particularly unsuitable undergraduate on to the books in exchange for a new building. The chapel was a jewel. Taken as a whole, it was a pretty, tranquil place in which to spend one's time.

Slowly I began to make a few acquaintances: firstly, other undergraduates with rooms on the same staircase as mine, then the people I shared tutorials with. It was all much easier and friendlier than I had expected.

However, perhaps due to the influence of my parents, or the dog-eared volumes they had stuffed in my trunk, at first I was nonplussed, disappointed even, at the characters I met. In my head everyone was going to be dazzlingly clever, full of political zeal in one direction or another, or at least possessed with some form of wit. In reality, many of the early, stumbling encounters I had in common rooms or local pubs made my parents' desultory cocktail parties seem like something out of *The Great Gatsby*.

Of course, we all subjected each other to long, earnest monologues on the unions, the Falklands, Ireland — or whatever the topic of the day was. There was never any shortage of opinion in the college bar. But what I thirsted for was different. An outsider to the country — and somewhat dazed — I didn't at first naturally align myself with either left or right. In fact, many of the noisily voiced orthodoxies I encountered seemed to me as delusional as the system they claimed to be reforming. In retrospect, I see that I was searching for someone who could explain the world to me, not as they wished it to be, nor as it lay sighted through one particular telescope, but as it actually stood, regardless of how uncomfortable that viewing might be.

Gradually I became aware of another class of human being in the college, who took great care to absent themselves from all this wrangling and political debate. These were members of a dining club called Merlin's. Sometimes one saw them gathering in the quad to take cocktails in the spring evening sunshine before one of their dinners, resplendent in black tie and their distinctive primrose waistcoat and forget-me-not cummerbund. The club was supposed to have been going for over two hundred years. For most of these it had existed in suspension only, banned by the authorities for various manifestations of over-exuberance. But five years ago, like a dragon's egg, it had unexpectedly hatched out again and so far had not been shut down. Perhaps these periods of suspended animation, followed by violent activity, had inspired the choice of name, I thought — the enchanted wizard roused from his sleep and riding out to reclaim England for King Arthur. I learned later that Merlin had in fact been the name of the club's first wine steward, who tore up various IOUs for the privilege of lending his name (and his credit) to the club. Membership was exclusive and considered to be the height of privilege in the college.

One day towards the end of the spring term, a

printed notice arrived in my pigeonhole in the porter's lodge. It informed me that my name had come up as a suitable candidate for election to Merlin's, and would I have any objection? Any objection? A few minutes earlier membership of Merlin's seemed as remote a possibility as being asked to become a Knight of the Garter. Now I was being asked to join. I couldn't understand it, but I didn't feel able to sidle up to one of the members and ask why my name had been put forward. It would be too embarrassing; especially if it hadn't been. The whole thing was probably an elaborate practical joke, the point of which I hadn't yet grasped. I returned the form, signing where asked, and addressing it to The Secretary.

Almost by return I received another printed letter, saying that I had been duly elected, and inviting me to send quite a large cheque to the Secretary for my subscription (breakages and fines not included), for the summer term. This was either a genuine bill, or a complicated fraud. In either case I couldn't afford it.

I rang up my father.

'My dear boy,' he said. 'Of course you must join. It's not the Bullingdon, you know, more Middle England than the House of Lords. But you will probably meet some good chaps.'

'Good chaps' was one of the greatest expressions of approval my father was capable of. His support was unexpected but welcome.

'But I can't afford it.'

'I'll stand you the cost for next term and then we'll see how it goes.'

Becoming a member of Merlin's was expensive. The dinners were not very cheap, the wine bills eye-watering, and the principle of collective responsibility was applied to any fines that followed a Merlin event. These might be simply a question of covering the cost of broken crockery, or a smashed window or two. However, on one legendary occasion they included rebuilding an entire Indian restaurant, which the club had hired for dinner. The guests had rendered themselves entirely insensible with strong drink, and then began shooting poppadoms as if they were clay pigeons — inside.

My election to Merlin's took place just before the Easter holidays. When I went home I discovered my father, too, had been a member, although the Second World War had rather interrupted the club's activities and he had only managed to attend one dinner. His enthusiasm for my membership was explained: it was a way of obtaining some vicarious pleasure from all the dinners I would enjoy and that he had missed. It also resolved the mystery of why I had been invited to join: the sons of previous members were automatically put forward for membership and, unless they were especially obnoxious, all were elected. My father studied the membership list that had been sent to me, with little grunts of recognition.

'Ackroyd-Smith. His father was there in my day. Not a man to be trusted. I believe they locked him up for embezzlement in the end. Illingworth Maxwell. Good family. Very well-off. Stockbrokers often are. Their clients less so.'

I also noticed that from the day of my election to Merlin's my father began to address me as an adult, no longer a child.

★ ★ ★

The first Merlin's dinner I attended was held on a sunny evening only a few days after the beginning of the summer term. It was a tradition of the club that new members should be led in by an existing member, so that they could be introduced and generally have the ice broken for them. I was in my room getting ready and had just finished tying my bow tie when there was a knock on the door. I opened it to see a tall, fair-haired man I had noticed about the college but had never spoken to.

'Good evening,' he said. 'I'm David Illingworth Maxwell. I've come to walk you into dinner.'

We shook hands, rather formally.

The rooms Merlin's usually hired were in the main college, near the Dining Hall. The club had its own chef and wine cellar, facilities of which the Senior Common Room was said to be very jealous. When David and I arrived small groups of people were standing about, almost as if they had been posed by a passing artist. Everyone was very well turned out, hair gleaming, bespoke dinner suits freshly pressed. They looked to me as if they were almost too grand to speak. Then a servant came in with a tray of the famous Merlin's cocktails. I can't remember the recipe for this toxic drink but it included champagne,

and a lot of Cointreau. Within minutes th
had livened up and the noise level in
tenfold.

Dinner was simple but very good. The wines
were excellent, including a Rioja, which was the
latest new fad. David Illingworth Maxwell sat
next to me and subjected me to a gentle
interrogation: what was it like being at school in
Switzerland, what did my parents do, and so
forth. With my tongue loosened by the cocktail
and the wine, I may have given him more
information than he expected.

'That sounds very interesting,' he said,
doubtfully, as I was explaining the attitudes to
tertiary education in different Swiss cantons. I
saw that we had better change the subject.

'Have you thought what you might do when
you leave this place?' I asked.

'Oh, it's already written in stone. I will join the
family firm in the City.'

'Won't that be rather hard work?'

David called for a steward to pour us both
another glass of wine.

'I don't know,' he said, after a moment's
reflection. 'I don't think you have to be in much
before ten, and you get a jolly good lunch in the
partners' dining room. Of course I won't be a
partner to start with, but as my pa is senior
partner I don't suppose anyone will object if I
turn up for the occasional session of browsing
and sluicing.'

'And do you have to take any more exams?'

'I haven't looked into that,' said David. Instead
he looked at his gold enamelled plate and slowly

congealing slab of beef Wellington. I shuffled in my seat uncomfortably. If this was the charmed world over which my father had reminisced so fondly, in which he hoped I would make my way, he might well be disappointed. To me, this network in the making seemed to have even less to say for itself than the armchair politicians in the bar. I studied my wine glass, thinking hard of something clever or funny to move the conversation along, but instead I found myself saying 'Well that sounds like a colossal shame to me.'

'I don't follow you.'

'I mean, you're presumably bright, otherwise you wouldn't be here. It seems a waste of that natural intelligence to put it solely to use suffering through long lunches in the partners' boardroom when you could be helping to solve some of the world's considerable problems?'

It wasn't just the wine. It simply didn't occur to me *not* to say it, because it seemed to be the truth. It would also be the first such slip of many. As if I had glanced in a mirror and noticed a change in my reflection, I suddenly had a sense of the person I might become. Or at least, a sense of who I definitely wasn't.

David Illingworth Maxwell's pale, taut and unsmiling face did not appear inclined to answer. He turned to his neighbour, in search of an escape, but found none.

Then, because he was very polite, he asked:

'So how about you? Have you thought about the noble path you might follow when you go down? Or perhaps you are so fortunate and enlightened you won't have to work for a living?'

26

'Oh, I'll have to work all right,' I said. It is a curious fact that until that evening I hadn't given a moment's thought as to how I would actually earn my living. I had no interest in the drug company that employed my father, and I am sure he would have been shocked if I had asked him to help me get a job there. I had felt free to challenge my neighbour on his inherited ambition without having a clear life plan of my own. Perhaps I was more naturally an observer than a participant in any of these worlds. There might even be some virtue in watching from the sidelines. I am making it sound more thought-through than it was, more of a conscious decision, but at that point a notion did creep into my mind. No doubt the idea had been gestating over the last few weeks, the realisation slowly dawning that no prophet was going to simply reveal to me the truth about the world. And certainly not David Illingworth Maxwell.

I was going to have to discover it for myself.

'I might try and get a job as a journalist.'

He raised a doubtful eyebrow at me. 'Indeed. Covering what, exactly?'

'I'm not sure. Politics, perhaps.'

And there it was. Once the notion had materialised, it felt perfectly right. From that moment on, I was clear about what I wanted to do with my life. It was an exciting thought.

* * *

Looking back, I still don't fully understand why I continued to attend Merlin's. In part it was to

27

prove to myself that I was not, as I had feared, an outsider, but an insider, a member of an elite. I did not then realise that a display of privilege is not always a sign of power. It is often no more than a reminder of where power once lay. They may have made a show of protecting their confidences from putative hacks such as myself, but in reality the other members of Merlin's were not powerful, either in the context of Oxford or, when they left, in the context of the wider world. When I left, in the mid-80s, it wasn't even something you dared put on your CV.

Of course, what happened with Andrew and the owl would change that perception for good. But I'm jumping ahead.

In any case, I continued to eagerly attend the club's gatherings throughout my first year. Through a chance meeting with a third-year student at one such drinks, I managed to secure my first piece of journalistic experience — writing some restaurant reviews for *Cherwell*, the university paper.

Admittedly, it was not quite the political essay slot I had in mind, but my years in Lausanne and New York, trailing after my parents on the international circuit, had given me a broader experience of restaurant dining than many of my contemporaries. Few of them had eaten out anywhere other than a hotel, and that was often limited to melon balls in a stainless steel coupe followed by duck à l'orange. There was not a hugely more imaginative range of food on offer at Oxford, but for a term or two my forthright and often unfavourable 500 word summaries of everywhere from the long-established Elizabeth to the local kebab van seemed to strike a chord.

Merlin's had very strict rules about revealing any conversation which had taken place at one of its events, so partly in search of that lead which might give me a break at the *Cherwell* beyond writing up curry houses, I took every opportunity to socialise with its members outside the formal dinners. This even extended to my accepting an invitation to join David and his family for a golfing week in Scotland over the long summer holiday. He derived great amusement by introducing me to everyone as 'Charlie, who wants to write about politics and change the world', which had the net effect of scaring them off, including his attractive elder sister. It rained for much of the week, and I spent the time mainly in my room, reading the early journalism of Winston Churchill.

★ ★ ★

That there might be people for whom membership of Merlin's was of no account, struck me as unlikely. Even the politicians at the common-room bar seemed to view it with slightly covetous eyes. But gradually I became aware that in my own small college there were individuals whose influence was of a different order, whose networks were wider than the college or even Oxford itself.

One such man whose star burned more brightly outside the university than within it was

Maldwyn Christie. He was in my year and also reading PPE. He was either never asked to join Merlin's, or rejected their invitation. Regardless, he seemed far removed from the often petty and juvenile preoccupations of that association. He was small, plump and quick of speech, whereas so many of my dining companions affected a languid drawl. I first met him at one of his breakfast levées, and remembered him mostly because of the thick tweed suit he wore whatever the weather. Maldwyn was often quick-witted and rather amusing, his eyes twinkling behind thick spectacles as he teased me about Merlin's. His banter was of a different order to what one heard at the club. It was more intellectual, more outrageous, and often referred to people who had the temerity to exist outside Oxford, who came from political or artistic circles in London and elsewhere.

It was not a huge surprise the following term to hear that Maldwyn had been elected President of the Oxford Union. I felt irresistibly drawn to write a profile of him, for the *Cherwell*. To my surprise, it was not only accepted and published, but created a brief sensation for its uncompromising and occasionally unflattering description of my friend. I found most student profiles in university rags reverential and naive to the point of fawning. There was a further stir when a staffer at Conservative Central Office came across the piece and invited Maldwyn to make a speech at the forthcoming party conference. He was barely twenty-one.

This feeling that the real world lay beyond the

circumference of Merlin's grew on me as my time at Oxford rolled by until, halfway though my second year, I almost began to regret having spent so much of my time with fellow members of what was, after all, only a dining club. I increasingly thought of the conversations we had not as the height of elegant discourse, but as shallow and uninteresting. That judgement might appear harsh, but it was strengthened when I met someone who was a member of Merlin's but had never bothered to turn up to a single dinner or cocktail party. The idea that you could be eligible to join the club, rich enough to pay its dues, and yet never bother to share in its social life, was a hard one for me to grasp.

The name of this unusual individual was Andrew Landford.

3

I first met Andrew Landford by chance. It was a dour, muggy afternoon in the early autumn of my final year, and I had nothing to do. That is to say, I had two essays to write for a tutorial later in the week, a lecture to attend, and a week's reading to catch up on. As I felt all these tasks could wait a little longer, I had arranged to wander up to the university rifle range and have a look around. The Oxford Rifle Club was on a recruiting drive. I had been promised that one of their star members, a third year with plenty of experience, would meet me at the range and show me how it worked.

The man who met me was taller than me, over six foot, with curly black hair framing a pale face, a strong mouth and nose and greenish eyes.

We introduced ourselves. He regarded me for a moment, as if weighing up a potential opponent. 'I know. You're the chap who wrote that profile of the mighty Maldwyn. Most unexpected.' It wasn't clear whether this referred to my ability to produce an article or Maldwyn's sudden elevation. He frowned, then broke into a friendly smile. 'Well, come and see how it all works.'

He showed me the gun cupboard where the rifles were kept. Most belonged to the club, but

32

Andrew had his own weapon, a Rigby which he took out and let me handle.

'It's beautiful,' I said. The polished stock and the dull metal barrel were the work of a master craftsman. I gave the gun back to him but instead of locking it away, he signed it out in the book and carried the rifle and a box of shells down to the range itself. There he showed me how to lie in the firing position, and how to squeeze off the shot, using a blank. He had an ease with the gun that was extraordinary to watch, cocking it open, loading, taking aim and ejecting the spent cartridge almost in a single movement, as if the rifle were merely an extension of his arm. I tried to copy him, in a ham-fisted way. He watched without comment for a few minutes.

Then he said, 'Right. How about some live firing?'

'Are you sure? I don't want to kill anyone.'

'I won't let you kill anyone,' said Andrew. 'Get yourself comfortable and put the ear defenders on, while I set up the target.'

Twenty minutes later, my ears still ringing despite the defenders I'd worn, we left the range. I felt rather shaky, but elated at the same time. I had hit the target several times, including one shot that clipped the edge of the bull.

'You did well,' said Andrew.

'Hardly.'

I'd just watched Andrew fire three quick shots into the bull. My face was flushed and my fingers were trembling with the focus and effort but Andrew remained pale and cool, as if we had just been sitting around reading books, rather than pumping rounds of live ammunition into paper cut-outs of enemy soldiers. His control and mastery gave me a strange thrill, but at the same time I felt uneasy. There was something about his white-knuckled grip on the gun, his determination to hit the bull every time, that I found unattractive, even alarming.

'I'll never make it to your level,' I managed to say.

'You can't know that,' he replied, adding, 'I taught myself. It's just a matter of practice. Most things in life are.'

I thanked him again and went back to my flat.

* * *

By that time I was living in rented rooms outside college, sharing a small flat with a law student called Mark Davidson. He was making tea and toast when I arrived. He handed me a slice and a cup and put some more toast under the grill for himself. I described my experience at the range to him.

'Oh, you met the College Swan, did you? You are honoured.'

'The College Swan?'

'That's what they call Andrew Landford. He likes to make it look as if everything he does is effortless, but underneath the water he's paddling away furiously. Did he tell you he's got a blue, or half-blue, or whatever they give you if you shoot for the university?'

'No, he didn't mention it.'

'He wouldn't. He cultivates an air of extreme modesty, but he is the most fiercely competitive man I've ever met. He's a bit much for most people.'

'Why do you think he never comes to Merlin's?' I asked. 'I know he's a member. I saw his name on the list.'

'Most people think it's because he's too grand. I don't agree. He's just bored by other undergraduates. He's too grown up for most of us. Did he mention that he was captain of the university ski team as well?'

'No.'

'You see? He never talks about himself. He knows we all do it anyway. He doesn't need to be a self-publicist when everyone else is gossiping about him.'

'Anything else I should know about this paragon?' I asked. I was already beginning to feel I disliked Andrew Landford, although he had done nothing to deserve such a reaction.

Mark took a contemplative gulp of tea and frowned.

'Why, are you planning a piece on him?' I shook my head. 'Still, I'd watch yourself with that. There is one thing . . . I don't know if it's true or not. But I heard this story in the college bar one night. Something about him poking someone's eye out with a punt pole.'

'That sounds improbable.'

'It does, rather. But apparently he was trying to impress some girl or other with his prowess on the water, and these tourists — who were drunk — kept getting in the way, bumping their boat, giggling and splashing them. The tourists followed them halfway up the Cherwell. Landford brushed it off at first, until one of them leaned over and said something to the girl in Spanish.'

'What?'

'I have no idea, but the story goes that Andrew's reply was in the language that needs no translation. He flipped his pole out of the water and sent the man head over heels into the drink.'

I laughed, but Mark didn't.

'It could have been much worse. As it was the poor chap clipped his eye on the corner of the boat and had to go to the Radcliffe. They say the surgeons couldn't save it, but I have no idea if that's really true.'

'Did he press charges?'

'If he did, I never heard about it. It's quite possible Landford paid him off. He's very rich, of course. Parents own a gold mine or a tea plantation or something. He doesn't have to work when he leaves here.'

'But you said he was competitive. Doesn't that mean he is ambitious as well?'

Mark wiped a drop of melted butter from his chin and grinned at me.

'Oh, he only wants to be the youngest prime minister since Pitt.'

★ ★ ★

A couple of days later I was in college for a tutorial. When it was over, I walked across the quad, heading for the library. As I passed the chapel I noticed that one of the doors was slightly open, and from within I could hear the sounds of the organ being played. Whoever had written the piece, it was faultlessly executed by the organist. He contrived to make the single instrument reproduce the sound of an entire orchestra. The beauty of the music was mesmerising. I stepped inside the chapel in order to listen. As I stood there, I realised it wasn't the college organist playing but a bigger, younger man. When he finished, I clapped and he turned on his seat to see who had been listening. It was Andrew.

'That was wonderful,' I told him.

'Oh, hello, Charles. I'm sure it was the most frightful racket. I still haven't quite got the hang of it.'

He stood up, switched off the lights and walked down the aisle towards me.

'Don't let me interrupt you,' I said.

'I'm finished anyway. I've got to get up to London this afternoon — dinner at the Carlton Club tonight.'

We walked out into the quad.

'The Carlton Club?' I asked. 'Isn't that a sort of unofficial headquarters for the Conservative Party?'

'Yes, it is,' replied Andrew. He looked annoyed with himself, as if he had committed an indiscretion.

'Are you after a seat in Parliament?'

He flushed, which made me feel my question, though frivolous, was close to the mark.

'Look, I'm sorry, I must rush. I've quite a lot to do before I catch my train. We must have lunch some time.'

Without saying anything further, he turned and strode across the quad. I wouldn't speak to him again for years.

★　★　★

The halcyon undergraduate days rolled past and became weeks in the blink of an eye. The weeks became months. Then the months became terms, and before I knew it, my final days as a student had pulled into the station.

I had sometimes tried to make time stand still, by telling myself, 'You'll never be this free or this happy again. Live for the moment.'

And I had lived for the moment a lot of the time. There were endless parties. There were picnics on the river. There were cricket and polo matches, and I played tennis for the college. Occasionally I would remember to attend a lecture. I managed to get to most of my tutorials although even I had to admit that my work was getting scrappier. In part, my studies were fighting a losing battle with the various romances I found myself embroiled in. They were initially, without exception, tempestuous and short-lived. But towards the start of my third year, I had begun a more satisfactory relationship with a girl I had met from one of the women's colleges.

Or so I thought.

Now finals were approaching and everyone was becoming more aware of the great divide between the fairyland we were living in and the obligations and opportunities of the 'outside' world. Everything changed when we both attended the wedding of some mutual friends who had decided to get married before they graduated. The occasion was riotous and even romantic, but at the back of all our minds questions were forming: where will they live? What will they live on? The couple concerned had only just turned twenty, and were good-looking and popular figures at Oxford. But how would they survive the cold glare of real life? Even then, some of us were showing signs of a survival instinct; others seemed happy enough to contemplate a penniless existence on some hippy farm in the Welsh Marches, with babies crawling around in the mud.

'That could have been us,' said my girlfriend, as we lay in one another's arms in the post-alcoholic haze that followed this occasion.

'No, it couldn't have been, not really. We're a little bit too realistic about life.'

'Why couldn't you have pretended just for a moment? You always want everything to be so literal.'

A tear ran down the side of her nose, sooty with mascara. I smudged it away and we comforted each other, but we both knew the end of one part of our lives was approaching, and that we would not go on together.

★ ★ ★

My exams took place during the first hot week of the summer and for five days I endured the torment of sitting in the Examination Schools, wringing out of myself whatever drops of knowledge I had absorbed in the last three years. The windows were wide open to try to keep some air circulating. The invigilators sat and nodded and then jerked awake again while the candidates scribbled away. Outside some thoughtless person was playing the latest hit from Frankie Goes to Hollywood, and the music drifted into the hall. Instead of concentrating on the question in front of me my thoughts strayed to images of grass lawns, cool drinks and girls. That in itself does not explain why I got a 2:2 instead of the 2:1 I had been aiming for. The truth is I hadn't done enough work, and maybe I wasn't as clever as I thought I was. The summer heat was just an excuse. For all I know that might be an invented memory. More than likely it was a typical English day in June: rain sheeting down.

★　★　★

A few days later I found myself in a punt in an alcoholic haze once more and, nearly for the last time, being poled along by a rather beautiful girl I had picked up at a drinks party. She was a good deal more competent at steering our craft than I had been; I was glad she had offered to take over after I became entangled in a curtain of overhanging dog rose, which had nearly pulled me into the water. As I watched her effortlessly guiding us back towards the place where we had hired the punt, I had one of those moments

40

when one thinks the meaning of everything is becoming clear at last. I lay with my head on a cushion gazing at the evening sky. I could hear the water lapping and gurgling a few inches from my head. I felt like Mole, in *The Wind in the Willows*. Here I was, another soon-to-be graduate churned out by the university. I had learned nothing of any great value. I would of course keep in touch with the close friends I had made, like Maldwyn, but might well never see many of my more casual acquaintances again. What on earth had the last three years been about? What would I take away with me, except for a few confused and mostly happy memories? What mattered now was what the next three years would bring. Where would I be in three years time? I might not even settle in this country — the demand for political journalists seemed to be scant, and I couldn't think of anything else I wanted to do. I might even be married by then.

I came out of my trance and looked at the girl standing in front of me. Her movements were elegant and economical as she steered us back towards the jetty. I realised that I was deeply in love with her and always had been, ever since I had first set eyes on her at five o'clock that afternoon. The air was warm. The river was still except for the ripples that flowed backwards from our craft. My life at Oxford was over, and what a perfect evening on which to end this period of my life and start the beginning of the next.

'Mary,' I said. 'Will you marry me?'

'No,' said the girl, with great decision. Then she added, 'You might at least get my name right. It's not Mary. I'm Sophie.'

Somewhere in the soft folds of the trees on the bank, an owl hooted.

Such an innocent sound.

4

1984

My notion of becoming a political journalist had only grown and deepened since I first found myself declaring it at a Merlin's dinner. Other than my unexceptional degree, a modest portfolio of reviews, columns and articles was about the only substantial product of my university years. The brief attention I had attracted over the Maldwyn profile in the small and incestuous world of student journalism had given me an inflated sense of my own talents — which was perhaps essential to making any kind of start at all.

Upon leaving I made grand applications to *The Times* and the *Daily Telegraph;* then, when they turned me down, the other broadsheets. After that I tried some of the weeklies, such as the *Spectator.* They seemed to be overrun with applications not just from people like me, but also those with first-class degrees or masters' from Harvard or Johns Hopkins. Other applicants had already made something of their lives: they had walked across Afghanistan; they had been ice-climbing in the Andes; they had studied the lost tribes of the Amazon basin. The newspapers had lots of bright, confident people to choose from. I had done nothing apart from reviewing a kebab van and interviewing one of

43

many student politicians. I had left university, found a rented flat in Muswell Hill, and had little else to offer except what, if anything, was between my ears.

'Have you ever thought of using your language skills?' asked one interviewer, more kindly than the rest. 'People are beginning to discover that not all foreigners speak English. Your Italian or your German might come in handy?'

But I didn't want to consider giving up on my chosen career before I had even started.

★ ★ ★

At last I was offered the position of junior reporter on *Mayhem*. You may remember it: it ran a series of dispatches from the front line during the Miners' Strike. These were full of descriptions of police brutality and the starving families of the strikers. At one point the magazine achieved a circulation of five thousand a month.

It was a strange world to find myself in, after the candlelit Merlin's dinners and afternoons spent on punts, but I think I wanted a change. By the end, I had found the gilded atmosphere of Oxford stultifying and I needed some fresh air. Perhaps, looking at my background and the friends I had made at university, it seems purely a matter of course that my politics would be traditionally conservative. But the truth was that, emerging blinking into the daylight of real life, I had no defining passion for either end of the spectrum. What did fascinate me was the way those who were driven by passionate ideologies attempted to communicate their beliefs to an often indifferent electorate. Then there was the gap between what politicians thought voters wanted to hear, and what they actually believed was the right direction for the country. I felt that gap was growing, and deserved closer scrutiny. If I was ideologically enthused at all, it was for those politicians who dressed up their message the least, rather than those who modified it according to the audience.

At least, that was what I said in the job interview, earnestly pressing my fingers to my lips, talking too quickly.

Mayhem operated out of the basement of a house in a Georgian square in Islington. The house was owned by one of our backers. The three rooms we occupied were cramped and were never cleaned until it became impossible to fight one's way into a room past the mounds of crumpled paper and piles of empty coffee cups. Then we would have a housekeeping day, and for the next few days the offices looked almost normal, before disorder took over again.

I joined at the end of September 1984, not long after the Battle of Orgreave, when NUM pickets clashed violently with the police. The tide — meaning the national press — was beginning to turn in favour of the government and *Mayhem*'s backing of the NUM was already beginning to look a bit futile. It had become important for the magazine to find a new cause to fight for.

My first assignment was to write an editorial

on the aftermath of the Brighton hotel bombing by the IRA, in which five people, including a Tory MP, had been killed. After a week of furious writing and rewriting and endless telephone calls, I handed in the article. I wasn't optimistic about its reception but even so I was unprepared for the swiftness with which my editor handed it back to me.

'On the one hand; on the other hand . . . ' he sneered. 'Your job is to get readers stirred up, not write a history essay. This is of no use to me.' He held up the two pages of typescript I had offered him. 'Thatcher had it coming. That's what our readers want to see.'

'But she seems to have come out of it more popular than ever,' I argued. It was the self-evident truth of the matter, whatever one's personal politics, and it seemed delusional to refute that.

Mike McFarlane wasn't an unpleasant man, on the whole. But he role-played the hard-bitten editor to perfection. He wore braces; he chewed on unlit cigars. Dark crescents of sweat dampened his shirt beneath the arms even on cold days. 'Who are you to judge who's popular or not? Leave that to me. Your job is to write articles that sell papers. My job is to tell you what sells papers, and what doesn't. I don't want journalists like spaniels. I want Rottweilers.'

And so, cold call by cold call, doorstep by doorstep, I set about transforming myself, if not exactly from spaniel into Rottweiler, at least into a reasonably interrogative terrier. I could no more replicate Mike's carefully crafted bark than

I could share his taste for cigars, but over time, my tenacity began to complement his more pugnacious approach. Hanging around at endless protest marches, party meetings and in the press lobby of the Commons, I began to build up relationships with the more approachable members of the various factions. At first, these were minor and of little consequence, but they provided an entry link into the chain of communication, and gradually I began to haul myself up.

★   ★   ★

Almost despite myself, I turned out to be much better at my job than I had ever expected. I overheard a rumour in Annie's Bar one night that a top civil servant in the Foreign Office had some classified documents regarding the Falklands that he felt the public should know about. Perhaps he was naive, as very senior people of his position and generation could be, or perhaps he thought a minor magazine such as *Mayhem* would be a less risky bet for him than the national press. Either way, I was astonished that after various approaches through an intermediary, he agreed not only to speak to me, but also to give us access to the documents.

'I've read some of your work,' he said to me at our first cloak and dagger assignation on a park bench. 'You don't dress stuff up much, do you?'

It was not through conscious effort on my part, but my refusal to take sides in my writing was gaining me trust, even amongst those who potentially stood to lose from such unbiased coverage.

In this case, the result was sensational. It was not so much the documents themselves — their contents only confirmed aspects of the war planning that had long been suspected — but the whistleblower was suspended and charged under the Official Secrets Act. He was eventually acquitted, but the trial provided one of the news highlights of an otherwise dull summer. *Mayhem*'s circulation exploded, and for a brief while the bigger beasts of the media jungle began to treat us more seriously.

I was promoted to Political Editor. My colleagues, who had only thinly disguised contempt for my non-committal position on many of the issues they cared so deeply about, did not exactly celebrate. Nevertheless, we managed to pull off a small scoop over an internal attempt to 'purge' the Labour Party of 'militants', and my coverage of the Westland affair was enthusiastically lapped up by our readers. When obvious incompetence or hypocrisy were involved rather than ideological judgement, I found it easier to twist the knife in the way my editor and colleagues demanded.

One day in the warm and thundery summer of 1989, as we were attempting to put our latest issue to bed, Mike and I nearly came to blows over the editorial line on a piece commemorating the closure of the last coal pit in Kent. I thought it might be a good idea to let him cool off for a while, and stepped outside to get some air. As I emerged on to the street, I literally ran straight into Maldwyn Christie. He spread his hands and goggled at me, the very parody of a man experiencing extreme surprise.

'Maldwyn!' I exclaimed. 'What's a hard-right Tory doing in a den of Bolshevism like this?'

'Has old Mike been giving you a bollocking?' he replied, ever adept at not answering a question directly. 'I can see that he has. Let's have a cup of coffee when I've finished with him.' Then, in response to an impatient roar from inside the office, 'I'm coming, dear! Keep your hair on.'

★ ★ ★

I had been back at my desk for about ten minutes when Maldwyn reappeared. 'Come on. There's a pub in Upper Street you ought to be introduced to.'

'I thought you said coffee?'

'You can have the coffee if you really want. I wouldn't recommend it.'

A few minutes later we were sitting at a table in Maldwyn's pub of the month — he had a passion for such places and then went off them, or else they went off him. He could be quite a disruptive force, in his way. Once we were sipping at our pints of Guinness, Maldwyn said, 'I saw the College Swan at a drinks party the other day.'

'Do you mean Andrew Landford?'

'Who else?'

'Where was this?' I asked. I had forgotten all about Andrew. We had been acquaintances at

Oxford, not friends. All the same, the mention of his name aroused my curiosity.

'He's bought a house in Notting Hill. One of those up and coming streets where the gentry are moving in and the locals are moving out. Actually, it's rather nice. I like rooms with high ceilings . . .'

'What was the drinks party in aid of?'

'Andrew is financing something called a think tank.'

'A what tank?'

'It's a group of people who are supposed to dream up new policy ideas. There were some left of centre politicians, and some of Labour's young rising stars too. A whole lot of intellectuals. A Rothschild or two. And, of course, me.'

'Why of course you?'

Maldwyn wriggled his shoulders in a display of false modesty.

'I'm hurt you haven't followed my own career more closely.'

'I have. That's why I was surprised to see you at our office today.'

Maldwyn already had a reputation as one of the brighter newly elected Members of Parliament. He had a remarkable ability to get himself noticed by the media and was being spoken of as a man to watch, someone who might be on the fast track to the Cabinet when Mrs Thatcher went — whenever that might be.

'The art of success is to know what your enemy is planning.'

'Ancient Chinese saying?'

'No, modern Maldwyn saying. I've been asked to do an article on 'Life after Thatcher'.'

'She hasn't gone yet,' I remarked.

'No, but it can't be long, can it? Anyway, are you yourself enjoying working for Mike's rag?'

We talked about the personalities at *Mayhem* for a while. Maldwyn claimed to have read and enjoyed my work, mentioning the classified documents, then praising my 'perceptive' take on some of the Conservative Party's more toxic scandals. It was a gift he had, making whoever he was talking to seem like the centre of his world. Maldwyn was unprepossessing to look at when he wasn't speaking, but when he spoke, which was most of the time, one found oneself caught up in his charm and his encyclopaedic knowledge of whatever subject was under discussion. There was no doubt about his intellectual powers, or his debating skills, and I could quite easily imagine him as a Cabinet minister one day. I couldn't quite imagine him going all the way to the top, but you never knew.

Suddenly Maldwyn looked at his watch, shook his head and said, 'I'm late for a meeting. I must go. Let's keep in touch, now we have met again. You can always get hold of me through my constituency office.'

He handed me a card.

★ ★ ★

I didn't get much work done that day. It wasn't the Guinness. Drinking at lunchtime was not so unusual back then and the habit of clutching a

51

bottle of water to one's bosom as if it were a comfort blanket was not widespread. Large glasses of white wine or a pint or two at lunch were a commonplace. So it wasn't the alcohol that had disturbed me: it was this sudden glimpse, through the person of Maldwyn, into a world other than my own, where people were beginning to do things with their lives. Maldwyn was surging forward in the political world. Andrew Landford must be doing incredibly well, even to think of funding a think tank. Perhaps he had inherited his parents' gold mine. David Illingworth Maxwell and I still kept in touch. He had been made a partner in his family stockbroking firm. I had read the other day that it had been bought lock stock and barrel for hundreds of millions of pounds by a French bank. Some of the proceeds had to be heading in David's direction.

All this was clear evidence, if evidence were needed, that my own career had become somewhat becalmed.

When I tried to examine myself in these rare moods of introspection, I came up a blank. I was happy enough at *Mayhem*, but the magazine lived on the edge of a financial cliff and might fold from one week to the other, if any of its backers pulled out. Rumours that we were a second front for the Socialist Workers Party persisted, although if there were hidden puppet masters, I was unaware of them.

★ ★ ★

Whatever way you looked at it, it was a precarious venture and I had no idea what I would do if the magazine fired me or else closed its doors. I had a reasonable social life. There were a couple of girls I saw from time to time; the relationships were cheerful and uncommitted on either side. I had a small allowance from my parents, which meant I should never be quite destitute. I saw little of them. My father was fast approaching retirement and was inclined to be grumpy at the prospect. My mother was falling under the spell of what we later realised was dementia. Long silences and disconnected sentences made one aware that all was not well.

But I realised I wasn't really going anywhere. Around me my former friends surged onwards like migrating salmon, their presence revealed by the occasional flash of silver. I, who had no idea what to do with myself next, no strong feelings for or against any political party, no relationships that might drag me out of my self-absorption — I just swam around in circles flicking up mud with my tail.

I see things quite differently now, of course. I see them for what they actually were.

5

1989

My flat in north London was near enough to Hampstead Heath, so that I could go running there every Saturday morning. I had persuaded myself that whatever was happening, or not happening, in my working life, I would at least keep fit — although perhaps my leisurely pace made it more of an amble than a run. I was jogging — gently — from the Heath towards Hampstead tube station on a calm, misty morning in early autumn, when I became aware of another runner overtaking me. As he moved past I saw a tall figure, moving easily and with longer strides than my own. He wore a blue tracksuit with a towel draped over his shoulders. His black hair curled over the nape of his neck, worn quite long. The profile was familiar.

I stopped, caught my breath and said, 'Andrew? Andrew Landford?'

It was indeed him, and he recognised me straight away.

'Charles. I was just thinking about you. I met Maldwyn the other day and he said you'd had a catch up.'

We stopped speaking, catching our breath, our hands on our hips. I was starting to drip with perspiration, not an entirely pleasant sensation, as my body cooled down.

'Look,' said Andrew. 'What are you doing now?'

'Doing now? I'm going to go home, take a shower and have a beer. Not necessarily in that order.'

As if by magic a large black Mercedes with a driver pulled up alongside the kerb next to Andrew.

'My car,' said Andrew, without any attempt at false modesty. It was an unexpected accessory in someone who could not be more than twenty-seven.

'Come home with me. You can take a shower in the guest bedroom. It's all en-suite. I can lend you jeans and a shirt; we're about the same size, bar an inch or two. It would be lovely if you stayed for lunch. I know that if you don't come now, we probably won't see each other again for years. Maybe never!'

Andrew looked so melodramatic as he said this that we both burst out laughing. Then he said, 'Phone, Bertie.'

Bertie the driver opened the window and handed out a phone on the end of a flexible lead, while Andrew gave instructions to someone concerning lunch and wine. Then we climbed into the car. Inside it was large and spacious. There were papers strewn across the back seat. Andrew stuffed them into a folder to make room for me and we moved off.

'This is the life,' I said. 'Is it mandatory for all former members of Merlin's? I never got the memo if so.'

'I don't know what Merlin's has to do with it,'

Andrew said, perhaps sounding more defensive than he meant to. 'I mean, I make a lot of money and I spend a good deal too. You probably think it's a bit flash,' he added.

I wondered if he was already beginning to regret his sudden decision to invite me back, so I reminded him of our last meeting outside the college chapel. 'You said we must have lunch sometime. And here we are, on our way to lunch. Only six years later.'

Andrew screwed up his face. 'I don't remember that . . . no, I do remember,' he said pensively. 'I was practising for a charity concert. It was a disaster. I kept turning over two pages at once.'

In an extraordinary way it was as if we were suddenly old friends, whereas in truth we scarcely knew each other. But the common ground of Oxford, and even in an odd way Merlin's, gave our meeting more significance than perhaps it might otherwise have had. What else would I have done that day? Gone home, had a shower, a couple of beers; grazed from the fridge; fallen asleep on the sofa; gone to see a film in Hampstead with some friends later on: a routine, aimless afternoon had awaited me and I was not sorry to be doing something entirely different.

★ ★ ★

Andrew's house was just what one might have expected. I could well imagine 'the occasional Rothschild' lingering in these high-ceilinged rooms. The place had an air of money, power and knowledge that came from being at the centre of things. Magazines and books lay in artless piles here and there, suggesting either the hand of a diligent interior decorator or, more likely, that Andrew really did read the *TLS* and the *New York Review of Books* and volumes on ballet and Tuscan architecture, international finance and modern geopolitics. He arrived downstairs and found me handling a weighty tome on the future of the Soviet Union.

'This fellow takes a gloomy view,' I said, putting the book down.

'In the short term. It's going to be a bit like the Wild West there before too long. Very little law, lots of oil and wheat and gold. It'll be a question of who gets the key to the larder.'

Andrew poured me a cool glass of Pils and another for himself.

'I've read some of your stuff in *Mayhem*,' he said in a neutral tone of voice.

'Like it? Hate it? Bored to death by it?'

'Oh, I like the way you write. No question.' A *But* . . . lingered unspoken in the air. I didn't pick him up on it. Instead I asked, 'And you?'

'I'm an investment banker. With a small New York firm. We've been going since the 1920s but there are only about a dozen partners. Slow and steady is our motto. I'm supposed to be helping grow our business in London and Eastern Europe. We've decided that a little bit of risk from time to time might be a good thing after all.'

Even I had heard of Andrew's firm. It was old New York money; never known to put a foot wrong. If you were chosen as a partner there you were made for life: you would become not just rich, but phenomenally rich.

'Including the Soviet Union?'

'Including that, or whatever that becomes.'

There was a silence while we sipped our beer. It was delicious and I felt I could quite easily sit here all afternoon. But at the same time there was tension in the air. It was Andrew: it was as if he felt a compulsion to analyse, to probe, to question. You could feel the lightest pressure of his will, like a percussion note too deep to be heard but which throbbed in the air.

'Maldwyn said you were backing a think tank of some sort.'

'Typical Maldwyn. He's not very discreet, is he? But one knew that. No — it's not a secret, really, and if you take someone like Maldwyn on board, you know his type, one has to expect that sort of thing. Don't worry. You haven't dropped him in it.'

I didn't quite know what to make of the reference to Maldwyn. What did Andrew mean by his type? I didn't feel like asking. I said, 'So tell me about this think tank?'

'Oh, it's an idea I've had for some time. We discuss factors likely to change the way we lead our lives. For instance, are we really going to have another ten years of Tory rule, or misrule, as some would say? What's going to happen to the bankrupt Soviet Union? Why don't we know more about what's going on in China and India, two of the most sizeable marketplaces on the planet?'

The room we were sitting in had long green velvet curtains and a pale green wallpaper with some sort of floral motif. In fact there was very little furniture apart from a large grand piano in the corner. I wondered if it was ever played now, recalling Andrew's musical skill from our university days. Overall the space had the curious feel of an aquarium, in which we swam around, our mouths opening and shutting to let out bubbles of air.

'What's in it for you?' I asked Andrew, regretting the crassness of the question as soon as I had spoken. There was something in his demeanour, as he sat ensconced in his enormous sofa, that made me want to nip at his heels. But he seemed untroubled by my question.

'One of the things we do in my business is wealth management. We look for unconventional investment opportunities for very high net worth individuals. We run what the Americans call a hedge fund. The think tank occasionally sheds light on some of the situations we are looking into, especially in Russia. So a think tank aligns with both my personal and my business interests.'

At that moment a maid in a black dress and white apron appeared in the doorway.

'Lunch is ready, Mr Landford.'

This was so beyond the realities of my world that it made me want to laugh. I composed myself as Andrew stood up and led me through to the kitchen. A contemporary of mine already endowed with a cook/housekeeper, a chauffeur, and heaven knew who or what else: it was just a little bit too much.

The kitchen was another large room with a table, made from some pale wood, laid with place settings for two and bowls of salad, plates of smoked salmon and saucers of quail's eggs. There seemed to be enough for six people, let alone two.

'Thank you, Marcia,' said Andrew. 'We won't need you to stay.'

Marcia disappeared like a genie back into her lamp. Andrew gestured to me to help myself while he poured me a glass of red wine.

The wine and the food were very good and we chatted away like the old friends we weren't until Andrew said, 'Why don't you join the think tank? A journalist with your background might be just the thing we need.'

'Me?' I asked incredulously. 'But I'm just a hack. I fear I'd be a bit underpowered compared with all the heavyweights you've got lined up.'

'We haven't really got anyone lined up as such. We want to approach George Soros — he's another of these hedge fund Americans, although really he's a Hungarian. Then Maldwyn's a possibility. He's very bright, and a darling of the left wing of the Conservative Party. I hope he'll join and I hope you will too. You'd bring all sorts of insight and information that others wouldn't.'

'When you said the think tank aligned with your personal interests,' I asked, 'what are those, exactly?'

'Oh, I intend to go into politics. I've always planned on doing that. But my observation is that you can either do it through a mixture of wit and charm — what they call 'charisma', I believe

60

— or else by making lots of money first. I am quite devoid of wit. Set me alongside Maldwyn and you'll see the difference straight away. But the House of Commons is stuffed with barristers, solicitors, teachers and social workers. A candidate with lots of money, a good, old-fashioned, self-made man, will always find his place if he shows he can be useful. Therefore the think tank, which will cost me a lot of money but which will, I hope, gain me access to senior people in the party . . . '

' . . . who will all want to know what you can give them.'

'Exactly.'

Andrew munched his way through a lettuce leaf. The thing about Andrew was that he appeared to deal in reality. I knew few people who did this: people who decided to act in the morning and by night had so acted, moved the world on a bit, changed something. I didn't deal in reality. I wrote speculative pieces that, as far as I knew, changed nothing. Maybe they influenced opinion, although I rather doubted it.

There was so much about Andrew that one could have made fun of. The trappings of considerable affluence, which would have appeared ridiculous if displayed by most of my other contemporaries, fitted Andrew like a glove. It would be pointless to mock: he just was who he was.

'Come along one evening,' said Andrew. 'Next Wednesday about six, if you can, and meet some of the others, see if you think you would enjoy it. If nothing else, you'll meet some unusual people.

It's worth an hour or two of your time, I should have thought. The ground rules are very simple and, as you are a journalist, I should mention them. Whatever is said on one of those evenings is spoken in confidence. People need to know that their innermost thoughts won't appear as front-page news the next morning. Chatham House rules and all that.'

'I wouldn't dream of it,' I said, a little nettled.

'I wasn't thinking particularly of you. There are other journalists who might join us.'

At this point a door banged and a cheerful voice shouted out, 'Hello? Anybody home?'

The voice held a familiar twang, but before I could even wonder where I had heard it before, a girl stood in the doorway. 'I'm back early,' she announced. 'Teacher was unwell.'

She was tall, about my height, which is five foot ten. She had dark hair curling over her shoulders and a plump, smiley face with bright hazel eyes. Andrew stood up and put his arm around her shoulder and kissed her on the cheek. Then he turned towards me, intending to introduce the new arrival, but I beat him to it.

'Caroline!' I said in surprise. I don't know how I recognised her but I did. At the age of seventeen she had been my nocturnal companion, invading my dreams as she sat beside me on the bed saying, 'Now then, Charles, here's what we do.'

Those last four words had formed the basis of many imagined embraces. Their memory may even have brought colour to my cheek as Caroline put her arms around me and said,

'It's my long-lost third cousin twice removed! Charlie! Charles Fryerne of Fryerne Court!'

All this required so much explanation between the three of us that it was some minutes before we all sat down again and resumed our lunch. Caroline Woodchester was just as I remembered her: maybe a shade heavier, but also more adult — a woman, in fact, not a girl. She and Andrew had met through a mutual friend from Cambridge, where she had been doing a course in Art History. This had all occurred three or four years after Caroline and I had first met.

'What are you doing now?' I asked Caroline.

'I sculpt. Or at least, I'm learning how to. You're in luck. An hour ago I was covered in lumps of clay.'

'How extraordinary that the two of you should know each other,' I said.

'Not extraordinary at all. As a matter of fact we met in New York, not Cambridge. I mean properly met.'

She glanced at Andrew, who glanced back at her with a look that was more proprietorial than fond.

* * *

I can't remember much more of the lunch. I think it broke up not long after Caroline arrived. The moment of intimacy, or faux-intimacy, that had existed between Andrew and me dissolved into something more general. But when I left in a taxi, it was agreed I should drop in on the next 'think tank'. When I arrived home I found that the car was pre-paid for. Some ungracious instinct forced me to make the driver wait, while I paid the bill myself.

Nevertheless, I did go to one of Andrew's think tank evenings. It was rather a let down if one was a celebrity hunter: no George Soros, no Rothschilds. The people in the room — apart from myself — were undoubtedly high-powered, but there was nobody who was obviously famous. At the same time, it was an enjoyable evening and I found, which would not have been the case if there had been somebody famous in the room, that I was able to talk quite freely. There was no agenda; nobody took any notes. From time to time Andrew threw in a prompt but otherwise it could have been any other gathering of men and women enjoying a glass of wine and chatting together.

Out of this mist some order emerged: there was to be a monthly newsletter starting in three months' time, and an (unpaid) editorial board was nominated. To my alarm I found myself amongst its members. Jeremy Cutler, who worked for a firm of parliamentary lobbyists, was another. We had met before, whenever he was trying to push a line to get coverage or comment in *Mayhem*. We agreed on some themes for the newsletter and some avenues for the think tank to explore. Sir Anthony Meyer had just mounted a leadership challenge to Thatcher. It was clear he wasn't going to succeed, but it was equally clear that his attempt would not be the end of the story. Change was in the air. It was a great time to launch.

That was about as far as it ever got. A few weeks later, Andrew Landford announced, via a round-robin letter and without any sign of embarrassment, that he had been asked to move to Moscow for a couple of years and that the think tank 'was on ice for a while'. But of course his departure was its death knell, before it had even got off the ground. I felt a curiously sharp sense of disappointment when I read his message. I had been more flattered than I realised by Andrew's seductive proposals. Even without the attendance of the famous names that had been promised, it sounded like an unparalleled opportunity to witness the machinations of real power at first hand, rather than picking up the leftovers from backbench MPs or party activists in tea rooms and bars. If I was to be an observer rather than a player, I wanted the best viewing spot I could find.

★   ★   ★

Andrew asked me to dinner with Caroline just before he left. I almost didn't accept. What would be the point? It was unlikely our paths would cross again once he left London. But in the end I went. I still felt an odd magnetic attraction to Andrew that was powerful enough to make me rouse myself and take the tube to Notting Hill.

'Are you selling the house?' I asked, as he handed me a glass of wine.

'No. Caroline's going to move in and look after the place for me. I'm only away for two years. It seems like a long time now, but it isn't really. Is it, darling?'

He reached across and attempted to squeeze her hand. She withdrew it and said with some asperity:

'It may not seem like a long time to you, buddy, with your busy and interesting life, but it is for me. I can't guarantee I'll want to stay here, rent-free or not.'

'Why wouldn't you?' asked Andrew. 'Many people would give their eye teeth to live in a house in this part of London. You'll love it. You practically live here now anyway.'

I could see the evening degenerating into a kind of low-intensity guerrilla war between the two of them, whilst I sat in silence watching them score points off each other. I was determined not to let that happen.

'So do you really hope to revive the think tank when you return?' I asked. 'It seems a hell of a long shot to me. We're heading towards a period of rapid change and you're going to be out of the country. You might even return to a Labour government. You might find yourself on the outside of everything looking in.'

'Andrew will never be an outsider,' replied Caroline. She was still angry. 'I expect in two months he'll have a dacha outside Moscow, a permit to drive in the Zil lanes, and a Russian hooker on his arm, with all those old Commies foaming at the mouth for an invite to one of his cocktail parties.'

Andrew and I both laughed a little nervously. I realised, as I had suspected before, that Caroline was an unusually direct person. She spoke her mind, which was not always the best course of action. At any rate, she was not dull. Andrew brushed her remarks away with a flick of the hand.

'Don't let's worry about old Commies. Let's have some dinner. We've got grouse tonight. I don't expect I'll see that on a menu for a while.'

Despite my best efforts, the evening was not a success and I rather wished I hadn't come.

'Look me up,' suggested Caroline as I left at about eleven. 'You know where I am, at least for now. I'll probably get sick of this joint in a few months, but keep an eye on your poor abandoned third cousin.'

'Yes, keep an eye on her,' agreed Andrew with a faint smile. '*Dasvidanya*, and all that.' He gave me a firm handshake. 'We'll meet again, Charles, and I look forward to it.'

6

Another, less predictable result of Andrew's abortive attempt at setting up a think tank was a mysterious phone call some months later from the lobbyist Jeremy Cutler.

'Can we talk?' he asked, when I picked up the call one morning in the office.

'Well, we're talking now,' I pointed out.

'No. Not on the phone. I need about half an hour with you.'

'What do you want to talk about?'

'Trust me, it will be worth the effort. Why not now? How busy are you? Could you slip out and meet me in Upper Street?'

I looked around me. It was, even by our standards, a quiet day in the office. Mike was out to lunch at *Private Eye* and unlikely to reappear that afternoon. My own desk was relatively clear. I was working up a piece about the decision to join the European Exchange Rate Mechanism, a proposition of the first importance and at the same time so staggeringly dull that I doubted my ability to write anything at all on the subject, let alone be entertaining about it. I agreed to meet Jeremy in an hour's time.

* * *

As I walked along Upper Street I wondered what this was about. I really knew very little about Jeremy. We had chatted for a few minutes at Andrew's think tank evening and I couldn't remember what we had talked about. I wasn't even sure that I would recognise Jeremy when I saw him. An impression of a man with a doughy, smiling face and sleek brown hair formed itself in my mind but that was all. So why was I now preparing to listen to whatever Jeremy might have to say? Perhaps he wanted to talk about a reincarnation of Andrew's think tank, without Andrew, in which case I wasn't interested. No, the thing that was pushing me along Upper Street, not pulling me, lay at my point of origin.

It was *Mayhem*. I was beginning to wonder what I was doing there, and where, if anywhere, it was leading. Before I could explore this thought more fully, I arrived at the coffee shop. In a street full of bright designer boutiques, jazzy kebab joints, noisy pubs with live music coming out on to the street even at that hour of the day, Jeremy had managed to choose an austere-looking café that looked something akin to a monks' refectory.

I had no problem identifying my host. A man in a suit with an open-necked white shirt sat at one of the tables. Other than him, the place was empty.

'Hi,' I said, sitting down opposite.

'Thanks for coming,' he said. 'Coffee?'

We ordered and Jeremy pushed a card across the table. It read 'CCC — Cutler Corporate Communications'. The design and font were elegant and understated, suggestive of large amounts of money somewhere in the immediate background.

'That's me,' said Jeremy, unnecessarily.

'As of when? I thought you worked for a parliamentary lobbying firm?'

I wasn't quite sure what that meant. I knew there was a dark side and a brighter side to the lobbying business. The dark side showed itself in murky attempts to influence policy through cheap holidays for MPs, gifts or even bribes. This was fairly unusual. The day-to-day business of lobbying was fairly transparent and probably a good thing as it allowed the occasional leakage of common sense, and even expertise, into the drafting of bills coming before the House of Commons. Jeremy was definitely one of the straight guys. More than that, I didn't know.

'I did. Then one of our corporate sponsors offered to back me if I set up a business in corporate communications. Same job, but a different audience: institutional investors, pension funds, people making big financial decisions who want to know more about what they are buying into. It's a bigger opportunity and while the ethical dimension is still there, you don't have to be quite so super-sensitive as you do when you are lobbying MPs.'

'And?'

Our coffee arrived.

'And now I have an office and a bag of gold, but no partner. I'm not allowed to take anyone from my old office with me, so I have to look elsewhere. You're it.'

'Me? I know nothing about the City. Nothing about PR. And I know nothing about you and you know nothing about me.'

Jeremy laughed.

'Well, that's fairly blunt. Which is why I want you to join me. You will join me, anyway, once I tell you the terms. OK, so why you? Because I've read your articles and I've noticed a rather odd thing. You can't avoid telling the truth. You spoke your mind at that meeting Andrew organised. Some of your pieces for *Mayhem* have been terrific, you must know that. They've really cut through to the heart of the matter and people are beginning to sit up and take notice. The trouble is, *Mayhem*'s last accounts didn't look too clever. Have you seen them?'

I admitted I hadn't. As long as my monthly salary cheque didn't bounce I didn't care. I thought that someone as financially illiterate as myself had no business writing stuff for a financial PR company, and said so.

Jeremy dismissed these concerns.

'That's not why we want you. Your truthfulness is why I want you. It will sometimes hurt us but mostly it will help. Trust is everything in this game. If people trust that you are giving them a true picture of what you are writing about, that will buy us more credit than any slick journalese.'

As we talked our coffee was left untouched and grew cold. Jeremy ordered some more 'to pay the rent'.

When he told me what the pay would be, I was hooked. It was a multiple of what I earned at

71

Mayhem, and I could double that if I earned a bonus. We shook hands and then at last sipped our coffee. It was bitter and cold, but, at that moment, it tasted like champagne to me.

★ ★ ★

I walked on air back to the office. Mike was still out, so I sat at my desk, refused to take calls, and tried to think straight. I didn't fully understand this 'truthfulness' business. Other people had accused me of being too literal; of never giving them any slack; of being the most boring man on the planet, because I was constitutionally unable to buy into other people's fantasies about themselves. Mike still complained that I would never write to an agenda: i.e., *his* agenda. If he wanted a hatchet job done, I was not the man to do it. I would always find good alongside the bad, or vice versa.

For some reason, and I thought I glimpsed why, Jeremy wanted this quality, and was prepared to pay for it.

There were no strings attaching me to *Mayhem*. The working conditions were cramped and sometimes, on warm spring days such as this one, they were intolerable. The pay was wretched. I didn't know anybody of my age and education who was paid as little as I was, and if it weren't for an allowance from my parents I wouldn't have survived. My father was recently retired and I felt sure I ought not to be taking any more money from him. Mike was an amusing character to work for but his fuse was growing increasingly short, and I wasn't sure how many more of his intemperate outbursts I could take. The rest of my colleagues were friendly enough but the gap in our political beliefs meant that we rarely mixed out of work beyond the odd drink in the pub.

Churning out pieces for *Mayhem* month after month had acquainted me with some of the shadier recesses of our political world; it had taught me to sniff out the stories lurking there and how to write these, but that wasn't enough. I was learning that to forge a career as a successful political journalist you also needed either to believe in something, or to know what you stood against. In truth, I could lay claim to neither position. Instead, the closer I found myself to the wheels of power, observing political operators at close quarters, the less I believed in any of their promises.

★ ★ ★

The decision to join Jeremy Cutler's business was perhaps as much a leap into the dark as any of my career decisions thus far.

But the money was good. In two months I would earn what it would take me six months to earn at the magazine. I was tired of always being a few pounds away from breaching my overdraft limit with the bank. And it might be more fun. It could hardly be less so.

Without a great deal more thought than that, I made a decision that would change my life. I composed a brief letter of resignation, which I left in an envelope on Mike's desk. I had no idea whether he would cheer when he read it, or whether he would try and persuade me to stay.

He certainly wasn't happy.

'Cur,' he said. 'Capitalist hyena.'

We both laughed, but not very easily.

'Why the hell are you doing this? You might have become quite good at this job if you'd had a bit more patience. You don't learn a trade like ours in five minutes.'

'It's been a bit longer than that, Mike,' I reminded him. 'The job's not going anywhere. And I can't afford to live on what you pay me.'

Mike gave a deep sigh. 'I can't afford to live on what I pay myself,' he said. 'I admit the pay is crap and the working conditions are dreadful. What happened to idealism?'

'I don't know,' I told him. 'I never caught any of that.'

There wasn't much more to be said. Mike couldn't begin to make a counter-offer even though I hadn't told him what my new salary was going to be.

'Your timing might be quite good,' he said. 'I don't know how much longer we can keep going. The circulation is flat-lining and we're being kept afloat by bank guarantees as it is.'

I didn't want to hear any more. I was beginning to feel guilty about my decision, although nowhere near guilty enough to change my mind and give up my new salary. We shook hands, and Mike told me to leave that afternoon.

'Bad for morale to have you dicking around if you've really decided to bugger off. I'll get Sheila to send you a P45 and a cheque at the end of the month.'

There weren't many other goodbyes to make. A handful of my colleagues accepted an invitation to a nearby wine bar, and we bought each other a few rounds, making cordial but non-committal promises to stay in touch. Nobody stayed long and I was back at my flat before nine.

Had I really made such little impression on this place? I wasn't one of their own, that was all. Nobody, least of all myself, knew what my true politics were, in a mazagine that was conspicuously on the far left wing of the Labour movement.

As I walked off down the street, I realised I hadn't thought about what working for Jeremy Cutler would actually be like, or fully considered what my job might involve. But I knew I was bored. Even the most strident editorials *Mayhem* produced were no longer tapping into the same undercurrent of popular rage they once had. The political centre was shifting, and Mike's uncompromising socialist views — which were not exactly cutting edge to begin with — now looked positively antediluvian. Yet I had learned the beginnings of my craft from him, and for that I would forever be grateful. But the world was moving on, and I was anxious not to be left behind.

7

It came as no surprise to hear that *Mayhem* had closed its doors a few months later, in the autumn. Somebody had pulled the plug. I heard Mike got a job at the *Guardian*. After that *Mayhem* was just a footnote to the political miscellanea of the Eighties.

Jeremy Cutler was entirely different to Mike. He was an operator, and he got the new business up and running within three months. We had a smart office in Bloomsbury; a glamorous receptionist and a small but growing team of account executives and writers. Our first few clients were already on board, including our original investors, and I had produced my maiden project for the business: a campaign to explain why banks had been buying stockbroking firms, wealth-management outfits, mortgage lenders and insurers, and why this was a good thing. More than a decade later, when we sold the company, we were still writing about banks, although by then we were trying to explain why they had managed to destroy value on such a momentous scale.

When we started, our main assets were a presentation suite with a glass boardroom table and an overhead projector which only Jeremy knew how to operate. By the time I left we had teams in London, Hong Kong and New York. We dealt in mergers and acquisitions; reputational turnarounds (as in, explaining why one CEO had left very quickly and why the new one was so much better); brand building for our clients; pitching in on one side or the other in a hostile takeover bid; using the new social media to reach an exponentially increasing audience online. It was all very different, and in the end rather alien to me. But I am jumping ahead.

* * *

For some weeks after leaving the magazine, I was utterly submerged in my new job. Jeremy's rather languid appearance concealed an enormous appetite for work. His network of contacts reached back beyond his days in parliamentary lobbying to a spell at the *Financial Times*. His address book was phenomenal. There was practically nobody he did not know, or had difficulty in gaining access to. The business grew very fast as a result.

We began at seven in the morning and it was unusual to leave the office before seven in the evening. Even then, our discussions sometimes spilled out on to the doorstep of the office and then continued for an hour in the pub before, our brains scrambled by everything that had happened during the day, we finally went home.

In my last few days at *Mayhem* the dowdy office seemed permanently clouded not just with cigar smoke, but with a draining inertia as piece after piece failed to land a single blow on its intended targets. By contrast, there was an energy at Cutler that was hard to resist. Multiple clients and accounts, all with differing demands. I had to summon every last reserve of energy I possessed to deal with the endless phone calls and faxes, piles of documents delivered by courier, meetings and presentations. At *Mayhem*, we had held small editorial conferences at the start of each week, then set about following our appointed leads with a steady diligence. There was focus and clarity, but also yawning longueurs, while one waited for calls to be returned and contacts to be exchanged. There was no such luxury in my new office. Half the time one forgot mid-phone call who the client was, and once I even sent a client's draft presentation to their rival.

But it didn't matter. Communication skills were becoming indispensable in every area of corporate life. The simple media-management techniques I had picked up while hanging around politicians for five years (diversion, distraction, going on the offensive) were lapped up hungrily. Even if our clients weren't always telling the truth, what I told them about the science of communication most definitely was. It commanded every ounce of my being, but in return, I was finally in a job where I felt I was actually doing something useful.

★　★　★

In the midst of this chaos I managed to carve out a couple of weekends in which I moved from my rented rooms in Muswell Hill to a ground-floor flat in Holland Park of which I, or at least I and the bank, were the owners. But weeks went by and I failed to make any progress in furnishing it. There was a double mattress in one room with a couple of sheets and a bedspread and a phone and a lamp on the floor beside it. There was a table and two chairs in the kitchen, some glasses and a few plates from Ikea in a glass cupboard. Not to mention an entirely empty fridge. And that was it.

'Jesus,' said Caroline Woodchester as I opened the bedroom door and then quickly shut it again. I hadn't remembered to pull the sheets back in place before leaving for work that morning. 'What the hell is this? Conceptual art?'

'No, I just haven't got a cleaner yet,' I told her. 'I'm not sure I can afford one. Anyway, now you've seen the place you can understand why I'm not offering to entertain you at home.'

We went out into the drizzly November night. I wasn't feeling as wealthy as I had hoped after trebling my salary. My vast mortgage ate up almost every pound I earned, leaving me with not much more spare cash than I had ended the month with at *Mayhem*. But it was all in a good cause. I was an owner, not a renter, and one day house prices would rise again.

All the same I could not afford to take Caroline anywhere smart, and I didn't see why I should. I had received a call out of the blue from Andrew Landford in Moscow. We hadn't spoken since the previous year, and now here he was, sounding concerned that Caroline was lonely, asking me to ring her up and take her out. 'She's feeling a bit low at the moment. You know where she lives, so give her a bell and cheer her up. Can I ask you that favour? Congratulations on your new business venture, by the way. Most unexpected of you, but I am sure you will do very well . . . '

So here we were, facing each other across a rather low, uncomfortable table in a restaurant that couldn't decide whether it was a bistro or a pub. A television sat in one corner with the sound turned down. There weren't many people about. We ordered wine and steak and chips.

'So how are you?' I asked Caroline.

'Exactly as you would expect, I guess. Boyfriend in Siberia, missing presumed in the office — I mean, I literally haven't seen him for nearly a year now. And sculpting turns out to be hard work. I know, who knew, right? Plus staying in Andrew's mansion feels like squatting in a five star hotel . . . I feel totally guilty about not paying any rent, but he says I'm helping him out, housesitting . . . and right now I'm not picking a fight on that one.'

'It's quite a place for someone of our age.'

'Andrew isn't just 'someone of our age', though,' said Caroline, laughing. 'I've met some of the guys he works with. They all have two endgame scenarios. One, they burnout on the job and leave in a bodybag. Or two, they stick it out and become billionaires. Not millionaires, *billionaires*. I don't see Andrew doing either, funnily enough. He'll get rich, for sure, but then he wants to go into politics, before he looks too old and grey for the cameras. He has it all planned out. Believe me, you'll be telling your grandkids that you used to know that Landford guy, and they'll be mighty impressed.'

Our food arrived. I waved a fork around with a rubbery chip on the end of it.

'Do you really think he'll make it as a politician?'

'I reckon. He said he wants to be prime minister by the time he's in his forties. He probably won't get that far, but you never know. I can't figure out if he's capable of becoming a crowd pleaser. There's serious steel in Andrew, and that could put off people who prefer their leaders a little more homespun. But if wanting something bad enough can get you anywhere, then don't go betting against Andrew.'

I enjoyed talking to Caroline. My few encounters with her in the past had made me feel that she, too, could be steely. Or rather, that she had a hard, down-to-earth manner that didn't entirely appeal to me. But tonight, perhaps tempered by Andrew's long absence, she was more relaxed and easier to talk to.

'Well, if Andrew's that good at planning, I hope he told you that Mrs Thatcher was going to resign this morning,' I said.

'Of course! He forecast it months ago: the event that is, not the date. He even put a hundred pounds on John Major as successor. He got terrific odds, you won't be surprised to hear.'

On the television, as if in tune with our words, they began rolling the tape — for the umpteenth time that day — of a tearful Mrs Thatcher leaving Downing Street for the last time and getting into her car for the drive to the Palace.

'Poor dear,' said Caroline.

'Not everyone would agree with you,' I remarked.

'I'm a Yank, I don't take sides over here. I can say 'Poor dear', though. Imagine. All that power and glory gone in a flash. It started when they blew up that hotel. She never got over it, if you ask me. But what a fall from grace.'

The phrase resonated with me: what a fall from grace. I began to revise my opinion of Caroline and found myself studying her across the table. She was an attractive girl, a little shapely and — if one was a purist — rather inclined to cover herself in bits of clay. But that suggested an intensity about her attitude to her art. I wondered if she was any good. She caught my gaze and our eyes met for a second. Then she broke off the eye contact, pushed her steak away and said, 'Do you mind if I light up? I can't eat any more of this.'

'It's tough, isn't it? Bad choice of restaurant. I'll try to do better next time.'

'Next time?'

I didn't say anything. There was a quizzical look on her face as she wreathed us both in cigarette smoke so that my eyes watered. I gave up trying to eat.

'I didn't mean to be presumptuous,' I said apologetically.

'You weren't. It's sweet of you to oblige an old pal like this.' She raised an eyebrow. 'I mean Andrew, of course.'

'Andrew's not really an old 'pal'. We were barely aware of each other's existence at Oxford.

We're new friends, if anything.'

'And I am your third cousin twice removed.'

I was getting tired of that joke.

'That is the furthest thought from my mind,' I said. 'The Fryerne clan gatherings mostly proceed happily without my attendance at them.'

I ordered coffee. We had successfully established that there was almost no possible connection between us and the conversation seemed to be running out of steam. After a moment I put my hand over the saucer containing the bill.

'Well, I'll just deal with this . . . '

As we stood up she said in a serious voice, without the teasing tone that sometimes crept into it, 'That was so nice of you. Thanks.'

'The steak . . . '

'Forget about the steak. I'm not normally Miss Picky with my food. Call me again sometime, if you don't believe me . . . and next time, it's my treat.'

I stood up and took the bill to the bar to settle it. When I turned around again, she had disappeared. I waited for a moment in case she had simply gone to the loo, but when she didn't reappear I went outside to see if she was waiting for me there. She wasn't.

She'd simply gone.

Even allowing for differences in culture, upbringing, views about social conventions, this seemed a bit abrupt. Of course she'd gone. She'd eaten her food, or rather some of it. She'd thanked me. She'd left. What was I looking for? A medal? I'd taken the poor girl out for a rather second-rate dinner in one of the few really unattractive restaurants in this part of London. I'd been my usual boring self, had failed to cheer her up and indeed I hadn't even really tried. Half my mind had been on her and half on a piece I would have to write as soon as I got into the office in a few hours time. I was tired. She was tired. We'd gone our separate ways.

Still, saying goodbye costs nothing and most people find the time to do it.

I decided I'd fulfilled any obligation I had to Andrew and I would leave it at that. This strange American art-student quasi-relative could get through life without further assistance from me.

★　★　★

The invitation to the viewing arrived at the CCC office address. I picked it up and studied it:

Caroline Woodchester
Has pleasure in inviting you to
A Private Viewing of her work at
6:30 p.m. on 10 December 1990
The Wylman Gallery, Clifford Street

I remembered Caroline saying she was struggling with her work, but that hadn't prevented her from putting on a show. I looked in vain for any personal message on the card. There was none. I was about to flip the invitation into the bin when Jeremy twitched it out of my fingers and studied it for a second.

'If you're not going, may I use the invitation?

I'd be quite interested to see what she's been up to. We might see something to buy for the office, show people we aren't just soulless money men.'

I hesitated for a second and then said, 'Let's both go.'

And so it was that, despite my decision not to bother myself any further with Caroline, I found myself walking down Clifford Street one frosty December evening. On the office television that night when Jeremy and I had tuned in to the evening news, there had been pictures of the country shrouded in a blanket of snow. Here in central London we were free of that, but not from the plunge in temperature. When we arrived at the gallery, we found there were already a dozen guests there, stamping their feet and blowing on their fingertips. Then they began fingering the catalogues and peering at the sculptures. These were not sculptures of the sort I had been expecting. As a matter of fact I didn't know what I had been expecting. In my mind's eye I had speculated on large formless shapes of stoneware or bronze, challenging and unsatisfactory. Caroline's work ranged from full-blown sculptures to simpler studio ceramics: porcelain bowls and pots with striking designs and deep glazes reminiscent of amphorae; vases; bowls that looked as if they belonged in a tea-ceremony. The pieces looked timeless and graceful, mostly not more than a foot or two in height. A few larger figures which, with a bit more self-confidence I might have labelled Rodinesque, lurked in corners and doorways as if unsure of their final destination.

Caroline came up to us, followed by a waiter carrying a tray of drinks.

'How sweet of you to come,' she said. 'So long since we last met.' Jeremy smiled and nodded. Turning to me she added, 'You too, Charles. Come find me before you go if you can. I'd love a moment of your time.'

'Yes, of course,' I said, for some unaccountable reason cross with myself and with her. More visitors were arriving and Caroline went off to welcome them. Jeremy and I studied the work. I was then much more ignorant of sculpture and ceramics than I am now, but even I could tell this work was rather good. The shapes and forms of the pots and the occasional figurine were elegant and subtle. The glazes were deep brown or blue, overlaying designs that looked as if they represented thousands of peacock eyes, or else an infinity of small wavelets breaking on a beach. Jeremy decided to buy one of the larger pieces, not a pot but a ceramic stone figure reclining on a black plinth.

'That would look rather good in the reception area,' said Jeremy. Without waiting for an answer he went off to find the gallery owner and start haggling over the price. The last thing I wanted was to have Caroline find me trying to shave a few pounds off her already no doubt slender profit — I knew a gallery in this part of London would take an enormous cut — so I left him to it. The outcome must have been successful, for a few minutes later a red spot had appeared on the plinth.

'Right. I've dealt,' said Jeremy, reappearing at

my elbow. 'It's getting rather hot and noisy in here. I think I'll push on. What about you?'

I said I'd stay a little while longer and Jeremy left, to be replaced by Maldwyn Christie who had just arrived.

'Did you see any of the coverage of my speech in the House last night?' he asked, not bothering with a more formal greeting. I was quite surprised to see him there, but then remembered that Maldwyn had also been picked as a possible member of Andrew's think tank.

'No.'

'You are always, by a very long chalk, the least rewarding member of my fan club. I talked about how ridiculous it was that a few inches of snow should bring the whole country to a standstill. I was rather funny about it. Even Neil Kinnock cracked a smile.'

'I don't doubt you had them rolling in the aisles.'

'Anyway, it's rather pointless talking to you because now you aren't at *Mayhem* you don't hear any decent gossip. Not that they ever let you in on any of their real secrets. They always had you down as a potential mole.'

'Really?'

'Mike did. He was just waiting for you to reveal yourself.'

'Poor Mike. I must have been such a disappointment to him.'

I disliked being reminded of what an outsider I had been, but it was true.

'What's it like, working with the extremely tough Mr Cutler?'

'Good. We get on. Why do you call him tough?'

'I've seen him operate,' said Maldwyn. 'He brought down more than one aspiring politico when he was at the *FT*. Fortunately he never had me in his sights.'

'Perhaps you weren't important enough?'

Maldwyn took off his spectacles and rubbed them with his tie.

'God, it's noisy in here,' he complained, placing his glasses back on his nose. 'For a moment there I thought I heard you say I wasn't important enough. I must have been mistaken because nowadays, Mr Fryerne, I am very, very important. There's even talk — although being you, you either haven't heard or don't care — of me becoming a junior minister one of these days. So, watch out. Now, enough about me. We won't talk about you, because you are far too reticent and shy. Instead, let's have a look at your dear cousin's work. From where I am standing, it looks a good deal better than I imagined.'

We started to circulate around the room once more. I followed in Maldwyn's slipstream as he chattered away. 'She is really quite good. I don't know what I was expecting — an installation; video clips; papier mâché images of Morecambe and Wise. Not many people doing really good work in porcelain these days . . . so unfashionable and yet so nice . . . '

Maldwyn didn't appear to need any comment or response. As I trailed behind him, I was again struck by the levels of proficiency Caroline had attained. Those glazes would be difficult to

88

reproduce. I wondered how much she had had to throw away when the firings didn't work. Caroline was with us again now.

'Darling,' said Maldwyn, 'Mwah! Mwah!' He kissed her in noisy self-parody on each cheek.

'Do you think everyone will decide it's time to go soon?' she asked me with a touch of pathos in her voice. 'I can't wait to leave.'

'Tell them to stop serving drinks,' I suggested. 'That usually does the trick.'

'A bit brutal,' said Maldwyn, 'but it will work. You've sold quite a few pieces tonight anyway. I should have a word with the owner — he's really the man picking up the tab tonight, although in the end, dear Caroline, it will come out of your pocket. And therefore,' he said, snatching a flute from a nearby waiter. 'I shall have one more glass of this rather disgusting champagne and then go.'

Caroline went across to talk to the owner, a small bearded man with the sleek features of an otter.

Maldwyn had used the opportunity of the fresh drink to abandon me and intrude upon another small group, amongst whom I recognised the face of a well-known member of the Shadow Cabinet. I decided to leave him to his networking and re-examine Caroline's ceramics. It was odd. The fragile formality of the small porcelain bowls, the subtlety of the colours, the intricacy of the wavy designs: all these had come from within her and therefore were, in some way, the essence of her. I had yet to grasp how art can distance itself from its creator: how someone like F. Scott Fitzgerald, absolutely broke and

89

drinking hard, could produce a work as lyrical as *Tender is the Night*, writing to stay alive and to pay for his wife's sanatorium expenses. These things I learned, in time. Just now I marvelled only that I had not foreseen Caroline's art in Caroline.

Her work invited me to re-evaluate her, to forget the awkwardness of her social manners. But then, it was just as likely that any awkwardness in our relationship was because of me. I knew that I was ignorant of much of what passes for social graces in ordinary life; I was tactless and distracted, living in my head too much, stepping from one cloud to another but overlooking the demands of life outside my work. I was working for probably the one person in London and in the one job where this detachment was acceptable, even valued. No, I reasoned, if there was anything gauche or untoward in Caroline's behaviour then it was a reflection of mine towards her. At this moment she returned.

'Hi,' she said brightly. 'All done. We'll close up in ten. Do you want to come out afterwards with Josh' — she indicated the owner — 'and me? I'm not sure where yet, maybe a few drinks, something to eat.' She glanced at the hangers-on still drifting round the gallery. 'It looks like there's going to be quite a crowd of us.'

The invitation was sufficiently uninviting. We all know that kind of evening. You begin by arguing for about twenty minutes about which restaurant to go to and when you get there it is full. You find somewhere else. It takes about twenty minutes for two of the party to catch up because they couldn't get a taxi. By now, nobody is in the least bit hungry and all anyone wants is a drink, followed by bed, with luck on one's own. But then the business of choosing food nobody wants takes another half an hour and by the time it finally arrives you have begun to wish you were dead.

I said no.

'Suit yourself,' she said, taking out a cigarette in defiance of the no smoking signs everywhere. 'Just thought I'd ask.'

'It was nice of you. You said earlier you wanted a word?'

'Did I?' she said vaguely, exhaling smoke all around me. 'I can't remember now. It will come to me later, but then you won't be there and I'll forget again. Sure you won't come?'

'Quite sure. Caroline . . .'

'What?' she asked as my sentence trailed away. She sounded fierce, as if I had offered her a present and then taken it away.

'I like your art . . . I like what you're doing. I am the last person in the world to judge, but I think it is really good.'

She looked at me in surprise.

'Why, thank you, Charles. I'll take that as a compliment.'

'Take it as the truth,' I said.

Then I left.

8

Visits to my parents had changed in character. Once I had considered them as a sailor might view a return to a much loved and well-remembered harbour. Now my parents had taken on the aspect of remote islands in a distant sea.

The journey to Uxbridge was not so daunting in itself. Their house stood at the corner of two identical-looking avenues of villas.

On the outside it presented a mixture of sooty brick and dark red paintwork. Some of the windows had been done in coloured glass: roundels set with figurines, perhaps saints. Inside, the house appeared to be larger than it had looked from the outside. Entering through the front door, one arrived in a cavernous hall, with a staircase leading up into gloomy silence.

Usually I was intercepted by my father before I could penetrate any further. He would appear in the doorway of his day room. He was always carefully dressed, in a cardigan, brown corduroys, shirt and tie. His other accessory was a rumpled copy of the *Daily Telegraph*, which he clutched, as if fearful that someone would remove it if he let go for longer than a second. He pretended to look enormously surprised at my appearance, as if either the day or the appointed hour of my arrival had been omitted from his diary. His first words were — nearly always — 'Good Heavens! Is it that time already?' before he beckoned me testily inwards, as if further delays or reluctance on my part would ruin the entire day. Then I would seat myself opposite him, and we would strive to obtain information from each other with very limited success.

Communication with my father had become difficult; with my mother it was all but impossible. She was relatively young, not yet seventy, but now sat shrouded in silence. Her very features seemed to melt as Alzheimer's took hold. Her firm mouth had become slack, with snail tracks of saliva glistening down one side. Her eyes were cloudy, not because of cataracts but because an habitual lack of focus made it impossible to know at whom or what she was looking.

There were carers to help, and my father angrily rebuffed suggestions that he could not cope. As a result most of my visits were spent in painful denial: denial by my father that his wife would not 'get better'; denial by me that I was fast losing any sense of connection with my own parents.

It hurt a bit. I remembered too well the happy summers we had spent sailing on, or walking above, Lake Geneva. Everything up to the point where we finally left Lausanne for the delights of west Uxbridge was clear and sharp in my memory. After that, it had all gone downhill. In the end my father had well and truly been 'put out to grass', as he had feared. He was given almost nothing to do and after a year or two he had finally taken voluntary redundancy, which I suppose had been his employer's plan all along. I believe he had once been considered as rather good at his job. Then suddenly he had found himself transplanted from a busy and useful existence in Switzerland, from the sunny shores of a Swiss lake, from Swiss coffee and French cooking, to this: a house that crushed the spirit even on a sunny day. The place stank of over-cooked food and unwashed clothes and a general airlessness I found increasingly difficult to tolerate.

* * *

At the beginning of 1991 my mother died, quite unexpectedly. There was no crisis: only dissolution. The carers went, my father having been assessed as physically and mentally fit enough to live on his own. At first I made an effort to be with him nearly every weekend. I don't think he appreciated my company, however. It became obvious to me, if not to him, that he was discarding any ties that bound him to life. At first I just went home anyway. But with each fresh visit I noticed further signs of deterioration in the house, and in my father, as if they were competing to see who could collapse first. Doors warped and got stuck; lights blew out all over the house and I had to keep replacing the bulbs. Supplies of coal and wood ran out because my father forgot to re-order them. I used to bring carrier bags of food with me to keep his fridge stocked; but as I threw out an almost identical quantity of spoiled or wasted food, I realised there was little I could do to make him actually eat anything when I wasn't with him. When my mother went, some vital component inside my father broke, and now the whole circuit was shutting down.

*　*　*

From June that year I became increasingly immersed in the new business. It became harder and harder to find time for anything or anyone else, to the point that I scarcely saw my friends, never mind went down to Uxbridge. So I told myself, and it was probably true. The awful and greater truth was that my father didn't really want to see me: he just wanted to curl up and die, without interruption or distraction. It is only an hour at most from my flat to his house, but it might as well have been halfway to the moon. The health visitors and carers started coming again, and my father was cocooned in the local support network. Each time I put off seeing him, or allowed him to talk me out of a proposed visit, I used to tell myself, 'I can go next week. After all, it isn't that far.'

Then, one quiet morning just over a week before Christmas, as I was wrapping a couple of pullovers for him — he had been complaining about the cold even with the central heating on — the distance became further than a few stops on the Underground. It became immeasurably further as the phone rang. I couldn't imagine who would be calling me at that time if it were not an emergency and therefore something to do with Dad. When I put the phone down the distance between my father and me was complete. I was an orphan.

I don't think I wept then; a few dry tears more like retching. I knelt on the floor amongst the pullovers and put my head in my hands. It didn't help. In recent years we hadn't been a particularly close family and now we weren't a family at all.

★ ★ ★

As I made my way over to Uxbridge that morning, I realised that I was now the Charles Fryerne of Fryerne Court. Another clan gathering; for a moment I didn't think I could go through with it. I could scarcely even contemplate the funeral. But I knew I had to do something. Something equivalent to the ceremony that had taken place on my Uncle Roland's death had been going on for several hundred years, if family tradition were to be believed. Messages — sometimes rather peremptory — started to arrive on my answerphone: 'Do try and let us know what the plans are for your father's memorial — some of us have rather busy lives and it would be nice to get something in the diary' — this from a rather bossy aunt on my mother's side.

For the first couple of days I tried to ignore it all in the hope that this mysterious clan feeling that rippled through the Fryerne family ranks like a wind through long grass would abate itself.

Quite the opposite occurred: I continued to receive more phone calls and even cards and letters from the Fryerne diaspora, urging me to set a date. Even then I don't know if I would have found the courage to do something if it hadn't been for Caroline. She rang my flat that Saturday morning saying she would be around in ten minutes, then hung up before I could think of an excuse to put her off.

She was with me in an instant, clutching a large Filofax and a box file in her arms. She wore a striped pullover and jeans and leather boots; only just enough protective layers for an icy blue December morning.

Within a few moments we were both sitting at the kitchen table, making lists. The Filofax turned out to be Cousin Brad's. He had acted as standard bearer for the American branch of the family, while the box file contained guest lists from Uncle Roland's memorial. I went out to buy a bottle of wine and some sandwiches and fuelled by these, we produced a tolerable invitation list by late afternoon.

'Now, where?' I asked.

'That adorable little St. Mary's-Without church, where we first met. Your famous Fryerne memorials have always been held there, so I'm told. Brad's got the details of the priest in his Filofax. Let's call him.'

Getting a date in the vicar's diary wasn't possible before Christmas, so we aimed for mid-January.

By the time we had completed all this, including a selection of lessons and readings, we were both exhausted. The wine was all but gone: I poured out just enough to wet the bottom of our glasses and then raised my own:

'To a good job well done — I couldn't possibly have done it without your help. I feel enormously relieved.'

'My pleasure. I never imagined I'd become quite so involved in your crazy old family rituals, but now it's done.

'You'll come, of course?'

'Yes, I'll come.'

Without thinking, I picked up her hand and then squeezed it.

'Thank you.'

For a moment her hand lay in mine: a good, strong hand with blunt fingers and short fingernails. A practical hand; an artist's hand. Then she withdrew it, not abruptly but with decision, as if a voice were whispering, 'This hand is reserved for Andrew, so this is where I draw the line.'

The moment of awkwardness, if it had been there at all, passed. A few minutes later Caroline left, and I didn't see her again until the day of the service.

9

Caroline went back to New York for Christmas. I spent a gloomy morning escorting my father through the due processes of the Kensal Green Crematorium, returning home with the ashes which, unaccountably, I put in the cupboard under the stairs — thus causing a huge panic when the day of the memorial came around and I couldn't remember where I had left them.

I had a low-key Christmas, most of the friends I'd managed to keep up with fleeing the city for family homes in the country or house parties with friends abroad. I saw Maldwyn for a drink. Jeremy invited me to a family lunch on Christmas Day, which I refused. It was enormously kind of him, because he saw me all day every day at the office and I think he was quite relieved when I said I just wanted to spend a couple of days with my feet up.

And that was what I did. I sat and watched endless old films sipping from a glass of white wine and occasionally heating up some ready-made mince pies and other assorted snacks. As a matter of fact I felt so tired I could hardly speak or move. The last few months had been more strenuous than I had realised, both mentally and physically, and it was wonderful to do nothing, to sit with an empty mind gazing at the flickering screen.

Not entirely empty, however. From time to

time I found myself thinking about Caroline. Andrew had been away in Moscow making his billions for well over a year now. He hadn't even come back to see her for Christmas. I began to wonder exactly what it was that she saw in him.

As far as Andrew was concerned I received the occasional call with odd bits of news. He rang me from Moscow on Boxing Day to say he'd just heard about my father from Caroline and sent his condolences. After quickly disposing of that subject he went on to give me some of his own news: cautiously phrased, I thought, Andrew clearly presuming his phone calls might be overheard by a wider audience than the pair of us. He seemed to be enjoying himself in what sounded like a dangerous place for a Westerner to be living at the time, although the expatriate community was growing fast in anticipation of the implosion of the Soviet Union, and the possibility that someone might leave the keys in the door to the sweet shop. Not only the keys to the sweet shop, but the oil and gas and aluminium and nickel shop. There was much debate about 'shock therapy' being administered to the Russian economy, the need for a rapid transition to a Western model: in other words a free-for-all. It didn't take much imagination to hear the sound of gunfire once that all kicked off. I admired Andrew for hanging on in such a fraught environment. I wouldn't want to be there myself. I wondered what his communications with Caroline were like, and how she was surviving on a fairly minimal diet of affection and shared moments.

Was I interested in her myself? I supposed I must have been, because otherwise why did I keep thinking about her — despite the fact I told myself she was not my type. But what was my type? Was there such a thing as 'type' and did the idea have any meaning? After all, I was just as much a 'type' as anyone else. I was often tactless, introspective: the patina of Englishness achieved at university overlaying a rather more complex upbringing as an expat child in New York and Lausanne. Whose type was I? I wondered. Either I liked Caroline (and she liked me) or I didn't. The fact I even had to ask myself the question was revealing. I just wasn't sure. There were times when I thought she loathed me; others when she adopted that quizzical look, as if she saw before her, not me, but a lump of clay that could be kneaded into a more acceptable form.

And did I like her? There was not the slightest tickle of sexual attraction between us — as far as I could tell. But I was usually rather slow when it came to that side of relationships. Indeed the few girls I had slept with had all been surprises — I was surprised that they would contemplate such an act with me and then even more surprised when it turned out they had been waiting for me to make a move. Apart from that one serious relationship at university, my liaisons had never lasted, and I hadn't even managed a fling since joining Cutler.

In many ways, I simply hadn't woken up. Some people remain in a form of sleepy trance for their entire lives. A few awaken, or are awakened by events outside their control. A small number — perhaps Andrew Landford was one — are awake from early on and realise that, in the kingdom of the half-asleep, the truly conscious person can carve himself an empire.

I told myself that, in any case, Caroline was Andrew's long-term partner. It was only a matter of time before he proposed, surely. The offer of a rent-free home while he was away in Moscow was a honey trap: difficult to refuse at the time, it would bind Caroline to Andrew long enough to allow him to recommence his wooing on his return. I didn't want to do anything that smacked of taking advantage of Andrew's absence, either. I thought that would make me look rather cheap, and I didn't want to put myself in that position.

★ ★ ★

January went on in the same manner as December had ended. A grey wind howled out of the north. My blood ran thick and slow. Everything seemed an effort. Even going to the office, which before had been as addictive as a drug, failed to excite me now.

The day of the memorial came at last. It was another bitter day, with half-formed flakes of snow swirling in the wind then settling for a moment on coats and umbrellas or dissolving into pinpricks of icy water on one's hands and face. Caroline and I took a taxi from the station to St Mary's-Without and went inside to greet the vicar. An attempt had been made to heat the church with two small blow-heaters reinforcing the ancient-looking central heating pipes that ran the length of the church. It was still too cold to take one's coat off, and our discussions were brief and businesslike. Perhaps because of the discouraging weather, the turnout was not especially good. There seemed to be far fewer people than at Roland's send-off, and the mood was more sombre. My father, I realised, had cut himself off from more than just me. To many of those attending it must have seemed as if he had been dead for years.

The vicar trotted through the service as fast as he decently could and the congregation dispersed. The idea was to have a buffet lunch at the Fryerne Arms, and for me to make a brief speech. Where were those notes? I patted my pockets but couldn't immediately locate them. By then we had arrived at the pub. A row of fairy lights draped across the entrance was blinking nervously. Only a few cars had turned up. I suspected that some of the family felt they had done all they needed to by turning up at the church and had chosen to pass on the cold buffet I had thoughtfully organised for a sub-zero afternoon. Brad had given Caroline and me a lift from the church. When we got into the car, which had a driver, Brad had levered himself around in the passenger seat and extended a huge hand to me. I grasped it and then found he wouldn't let go.

'Your father was one helluva guy, Charles. I miss him. We all miss him.'

'Thank you,' I said faintly. The circulation was

beginning to go in my right hand but still he clung on.

'It's been an honour to act as marshal to the American side of the family. We value our history, Charles. We surely do. This is one special relationship that will remain intact, as it has done over many, many years.'

Inside the pub a fake gas fire with imitation logs burned merrily in the hearth, giving out no heat whatsoever. A dispirited looking waitress began handing out drinks. Nearly everyone went for the orange juice rather than anything alcoholic. When she had done this she returned with a gilt silver tray on which sat a few sandwiches surrounded by wilted lettuce and crisps. It wasn't what I'd arranged but as there were at best a dozen of us in the room, ordering yet more food seemed pointless. Brad introduced me to an elderly gentleman called Alan Fryerne-Smith. His was a face distantly recalled from earlier gatherings. I couldn't remember whether I had last seen him at Roland's memorial. He was tall and thin and of military bearing; a solicitor from a country town in Dorset.

'I was just saying to Charles here,' said Brad, 'that his father was a damned fine fellow.'

'Oh yes, very much so. You won't find many like your father on the average London bus, Charles. He was a different kettle of fish altogether. A very special sort of chap. I forget what it was that he did. Was he in the dry-cleaning business?'

I explained that my father had worked for a

global pharmaceuticals company.

'Exactly,' replied Alan Fryerne-Smith. 'I knew it was something of the sort. A very fine chap. We'll miss him.'

Brad, who had looked somewhat winded when his friend suggested my father had been a dry-cleaning executive, now broke in and said:

'But the person who'll miss him most will be you, of course.'

'Yes, I do miss him,' I agreed.

'You must miss him very, very much.'

'Exactly,' said Alan Fryerne-Smith. 'Very, very much.'

At this moment Caroline elbowed me sharply in the ribs and said to Brad sweetly, 'Do you mind if I borrow Charles for a moment?'

'Of course. I'm not sure he's ours to lend, but you may borrow him.' Brad laughed explosively and we withdrew to a table a few feet away.

'If you don't make your speech in the next thirty seconds I shall kill myself,' she said in a low Voice. 'I'm not sure I can take any more of this.'

'What? Me? Now?'

'Yes, goddammit.'

Without waiting for a reply she picked up a knife and dinged an empty wine glass. What little conversation there was faded into mutterings and then stopped.

I had rehearsed my speech briefly and consigned it to a few cards on which I had written out the main bullet points, e.g.:

• Long history of family reaching back into the

105

late Mediaeval period
- Astonishing loyalty and cohesiveness of the Fryerne family over hundreds of years
- No house, but the tradition of Fryerne Court preserved, which is the thing of greatest value . . . and no tax to pay on tradition yet, thank God (wait for laughter)
- Now honoured to become the Fryerne of Fryerne Court and hope I can bring what credit I can to the title and tradition etc. etc.

But in the panic that morning when I was looking for my father's ashes — which were to sit at the foot of the altar during the memorial service — I had left the notes on the kitchen table. Perhaps it was just as well. By now the dozen or so people in the room were looking at me expectantly. I began to speak without the least idea of what I would say next.

'I feel far too young to have become the bearer of the title that my father held. Today we are honouring the man who held the title as much as the title itself. My father was a good hard-working man whose job was taken away from him. Personally I think that's what finished him off at such a relatively young age — he was only 71 this year — that, and the premature death of his beloved wife, and my mother, Emily. So, he has left us too soon and I for one regret that I never really had the time to get to know him properly in his retirement. I feel somehow that he and I have been robbed of each other's company — that we might reasonably have expected to have another ten or fifteen years to enjoy together. But that was not to be. So now we must recall why we are here: I would like to propose a toast to my father, and to all of you who have taken so much trouble to be here. To my father Charles Fryerne and to all of us, the Fryernes of Fryerne Court!'

All this gushed from me as effortlessly as if I had written it down. Where it came from, I do not know. But after all, I am in the communications business and I must have learned something over the years.

'When did you make that up? asked Caroline a few minutes later.

'I don't know. I forgot the notes I had prepared. I think it helped that you pushed me in at the deep end.'

'You really are full of surprises, Charlie boy. I nearly wept when you talked about your dad. Brad was gushing tears. Gushing.'

One by one the guests finished their orange juice and crisps and took their leave. I felt slightly ashamed that I hadn't been more generous but perhaps on a day such as this, it didn't really matter. Thin pickings after the feast at my Uncle Roland's memorial, though. Brad left issuing many, many invitations 'to come visit with him' in New York. Then barely forty minutes after we had arrived, the dining room was empty of all but Caroline and myself.

'What you and I need,' I said to her, 'is a proper drink.'

I called the waitress over and ordered a bottle of the nicest looking Bordeaux on the list, which wasn't saying much.

'This is where we first met, isn't it?' I said to Caroline, handing her a glass.

'Was it? I don't recall. Oh yes, I do though . . . '

I was not at all sure she did not blush and I couldn't resist reminding her.

'You offered to take me upstairs to have sex, right in front of my mother. I mean you spoke to me in front of my mother. The other event was to be a shade more discreet.'

'I didn't, did I?'

Now there was no doubt that she was blushing, all the way to the roots of her hair. We caught each other's eye and then looked away again. I wished I hadn't raised the subject. At the same moment I became aware for the first time since that long ago day, of a surge of desire for her. I remembered all the dreams I'd had in the months immediately following that first meeting, when I dreamed that we had in fact gone upstairs together in that pub; that we had in fact found an unlocked bedroom, where she had sat on the bed and patted the space beside her. I still remembered the words she had spoken, only ever in my dreams and never in real life:

'Now then, Charles. Here's what we do . . . '

The dream had always ended there and had faded over time.

I didn't dare look at Caroline or touch her for fear of giving myself away. Still blushing, she managed to say:

'That was wicked of me, Charles. What a tease I was. I take it you've forgiven me?'

'There was nothing to forgive. You made me

feel rather wonderful for a moment, I do remember. I couldn't believe someone like you would take any interest in a prissy, pompous youth like me.'

'You sure were pompous. I remember that, all right. That's probably why I behaved the way I did. But still. What happened next?'

'You went outside to smoke a cigarette, and my father made his speech. It was much better than the one I just made. Certainly longer. And you left, or at any rate I didn't see you again until you turned up that day in Andrew's house.' I looked very hard at my wine, trying not to give anything away. 'You must miss him.'

Caroline's shoulders sank. 'You could say that. He's been away so long I don't really know what I'm missing. We speak once a week, or at least we try to, his schedule permitting . . . And then all he can talk about is his precious job. Double-crossing Russians, lawyers on the make, caviar and lobster filled banquets in old haunts once reserved for the KGB . . . I try to sound interested.' She took a large gulp of her drink. 'Don't get me wrong, he's sweet enough. He sent me some sensational jewellery on my birthday, and he's always telling me how he's going to set me up with an art dealer in Moscow . . . apparently the art market is really taking off there now as well, but . . . well, when push comes to shove, the guy's just never around. And that's hard.'

I didn't know what to say, and we sat there in stunned silence for a moment. In a determined effort to heave the conversation on to a fresh

109

track, Caroline asked me, 'Anyhow. That guy, Alan Fryerne-Whatever, he was something else, wasn't he?'

'The weirder fringe of the Fryerne clan . . . Caroline, why do you think all these people come here every time someone dies or gets married or christened? The same people don't always show up, but at all the gatherings I have been to there have been at least forty or fifty people. Some of them are from just down the road in Petersfield or Alton. But some of them rock up from South Island in New Zealand, or the Upper West Side in New York. They spend thousands getting here. It's like a herd of elephants gathering from all over the plains at the ancestral burial grounds. What makes us all do it?'

She was silent for a moment, thinking.

'I honestly have no idea. Maybe it's like a chain letter. People feel they have to pass it on and keep the chain unbroken, or there will be seven years bad luck.'

'No . . . that doesn't explain it to me,' I replied after a moment.

We sat in the quiet dining room. The waitress had disappeared without bothering to tidy up and we sat amongst a litter of plates bearing half-eaten sandwiches, unfinished glasses of orange juice and club soda. The reason for the continued existence of a pub as dreary as this was as much a mystery as the rituals of the Fryerne family. And yet, in that strange place, I saw for the first time the beginnings of intimacy between Caroline and me. Until now there had always been a barrier between us: a combination of her defensiveness and my own diffidence. That had disappeared now. I felt more at my ease talking to her than I had done with anyone for a very long time.

'My own theory,' I said after a moment, 'is that we are a group of very ordinary people. Not a group in the sense that we have something in common, as if we were all members of the same religious sect or political party. But we do have one thing in common: we all believe we are the dispossessed. The American Fryernes and the New Zealand Fryernes use our name as a link to the old country because for whatever reason they have not rooted well where they are. The English Fryernes cling to a title that was invented by themselves, for themselves, as a way of creating an identity — they received land from Henry Tudor but no other form of recognition, so they've had to invent one. They were on the cusp of glorious things, but whatever our ancestor did, it was only quite good and not good enough. But why we have kept going since the house was sold and pulled down, I don't know.'

'I kinda like that,' said Caroline. 'The dispossessed . . . I'm not sure that we ever owned very much we could be dispossessed of, but hey, that'll do for me.'

I poured some more wine for us both.

'Maybe nobody dares to break the chain. That part might be right. There aren't many younger people coming to these things, I've noticed. I don't go often myself. Maybe it will just peter out.'

111

'I won't weep too many tears if it does. But, you now — you're the official head of the family. It's up to you to give us our battle plan, restore our global dominance.'

She was mocking me again, but not unkindly. We sat for a while longer, until the wine was gone, and then summoned a taxi to take us to the station.

On the train we sat side by side at a table opposite an old lady, who gently removed herself at the next stop. The dark grey afternoon was turning to evening, enfolding itself around us while occasional sleet showers rattled against the windows. The temptation to close my eyes was overwhelming. Caroline fell asleep first, her head reclined on my shoulder. Shifting to get comfortable I put my arm around her and the two of us dozed until the bright lights of London and the robotic cries of 'Mind the Doors' awoke us. I was the first to fully awaken and disengaged myself so as not to embarrass her, but an eye opened and she smiled sleepily.

'That wine certainly did the trick. I'm sorry. Does your shoulder have any feeling left in it?'

'I've been asleep until this very minute.'

She nodded and, yawning, stretched herself like a cat.

'Will I see you soon?' I asked her.

'I guess so. If you want to, that is.'

'Oh, I want to. I'll call you.'

We said our goodbyes at Waterloo. That night, for the first time in many years, I had the dream again: I was following a girl up the staircase that led from the dining room at the Fryerne Arms to

112

an upper landing. There we found a bedroom door unlocked. The room was clean, the bed made up. Caroline sat down on the bed and then looked up at me with bright, teasing eyes.

'Sit down beside me, Charles, and I'll show you what we do.'

The words were somehow different but even in my sleep I was aware that the gates of dreamland had opened again and welcomed me into the land beyond.

10

The first I heard about it was a call from Caroline, cancelling an arrangement we had made to go and see a film together.

'I can't make it,' she explained. Over the phone her voice, normally cool and collected, sounded a little breathless. 'Andrew is coming back from Moscow today.'

'Today!'

I don't know why I should have been so surprised. I struggled to keep the disappointment from my voice, but Caroline picked it up.

'He just comes and goes as he pleases,' she said. 'I'm going to have to spend the next few hours getting his palace in perfect condition. He lands at Heathrow tonight.'

'You'll be very pleased to see him again,' I said. I intended no sarcasm or bitterness: why should I? But again she picked up a note in my voice I hadn't even heard myself.

'Don't be difficult,' she said. 'Think what it's like for me.'

We hung up, making no alternative plan. From now on, or for however long Andrew planned to be in London, I would only see Caroline if it suited Andrew.

* * *

The next few days were surprisingly painful.

114

Caroline was not my lover, or my girlfriend. She was barely even my friend. And yet now that I couldn't see her — at least not without Andrew, because anything else was unthinkable — I somehow felt a little denuded and empty. I found I actively missed the warm sound of her voice; the quick, interrogative flash of her eyes as she picked me up on some remark I had made. I realised I missed her. And yet she and Andrew were living together only a few streets away. I could go around tonight, now, and it wouldn't cause any consternation. But for some reason, I just didn't want to see them together. I presumed they would also have gone back to sharing a bed and suddenly the thought of that upset me more than it ought. The whole thing was ridiculous.

I did my best to forget about them and for a few weeks was able to immerse myself in work. But even there I was challenged one morning by the arrival of the sculpture we had bought before Christmas at Caroline's exhibition: a reclining figure in ceramic stone, which sat upon a polished granite plinth.

'It fits the space well, doesn't it?' said Jeremy, who had come into reception behind me.

'Yes. Good choice.'

'She's a talented girl, your friend.'

This felt like dangerous ground, and I was keen to steer us away from it as quickly as possible. 'She's been helping out with a lot of family stuff since my father died.'

'Well, you'll be seeing less of her now, I would have thought. Andrew's back,' said Jeremy. 'But you probably knew that anyway. I spoke to him on the phone. He sounds pretty pleased with life.'

* * *

A couple of days later Andrew phoned me to invite me to dinner. He sounded exactly as Jeremy had suggested, very satisfied with his lot.

'How are you?' I asked, with as much enthusiasm as I could muster.

'Never better. Things are a bit hairy in Moscow, though. Lots of tanks and soldiers all over the place. There's been talk of a coup against Yeltsin by the old guard. He's rushing through his economic programme at some speed and not everybody is quite as keen as he is.'

'How long are you over here for? Or is it a permanent move?'

'Come to dinner on Saturday night and I'll tell you all about it. We've a few friends coming. Jeremy and his wife will be there, so that's two familiar faces.'

I couldn't really refuse.

* * *

Saturday night came and I made my way to Andrew's house. The curtains were open and I could see people in the drawing room, picking at canapés laid out on top of the grand piano. The maid, who had disappeared during Andrew's absence abroad, was now re-established as part

116

of the household and met me at the door to take my coat.

Andrew seemed unchanged: tall, good-looking in a cold sort of way, and quite uninterested in small talk. He handed me a glass of champagne without asking me what I wanted and said, 'By the way, before it goes out of my mind, thank you for keeping an eye on Caroline while I've been away. She appreciated it. As did I.'

'It was a pleasure,' I mumbled.

'Sorry about your dad.'

'Caroline was a great help with all of that.'

Perhaps there was a flicker in my eyes, or some unwanted colour in my cheek, but Andrew changed the subject abruptly.

'Of course the great thing about Yeltsin is that he's completely uninhibited. He's going to change Russia, and he doesn't care who or what gets in his way. He'll just steam-roller right over them. Things might get a bit messy.'

'Is that why you've come back?'

'Partly. The threat level has gone up slightly and my partners wanted a briefing. I'll probably be here for around six weeks and then see if it's OK to go back.'

He handed me on to somebody and went to greet his next guest. I looked for Caroline but she wasn't in the room. Then, suddenly, she was, wearing a dark blue evening dress, much smarter than the rest of us who were all decked out in the usual miscellany that is known, for some mysterious reason, as 'smart casual'. For this reason, if no other, she now looked like an attractive interloper, an unknown but intriguing addition to the party. She went around the room saying hello to people. When she came to me she gave me a cool smile, the smile she used to give me when we first met. It was as if the growing intimacy of our last few meetings had never existed. Perhaps it had all been my own imagination? How could this stranger be the same Caroline whose head had rested on my shoulder as we sat in the train to London? We were standing in a space of our own, for a moment, as members of the party began to collect around Andrew who was telling some anecdote about Moscow. Without the least forethought I said to Caroline, 'I miss you. I don't like seeing you back with Andrew.'

She went white, then red. Her eyes began to brim.

'How could you?' she whispered fiercely. 'You bastard. At my own dinner party?'

Then she was gone, flicking away a tear with an unobtrusive gesture that I think only I noticed. I felt as if I had been in a car crash. My legs were so wobbly I had to pull up a chair and sit down for a second.

I really don't remember much about the rest of that party. We moved into the dining room and I must have been hell to sit next to. I doubt I spoke a coherent sentence all night. I left as early as I could, pleading some excuse about a headache. Andrew came to the door with me.

'We've hardly said a word all evening,' he complained. 'We must have a proper chat sometime.'

'I'm sorry I was in such bad form,' I

apologised. 'I think a couple of aspirin will sort me out, but yes, let's speak soon.'

Caroline didn't say goodbye.

* * *

I was to see Andrew again much sooner than I had expected, in our own boardroom. Jeremy had buzzed to ask me to come through without offering any further explanation.

'Andrew!' I said, in surprise. For a moment I wondered if guilt was written in every line of my face, but it couldn't have been because he shook my hand warmly.

'I hope you're feeling better.'

'Absolutely.'

Jeremy handed coffee around.

'Andrew might want us to do some background stuff on the new Russia, to try and explain what his bank is doing there.'

'It's certainly not there for the fun of it,' said Andrew. Now that we were in daylight I could see what I had not noticed before: lines of strain around his eyes and mouth, a dusting of grey along the edges of his neatly trimmed black hair.

'How bad is it?' I asked.

'Oh, it's perfectly OK ninety per cent of the time. Then you hear of someone working for a law firm or another bank who's had a run in with the FSB. Tossed out of the country at five minutes' notice. Some of the locals have been beaten — nobody who works for us, I might add. It makes you wonder just how long it can go on without some kind of catastrophe. Yeltsin is

119

parcelling up the economy and handing out chunks of it to crony investors and it's not a popular policy if you're not on the inside track.'

'So how can we help?' asked Jeremy.

'We want to explain why our bank is there and why we believe that in the long term — in the very long term — whatever replaces the current set-up will work. Huge mineral resources, a well-educated population, vast internal markets, an emerging middle class . . . '

We talked for some time and Andrew agreed to commission some work from us, which I would write.

'We tell it like it is,' I warned him. 'That's our house style.'

'Is there any other way?' asked Andrew. 'I'm planning to go back to Moscow in about a fortnight. Can you deliver me a first draft before then? We want to present it in the form of a client newsletter. I'll fax you a sample.'

We parted, and I agreed to get in touch as soon as I had something on paper.

★　★　★

I did my research and over the following days prepared a draft article for Andrew. I went through it with Jeremy and then, my pulse raised, I rang Andrew's number. He answered almost instantly.

'Oh, it's you,' he said, sounding disappointed.

'Were you expecting a call? I can ring back later. I was calling about the newsletter you commissioned.'

'Of course. No, fire away.'

'You did say you wanted a look at this before you went back,' I reminded him.

'Can you bring it round?'

I hesitated a moment, then agreed.

'OK. See you in a few minutes,' he said.

I hadn't quite meant that I would drop everything that second but Andrew was the client. I took a taxi to Notting Hill and Andrew met me at the door.

'Come in,' he said. 'Everything's a bit of a shambles — I'm in the middle of packing.'

Apart from a couple of suitcases in the hall the place looked as tidy as ever.

'Is Caroline out?' I asked. I had been mentally preparing myself to face her on the way over. I don't know what I had been thinking at the party. Perhaps I had drunk too much champagne on an empty stomach. My words had been reckless and I cringed every time I remembered her furious reaction . . . And yet, at the same time, what I had said had the ring of truth. There were no two ways about it. I really was beginning to feel something for her. But who knew how she might react the next time we met?

'Caroline's out, all right. She's walked out on me.'

I couldn't have been more surprised and it must have shown in my face.

'What do you mean? Have you had a row?'

Andrew looked irritated but then composed himself.

'We'll look at your article in a minute. I've some coffee on the go — do you want a cup?'

We sat at the kitchen table with our cups of coffee. Andrew ran a hand through his hair. He looked exasperated but did not have the air of a man who had lost control. For him, having his girlfriend abandon him instead of welcoming him back from his self-imposed exile was a glitch; nothing more.

'What do you mean, Caroline's walked out?' I repeated.

'After that dinner party you came to. The next morning. She was sleeping in one of the spare bedrooms — we haven't shared a room since I got back, she says I'm taking her for granted — and by the time I awoke she had packed and was on her way out. If I hadn't caught her she mightn't even have said goodbye.'

My mind was in such turmoil I could hardly speak, but somehow I managed to squeak, 'How odd.'

'Yes. Very odd. The truth is, Charles, I'd planned to ask her to marry me on this trip home. I thought it was only fair to give her a reason to stay with me while I still have this commitment to be in Moscow for at least another year.'

'Perhaps you should have come back earlier.'

'Did she mention she was finding it difficult? I know you saw her a couple of times while I was away.'

I felt myself going red.

'She didn't really confide in me.'

'Sorry. Unfair of me to ask, but I just wondered. I can't understand why she should walk out on me though. I'm aware she's a very

122

special girl, talented, and I'm proud of what she's done. You went to the exhibition, didn't you? I saw that piece Jeremy bought.'

I nodded.

'But I'm going to be very well-off if I stick it out in Moscow. The bank will make me a partner, and when that happens, it's a very big step up in terms of salary and bonuses. A massive step up. Why would she turn her back on all that, or put me under pressure to do the same?'

'I don't know. She never mentioned anything to me.'

Andrew seemed reluctant to believe that Caroline and I hadn't spent all our time talking about him. It simply didn't seem possible that he wasn't the main topic of any conversations we'd had.

'Well,' he said after a while. 'I don't see how I can propose now. I'll try and see her before I go, of course, although I have a lot to do and not much time to do it in. I still keep in touch with the political world over here. I'm not sure that Major can win an election. There are some interesting people on the Labour benches and I want to meet them.'

I didn't see how he could sit there talking about politics, when his whole world should have been crashing around his feet. But that was Andrew: steely, self-absorbed, allowing nothing to deflect him from his life's goals, even the — no doubt temporary — absence in his life of the woman he had decided to marry.

'Look,' I said. 'If there's anything I can do to

help, let me know. But can we look at this article now?'

Andrew smiled.

It was the kind of smile I imagined he must have given over many boardroom tables, to partners, colleagues and competitors alike. The kind of smile that closed down a conversation, sealed a deal, won an argument or even threw down the gauntlet. I felt unnerved. There was nothing dangerous in his tone and his expression seemed sincere. Yet there was something in his eyes, a splinter of pure ice, that made me feel uncomfortable.

'Quite right, Charles. We must deal with the matter in hand. I apologise for dragging you into my personal affairs.'

* * *

We spoke several times on the phone after that but didn't meet again before he returned to Moscow. On our last call, a verbal sign-off on the work we had been doing for him, he surprised me by saying, 'I don't suppose there's any particular reason for you and Caroline to be in touch but do me a favour, please? Look her up and let me know how she is. I'm particularly interested in her state of mind with reference to myself. Anything you can report along those lines would be hugely appreciated. I'm sure you know that I am determined to marry Caroline, and if you can assist me in understanding why she's being so difficult at present, that would help me enormously.'

Andrew wasn't given to using words like 'hugely' and 'enormously', which I imagined were designed to make me feel important, otherwise his request would have sounded like an instruction to one of his staff. I gave a vague reply and rang off. I was rather fed up with Andrew, and as for Caroline, I no longer knew what I felt for her. I wondered if she would simply go back to New York, although on reflection that would have been a perverse decision, since her career was just beginning to take off in London. I didn't know who Caroline's friends were and whether she would be staying with one of them, or whether she had found a room in a hotel or a furnished flat.

Andrew went back to Moscow and we exchanged letters and faxes as we continued our work for his bank. Caroline stayed hidden from sight.

* * *

All this changed when Caroline rang me one evening to ask if she could come and see me.

'Of course,' I said, with a feeling in the pit of my stomach that was either excitement or dread. 'When?'

'I'm in some pub up the road. I've been waiting for you to get back. I can see the lights in your apartment right from where I'm sitting.'

This sounded so forlorn that I told her to come around immediately.

'Charlie, now don't freak out or anything, but I've got my bag. I swear I'm not coming to stay,

I'm just on my way to a girlfriend's for the night.'

A minute or two later she was with me. We embraced at the door. She felt tense and stiff, yet yielding at the same time.

'Come in. Have a drink. You look shattered.'

'Thanks, buddy. You always did know how to make a girl feel good.'

Caroline came into the kitchen and looked about awkwardly, as if unwilling to commit herself to the act of sitting in one chair rather than another. I put a glass of wine on the table and then took her by the shoulders and guided her down on to the nearest seat.

She did look shattered: tired, haunted, mixed-up, all those things.

'So I guess Andrew told you about us?'

I explained I'd seen him but she cut me off.

'That accounts for this week's look. The shattered look. Recommended for all women who have brutally dumped their long-term lover when he has been nothing but kind, generous and supportive.'

'Kind, generous and self-centred, more like it, not to mention controlling. He's not interested in you, Caroline. He wants a wife to go with the millionaire toy kit he is building himself: dream job, dream house, dream wife.'

I didn't know where this had come from. Still, it was true.

Caroline looked at me with interest.

'So you *do* have a bitchy streak in you after all. And I'm nobody's dream wife, I can tell you.'

'You might be,' I told her. 'And I'm not bitchy.

126

I'm just saying what I believe.'

There was a long, long pause.

'Does that apply to what you said at our dinner party?'

'Look, I'm sorry. That was hugely out of line, I don't know what I was thinking. Perhaps it was the booze. I don't even know what I was trying to say.'

Sometimes honesty is not the best policy.

'You don't even know what you were trying to say? Jesus, Charlie, you're really charming the pants off me tonight.'

I flannelled, buying time while I tried to get my jumbled thoughts in some sort of order. 'I suppose what I was trying to say was . . . it upsets me, the way Andrew treats you. As if he has abandoned you. I can't understand why he would do that . . . and why you would let him.'

Caroline drummed her fingers on the table.

'Mind if I smoke?'

'No — I'll get an ashtray.'

She lit up and inhaled, then blew a long stream of smoke towards me. It calmed her and made my eyes water.

'You know, he's never even told me that he loves me,' said Caroline. She sipped some wine. The tension had gone out of her face and she looked less haggard. 'Andrew used to say 'what a great couple we'll make'. As if he was my brand manager and I was some kind of product he was going to promote. He also liked saying that when he was a partner he would find sponsorship for my sculpting shows, as if that was the only way I could ever possibly make it. Like a little girl's

127

game, pretending to be an artist, propped up by some stockbroker's cash.'

'Why are you telling me all this?' I asked, without conviction.

'Because you once told me, Charlie boy, and for this I will always be grateful, that you thought my work was good. You then ruined it by qualifying yourself as incapable of judging good art or bad, but all the same, it gave me one helluva boost when I needed it.'

She stood up with a yawn, and then stretched, as if she was about to go. The evening was drawing to a close quicker than I had hoped.

'Where were you going with that suitcase?' I asked her rather too quickly.

'Where I am going with that suitcase is to stay with a girlfriend until I can find a new place to live.'

'Andrew's been gone for weeks. Have you been living in friends' flats ever since?'

'You don't make much money sculpting, believe it or not, and my father cut my allowance when I broke loose from the law firm. So it's going to take a while to find somewhere within my budget.'

I asked her how much that was and she told me to mind my own business. I thought for a moment and then told her:

'Top of the stairs on the right is my spare bedroom. That's yours for as long as you want it. No strings. It's not good for you to keep moving around and it can't possibly be good for your work.'

Of course the answer was no, at first, but as we

sat talking companionably I knew in the end that it would be yes. It was not complacency that made me think that: far from it. It was the sense of inevitability that had surrounded us ever since we met at Andrew's house; or perhaps even further back, to our meeting at the Fryerne Arms and her light-hearted teasing of me then. Maybe that was stretching it, but before an hour had passed she had phoned her friend to explain and gone upstairs to unpack. She reappeared at the head of the stairs in her pyjamas.

'I won't come down again,' she said. 'I'm too tired to talk any more. I'll see you in the morning.'

'I leave early,' I said. 'I won't wake you. I'll leave a note and some spare keys on the kitchen table.'

It felt strange, going to bed in my flat knowing that Caroline was sleeping only a few yards away. I thought I could hear faint snores coming from that direction and I smiled. I wasn't quite sure what I had just done or where it would lead, but I felt more contented and at peace that night than I had done for a long, long time.

* * *

There are watershed moments in life and that was one. Before me stretched the endless prairies of time that you think you own when you are in your thirties. Decisions can always be postponed; life will go on and your youthful energy will never dissipate. But those prairies can be lonely, pointless places to wander on your own.

129

Caroline never did go to her girlfriend's flat. She moved in, and stayed for good. Over the following months, we grew closer, until she was no longer sleeping in the spare room. By the following year, there was no more confusion or ambiguity in our feelings for each other. It seemed as plain as day that we should spend the rest of our lives together.

And so I proposed, a second watershed moment.

Others would follow. The betrayal of a family name. Careers destroyed and lives ruined.

* * *

Later, many years later, as I lay beside Caroline in bed one night, her small snores reminded me for a second so vividly of the very first time she had slept under my roof all those years ago. That flash of recall triggered thoughts in me, taking my mind away from the book I was trying to read. My light was still on, and I was attempting, without much success, to stay awake long enough to finish a chapter.

The sound of her snores, the noise of a small, contented animal, might have been a vignette of marital contentment. A well-off, middle-aged, slightly overweight husband nestles up to his beloved wife of many years. Outside, the orange glare of sodium street lighting penetrates through the curtains as they move in the draughts that flow and eddy everywhere in this ageing, restless house. The house sits in a leafy suburb of Newcastle, a city I came to when I accepted a job in the newly formed Department of Strategic Communications at the university.

I like this house. It has big rooms, high ceilings. A merchant's town house, once upon a time.

Once upon a time.

Once upon a time a professor of Strategic Communications, his wife the sculptor Caroline Woodchester, the deputy leader (and some would have said future Leader of the Opposition) Andrew Landford, and Andrew's beautiful, sexy, intelligent wife Helen, all went for a journey in a car together. Not a car really: it was a three-tonne package of gleaming metal and glass. What happened next was not the fault of the car. That much, at least, is clear. The rest isn't.

I had always prided myself on my ability to discern the truth. It was my one marketable asset. But on the one occasion in my life when it really, really mattered, truth became the victim of circumstance; and other things, too.

I close my book and put it on my bedside table. Outside an owl hoots. I switch off the bedside light.

Click.

2

GILCASTER HEAD

1

2010

Clunk-click.

'Are we all strapped in?' said Andrew cheerfully, as he pulled shut the door of his car. 'Otherwise this wretched vehicle whines at you until you give in.'

Just like old times: Andrew taking control of things again, or in this case, his car. It was the newest of the new Range Rovers: enormous, luxurious, an emblem of success and power. I sat in the front beside Andrew while Helen and Caroline sat in the back, making bright, awkward conversation as we drove out of Newcastle Airport. Considering that Caroline had once nearly become Andrew's wife rather than mine, I didn't think they were doing too badly. But then Helen had charm, lots of it. I'm not saying that Caroline didn't, but she didn't have all those little upper-class English tricks designed to make the other person in the conversation feel flattered, needed and inferior. As for Andrew, having the girl he might have married and the girl he did marry in the back seat of his car must have made him feel good about life. I could almost write the subtext for him:

'Pity Caroline's let herself go — she always used to be so careful about her weight. She ought to ask Helen where she gets her hair done.

135

Helen has a man in Mayfair who does her hair. Looks a million dollars. Costs it too.'

But that was my subtext, really, as Andrew would never bother himself about where people got their hair done. I was the one worrying that my wife looked rather ordinary sitting next to Helen.

A worry that in itself was indicative of how we now felt about each other, I suspected. As marriages go, ours had been happy to start with. There had been holidays, and explorations, adventures across golden sands and frozen seas. I had discovered a taste and modest ability for cooking Caroline's favourite Far Eastern dishes to her satisfaction, even daring to experiment and create new ones of my own. We shared memories of countless private views, gallery openings, warm speeches, even warmer glasses of wine, the high-frequency and highly forgettable chatter of a successful night trailing off into the dusk. The occasional Fryerne clan gathering. Walks in the hills, sitting alone together in a deserted cinema on a Monday night, lying in bed while the smells of breakfast drifted in from next door. That, at least, had not changed.

Yet much also had.

Caroline had struggled to get her work recognised in the way it deserved. This was not for want of trying, she never seemed to be out of her studio, and exhibited on a regular — some might say too regular — basis. She had her buyers and admirers, but they were rather too select a group to propel her to the stellar career we had both envisaged. I found much to be proud of — her inclusion in a new EU-funded sculpture garden for Durham, several appearances in the Royal Academy Summer Show and winning a commission to create a permanent exhibition for the new languages centre at Newcastle University. But for some reason these seemed to deflate Caroline rather than inspire her. She took criticism personally, and dwelt upon it. What the critics often said I secretly agreed with; she had so much innate talent and imagination, yet even her best work often felt constrained, self-edited, as if some invisible barrier was holding her back.

None of this was helped, of course, by my relative success in my chosen field. To my slight embarrassment, I was now regarded as something of an industry guru. Jeremy and I had sold our business to a global media agency a couple of years back. Jeremy stayed on, but I had been offered an academic position at Newcastle University as Professor of Strategic Communication Studies. It wouldn't be going too far to say they practically created the department around me.

The change of location did more for me than it did for our marriage or Caroline's career. We found an old Georgian house in one of the city's leafy suburbs, in which we rattled about well enough, but she kept on her studio and our old flat in London, which is where she bolted when she needed to work. These days, that seemed to be nearly all the time.

I can't remember when things started to go wrong. Perhaps it was the question of children.

137

In our early years, focused on our careers, we had both agreed that starting a family wasn't a priority. Occasionally the odd Fryerne at a memorial service or landmark birthday party would remind me of my supposed duty to the clan, with questions that were as sharp as they were teasingly phrased. So much so that when, in more recent years, Caroline broached the subject again, I was more receptive to the idea. Alas, in some never fully diagnosed way, our bodies were not. We tried and tried, every treatment, every old wives' tale. We never formally admitted defeat; we just stopped talking about it.

The new Mrs Landford, of course, had already provided our host with a son and heir, a child that had been packed off to boarding school as soon as he was of age. That was about the sum total of my knowledge about Helen. She could have been a model. Maybe she had been. I think in fact she had been a successful corporate lawyer until she met Andrew. Then, by degrees, she had abandoned her career and became a lady of leisure. I suspect it would have been difficult for Andrew to deal with two high achievers in the same marriage. Somehow he had managed to persuade Helen that she could be more of a help to him in his career just by being glamorous and intelligent, and making middle-aged bankers and politicians feel good about themselves. She seemed to have accepted her new role. Physically she was a perfect specimen: long legs, good hair, made up to perfection so that she really did convey the impression of someone who had just jumped off the front cover of Vogue — and certainly not someone who'd had a child.

Beside her, Caroline did not look exactly frumpy, but she was . . . just Caroline: a little thickset these days, but still with a good figure. Hair not Mayfair, but still plenty of it. Clothes bought mostly online. The difference was probably in her face: Caroline wore a look of determination, experience and humour, which more than made up for any other inadequacies as far as I was concerned.

I don't suppose physical comparisons worked in my favour either. Andrew was one of those people who liked to tell you he could still get into the clothes he wore at university. Tonight he wore a beautifully tailored charcoal grey suit with a peacock blue silk lining. I wore what one wore in my job: a blazer and rumpled chinos, nothing too smart. Smart suits and big cars were not the way to ingratiate oneself in the academic world, or at least my corner of it.

Making a low hum like a spacecraft the Range Rover pulled out on to the motorway.

'Good luck you two girls being on the same flight from London,' said Andrew, cheerfully. I had taken the Metro from Newcastle and Caroline had come straight from her studio in London, where she had been working all week.

'Yes, wasn't it?' said Helen. 'We could have made a plan to sit together if I'd known.'

Caroline's reply contained the bare minimum of enthusiasm and regret. She wasn't sure about this whole weekend. Neither of us had seen much of Andrew over the fifteen years or so that had passed since the rather awkward letter I wrote to him announcing my engagement to Caroline. Neither of us had met Helen before. And other than that very uncomfortable conversation in his house after the day Caroline left, he and I had never discussed the matter.

Regardless, Andrew had remained a client of our firm; he wasn't going to let a little thing like the break-up of his relationship affect a business arrangement. But Jeremy had tactfully put someone else on as account handler, so Andrew and I had only met on his occasional visits to the office, with a quick handshake in the corridor or the occasional cup of coffee.

Maybe his self-esteem was wounded by what had happened; maybe it wasn't. Andrew was very good at rationalising and I imagined he would have taught himself to believe that being abandoned by Caroline wasn't a setback, but an opportunity. And so it had proved. He had gone out and found himself a new wife who fitted the job description perfectly. If he became leader and Helen was allowed her share of the limelight, the press photographers would love her.

We were now heading towards Gilcaster Head. At Oxford, people had spoken of Andrew's parents as being rich expats who had owned, variously, either a gold mine or a tea plantation. How these rumours had got about, I don't know. I can only imagine that Andrew had started them himself out of some warped sense of mischief. The reality was more prosaic: his parents owned several manufacturing businesses, amongst them a factory that made the edible wrapper that contains our morning sausage. On retirement, they had sold out and bought a small farm at Gilcaster Head, not far from Hadrian's Wall where it crosses from Northumberland into Cumbria. Their choice of location was hard to fathom: perhaps it represented some kind of rural idyll. They grassed over their few acres and settled down, dying one soon after the other only a few years ago. Now Andrew had taken over Gilcaster Head. It was an odd decision. The farm was in a most inconvenient place and with few neighbours. But he liked the idea of 'a place in the country', and spent a good deal of money doing it up.

The weekend was not planned as a reunion between the four of us, although in one sense that was what it was. Andrew had gone part-time at his bank a few years ago and had become an MP. This was something I believed he had been manoeuvring towards ever since his university days. At any rate, he now had a safe Conservative seat in a constituency in the North West of England. Time spent migrating between London and Gilcaster Head must have put a strain even on someone as resourceful as Andrew. But it hadn't interfered with his rapid rise through party ranks to a position on the front benches. At that time this was the Opposition front bench, after a tight general election, but Andrew was hopeful all that would change in the next year or two. Political parties were as noted for what they disagreed about amongst themselves as for the policies they claimed to be fighting for.

141

Andrew told me all this when we met one night in London. He wanted me to join his Praetorian Guard: a group of 'special advisers', the energetic bright men and women who would protect him and write his speeches and think his thoughts for him and generally help him in his plan to become party leader. Just now all was going well for him. The current incumbent had been weakened by a poor general election result. But Andrew wasn't the only person dreaming of running the party. Maldwyn Christie was interested too, and the public warmed to him rather more than they did to Andrew. This was what we were going to talk about that weekend, I supposed.

My role could only be guessed at, but I was interested, and I must admit, flattered as well. I was also intrigued to see a bit more of Andrew. Had he changed over the years? How was his master plan (become a millionaire, take charge of the Tories, then become prime minister) progressing? So far it sounded as if it was running like clockwork. In addition, I was lured by the idea that I could have a part to play on the periphery of power, however brief and minor it might be. It could be an interesting experience for a few months, just observing political life on the inside track, rather than from the outside. It was exactly the sort of project the university would encourage me to become involved in, as long as I was discreet about it.

All in all I was looking forward to our weekend. I didn't expect it to be comfortable — in the sense of easygoing — but it had to be better than some of the long silences that Caroline and I endured in each other's company, especially over recent months. I hoped this weekend would cheer her up, or at least lift her out of what seemed to be a long-lasting depression; anything that might buoy her in some way. There were too many retreats and silences in our relationship, too much entrenchment. We had backed ourselves into a series of dead ends, and any change in scenery that might offer a way out was to be welcomed.

★ ★ ★

The light was fading fast as we drove past the escarpment along which the wall stood. To the south, a red-rimmed sky cast its autumnal light over the empty landscape, which was broken up only by a few hill farms (mostly now trading as bed and breakfasts) and scattered blocks of conifers. To the north of the road stood the wall. Few of its mile castles still remained, but in the gathering gloom one could easily imagine what it must have been like once: the edge of the known world. It hadn't ever really been the last outpost, even in its hey-day — Roman castles and earthworks ran up through the borders and right into the Scottish Lowlands. But on a quiet evening like this, one could fancy oneself on the brink of nowhere. We passed a larger set of ruins where the outline of a fort and troop-houses could be seen.

'That's Housesteads,' said Helen to Caroline. 'We can come and look over it tomorrow if you like, while the men are talking business?'

'Really?' said Caroline. 'I hope the men aren't going to be talking too much business.' She sounded as if she was on the verge of an outburst of bad temper.

'Not at all,' said Andrew from the front. He could read Caroline's mind as well as I could, for what that was worth. 'We will try not to be dull. Never let it be said that I bore my guests.'

'You're about the only man I know who could get away with a remark like that,' said Caroline, and everybody laughed. The shadow of hostility lifted and then our attention was diverted as we turned off the main road on to a single track with passing places. 'God help us if we meet another car on this road,' said Helen nervously.

'Do you come up here much?' I ventured.

'Not as much as Andrew would like me to. Of course I've got to show up in the constituency from time to time and wave the flag. There's been a lot of flag-waving recently, hasn't there, darling?'

Andrew grimaced but did not answer.

We passed a crossroads. The scenery around us had become wilder: low hills and rocky outcrops clad with gorse and pine. There were few other houses — the odd farmhouse with a gleam of light in the kitchen window, and the glow of a village over to our right. Wind swirled fistfuls of leaves across the road, and in the distance there was the rumble of a late summer storm.

'Not far now,' said Andrew. 'I feel a gin and tonic coming on.'

★ ★ ★

He turned his head and smiled at Caroline. As he did so, something appeared in the dusk, just beyond the windscreen — a flurry of beating wings and burning eyes staring in at us.

'Andrew!' I called out, but it was too late.

There was a thud against the windscreen; a crescendo of white wings. A screech, as the car swerved then stopped without going off the road.

'Oh Christ!' shouted Andrew. He sounded rattled. 'Is everybody all right?'

'You hit an owl,' I told him.

'I never had a chance. It just flew straight at the car.'

'It's the owl you should be worrying about.'

'Hang on,' said Andrew. He opened the door and jumped out. I could see the owl in the light from the headlamps. It was still conscious and was hopping around in circles, dragging a wing.

'Oh God,' said Andrew. 'What should I do?' He sounded in a panic, quite unlike his usual self. He hopped around the owl and the owl hopped away from him. Eventually he picked it up by a leg and then let go with a yelp as the bird pecked him viciously.

'You little bastard!'

'It's not the poor owl's fault, darling,' said Helen. 'Oh, somebody please do something. Andrew's so useless at things like this. Can't you help, Charles?'

'I'm not useless,' shouted Andrew, with alarming fury. 'I didn't ask the sodding thing to fly into my brand new car.' He made another grab at the creature. There was a brief tussle of man and bird and then Andrew, seizing both its legs this time, lifted the owl up and slammed its head against the top of a dry stone wall. There was another screech and a frantic flapping of wings. Then they began to tremble.

'There! That'll shut the fucker up!' He slammed the owl again and again against the wall until the bent and crushed upper parts of the bird and its twisted head indicated that the unequal battle was over. 'Little fucker!' Andrew repeated again, bending down and wiping his hands on the grass. We all stared at him in mute horror. As he straightened up he caught our look and said, 'Well, what was I supposed to do?'

'Take it to a vet and get its wing pinned?' I suggested.

'What a carry on that would have been. I've no idea where the nearest vet is. And can you imagine Helen and Caroline holding on to that vicious bird while we looked for one?'

I looked at Caroline. Her expression was one of revulsion. 'That was so horrible,' she said, almost inaudibly.

Andrew ignored her, speaking to me, 'And then, can you imagine the vet phoning the local paper — Andrew Landford runs over protected species?'

In a tone unlike any she had used before, Helen Landford said, 'Andrew, will you stop buggering about. Get rid of that poor bird, drive us home, and pour us a drink.'

Andrew held the bird up. 'What should I do with this?'

'Take it home?' I suggested.

'I'm not having that in the car,' said Helen. Andrew tossed the corpse into a field.

'Someone will see that,' I told him.

'So what? It's like dead badgers. Everyone thinks they're roadkill but half of them have been shot by keepers or farmers and then been reversed over.'

He climbed back into the car. Nobody said a word until we arrived at Gilcaster Head a few minutes later. We got out of the car in silence and then Helen, with an effort, remembered her role as hostess and directed us to our room.

'Come on down in five minutes when you've had a chance to freshen up, and we'll have a drink. I'm sure we all need one after that.'

★ ★ ★

The house had been turned around at some point in its history so that we arrived at what must once have been the back door. I had an impression of a jumble of low, sloping slate roofs, gable ends and high chimney stacks. Inside any notion that one was entering a rural farmhouse was dispelled immediately by the fact that the house was not only warm, but hot. A wood-burning stove glowed in the small entrance hall and the central heating was on even though it was still only mid-September.

When we got to our bedroom I managed to open a window and let in some fresh air.

Caroline looked around the room and said, 'God, everything's so London.'

It was true. The six pillows on our bed, the overstuffed duvets, the luxurious wallpaper, the swagged curtains all indicated the fairly recent presence of an expensive interior decorator who had been assigned the task of making the occupant of the room feel that while it might be Cumbria outside, inside it was Knightsbridge.

'Are you all right?' I asked Caroline.

'Yes. I'd clean forgotten about Andrew's charming psycho side, that's all.'

I looked at her across the bed. She had never described him like that before. Controlling, perhaps. I had seen him use a rifle as if his brain was wired directly to the trigger, and noticed his brusque manner with those who worked for him, but I had never witnessed him behaving as savagely as he had with that bird.

Caroline turned away to get dressed and a few minutes later we went downstairs into the drawing room.

Another fire blazed here, and the sofas and armchairs had all been upholstered in a golden yellow damask with blue piping. We found Andrew opening a bottle of wine.

'What'll it be?' he asked. 'Wine or something stronger?'

'Gin for me,' said Caroline.

'Whisky.'

Helen appeared with a flute of champagne. Her hair was perfect once more, and she had fully recovered any composure she had misplaced in the car.

148

'Well, our trips here aren't always quite so dramatic,' she remarked.

'I'm sorry you had to see that,' said Andrew to Caroline. 'There really was nothing else I could do. I couldn't leave the poor thing to die of its injuries.'

'No. Quite right,' said Caroline, with a completely straight face. At first I couldn't tell whether she was being ironic. 'One dead owl. Problem solved.'

'The funny thing is,' said Andrew, 'I'm on the parliamentary Committee which just toughened up the Wildlife and Countryside Act.' He paused, thinking about it. 'I say, I wonder if I've put myself in a rather awkward position?'

'Least said, soonest mended,' I told him.

'Is that your strategic advice?' asked Andrew, laughing without much enthusiasm.

'I'm off duty tonight.'

'Yes,' said Helen. 'Let's not talk about death and owls tonight.'

★ ★ ★

Dinner was cooked and served by a couple who lived in a flat over the stables, Gurkhas from Nepal. They were known as John and Mary, although I doubted those were their actual names.

'Frightfully loyal and hard working, and so keen to please,' murmured Helen between courses. It was obvious she didn't have to do a hand's turn to keep Gilcaster Head going. She simply arrived, told them when to run her bath and when dinner was to be served, and that was more or less that. 'We couldn't possibly cope without them,' Helen told me, and I believed her. At any rate their presence left her free to look after her guests and after the very unpromising start to the evening, things showed signs of being back on an even keel.

I felt myself mellowing under the influence of all this luxury and Andrew too had lost some of the tension I had sensed in the air even before the accident. After dinner we went back into the drawing room. Helen and Caroline sat on the floor in front of the fire. Our host and I sat in two armchairs opposite them, on the other side of the room.

'You know,' said Andrew softly, as he handed me a whisky and water nightcap, 'it's a pity that we allowed your marriage to Caroline to come between us. We should have been more grown-up about it. I blame myself.'

He had a unique gift of making an admission sound like a veiled threat. I shifted in my seat.

'If anyone is to blame that would have been me. But let's agree to forget all that now.'

'I'll drink to that,' said Andrew, smiling.

★　★　★

That night, as Caroline and I undressed for bed, I said, 'You know, I quite enjoyed seeing Andrew again. How did you get on with Helen?'

'Oh, Helen. She's sweet, really. I don't know what she does with herself all day.'

'Organises Andrew's life for him, I expect.

Anyway, I'm glad we've all got together again.'

'Mmm.'

'You don't sound convinced. Andrew's not such a bad chap, you know.'

'Unless you're an owl.'

2

We were woken next morning by the smell of bacon cooking, one of the surest ways to tempt me out of bed. After a good cooked breakfast, Andrew and I decided to go for a walk and chew over the implications of the previous night's events.

Daylight revealed the full extent of Gilcaster Head. The back of the house was made up of an array of old farm buildings that had been merged into one over the years and converted into living space. The rest of the house had a handsome Georgian exterior, and a back door with three steps leading down from it into the garden.

The garden was rather scruffy in comparison with the immaculate interior of the house. Gardening was either not an enthusiasm of Andrew and Helen's, or it simply was not practical here, but the bare minimum of work had been done. The mostly unkempt lawn was bordered by a ha-ha, more like a ditch, and protected from marauding sheep by a few strands of barbed wire. Beyond that, fields of rough pasture heavy with dew and dotted by clumps of thistles led up towards a long plantation of conifers. They were not trees I had ever liked. Planted in blocks I found them more like black holes than forests, sucking the light out of everything around them. But these spruces were different to the huge swathes of neat commercial forestry a bit further up the valley. There was something ragged about them, their branches twisted with age. I wondered if they were the oldest thing about Gilcaster Head, although of course, their longevity would still be nothing compared to the remains of the Roman Wall a mile or two away.

Andrew pointed out the extent of his grazing, a hundred or so acres that he let to a local farmer, and then we set off down the lane for a walk. As we strolled along I became aware that another walker was approaching us from the opposite direction.

'That's a neighbour,' said Andrew. 'He's called Tom. I've forgotten what his surname is. He's one of those townies who've gone native: grows his own vegetables, drives a hybrid car — extremely impractical decision living somewhere like this — anti-fracking, pro-badgers, you name it. He's even got a bee in his bonnet about the remains of some ancient Roman temple near us that hasn't been properly excavated. As if this part of the world needs any more Roman ruins ... He's not a bad chap, just a bit over-enthusiastic, like a born again missionary.'

We stopped and greeted each other.

'This is Professor Charles Fryerne,' said Andrew, introducing me.

'Tom,' said the newcomer. 'Tom Gazelee. Are you staying the weekend?'

'Yes, we all got up last night. We're just getting some good Cumbrian air into our lungs.'

'Ah, I've been doing that for a few years now. You should try and spend more time here,

Andrew. God's own country.'

Tom Gazelee wore a woollen cap on his head and a Carlisle United scarf over an ancient Barbour, jeans and walking boots. He was like a hundred others you might meet on a country lane.

'Did you notice anybody about when you came home last night?' Tom asked Andrew.

'How do you mean?'

'I'm not really sure. Poachers, maybe. It's just that on my way to get the papers this morning I spotted a dead owl just inside a gateway off this road. About a mile further along, near the crossroads.'

'A dead owl?' said Andrew, his smile frozen on his face. I, too, felt awkward.

'Yes. Poor thing. It was a barn owl. Someone had battered its head in. Amazing how savage people can be.'

'Where is it now?' asked Andrew.

'I took it to the police station in Brampton and reported it. It's a crime to kill an owl, as I'm sure you know. You're on that parliamentary Committee.'

'How on earth did you know that?' said Andrew. He was struggling to remain calm.

'Oh, I Google you from time to time to see what my famous neighbour is getting up to. We're proud to have such a leading politician spend some of his time in a remote spot like this.'

Tom appeared to be perfectly sincere in his praise.

'But to go back to the owl — you must have

154

come that way last night. Did you see anything unusual on your travels?'

There was a pause, and then Andrew said in a dry voice, 'No, I can't say that we did.'

'Oh well,' said Tom. 'Of course they will get away with it, whoever they were. All I can do is to tell people to keep their eyes open. There are some evil bastards walking the earth, aren't there?'

'Yes indeed, Tom.'

We parted and walked on slowly in silence. After we had gone a hundred yards or so Andrew said, 'Model citizen.'

He laughed humourlessly. I waited for him to speak again.

'Calling in a crime even though it's only a dead bird, even though the police will no doubt have to go about interviewing people and chasing around after non-existent poachers and filling in reports. Do you know how big a problem drug abuse is in country schools, Charles? It's massive. The police don't have the resources to deal with something as serious as that and yet here's good old Tom diverting them to find the killer of a poor bird that was more than halfway dead already.'

We strolled on and Andrew said, 'You're not giving me any advice, I notice.'

'It's a bit difficult to know what to say.'

'You're telling me. What to say or what not to say.'

We faced each other. Andrew didn't look angry, or tired, or anxious, just preoccupied. There was a problem to be solved, and he was

155

going to solve it. And I was expected to help him.

The trouble was, Andrew's version of events was factual yet also omitted to tell the full story.

'In a way,' said Andrew, 'I've missed the boat. I suppose I should have told Tom Gazelee all about it. But I really couldn't. I mean, can you imagine me saying, 'Oh, by the way, yes, it was me who smashed that bird's head to bits on a stone wall, I'll just hurry along home now and ring the police.''

'A difficult line,' I agreed. 'But what you could do is go to the police station now, with me, and say that the owl flew into your windscreen and that it was virtually dead when you picked it up. You put it out of its misery. I can corroborate all of that.'

'What, go right now?'

'There's no time like the present. Get it over with. It was an accident.'

There was a long pause. Then Andrew said, 'No. There's too much downside and not enough upside. I've already told Tom I saw nothing. I didn't quite mean it but that's how it will have sounded to him.'

That's how it had sounded to me as well, but I said nothing.

'It will all blow over, anyway. One dead bird, for God's sake. I know it's an owl. I know barn owls have protected status under the Wildlife and Countryside Act because I'm on the damned Committee. It's very unfortunate that the bird should have flown into my car but that is hardly my fault and I don't see why I should deliberately put my head on the block and let them chop it off because of one unfortunate bird. No, I'll take your original advice after all, I think.'

'What advice?' I asked in alarm. I didn't remember advising him about anything.

'Last night you said: least said, soonest mended. That's the line I'm going to follow.'

'That was in a slightly different context,' I reminded him.

'Nevertheless,' said Andrew firmly.

I was an adviser; I had advised him; he had taken the advice. That was the end of the matter. We walked back to the house in silence. In my mind were his words: too much downside and not enough upside. He was thinking in terms of risks and benefits, not in terms of truth or lies.

* * *

After lunch Helen went off to 'do her household accounts', which I suspect meant a snooze in a back sitting room somewhere. Caroline decided to go out for a walk, leaving Andrew and I alone together in the drawing room.

'I've been following your career with great interest,' Andrew began. 'And Jeremy's too. CCC was a tremendous success and I gather Jeremy is quite happy working in a bigger firm now you've sold it.'

'Seems to be,' I agreed.

'But your move was interesting. Did they create that Chair especially for you?'

'Not exactly, but the timing was right: I was

157

free and they were looking to build up the department.'

'And you do what?'

'Provide the training and groundwork for people who want to do what Jeremy and I did, or who want to go into lobbying, or brand management.'

Andrew stretched his legs out in front of him and steepled his fingers on his stomach. We chatted for a while before he got to the point.

'Making me into an acceptable candidate for party leader is what's on my mind. Do you think you can do it?'

'Do you think *you* can do it?' I asked him. Andrew laughed.

'Answer a question with another question? That's the guru technique, right there.'

'I'm not the one who is going to have to sell himself to the party at the conference. You are. If you don't believe it, let's stop now.'

Andrew frowned.

'Of course I believe it. That's a given. But it's what's in the speech that counts. That's where you come in.'

'You've got a speechwriter for that, haven't you?'

There was a silence, during which we heard a car drive up. As Andrew rose to his feet, the doorbell rang. Andrew went into the hall and I heard him talking to someone. Whoever it was wasn't invited in. Then the door was shut and, after a moment, the car drove off. Andrew came back into the drawing room and sat down. He seemed a little paler than before.

'I'm sorry for the interruption. What were we saying just now?'

But he had lost his composure and when I said, 'Who was that?' with a strong feeling that I knew the answer, he answered irritably:

'Well, if you must know, it was the police. Can you believe it? Two of them in a patrol car on a Saturday afternoon, when there's a football match on in Carlisle. How can they spare the men to go on a wild goose chase like that?'

I waited. When Andrew could see I wasn't going to comment, he said, 'Maybe it's better if you don't know any more about this.'

'Well, I already know that they've driven away without taking any notes or photographs of your car.'

'One of them was examining a chip on the windscreen,' said Andrew, 'nosy bastard. They'll be looking for owl DNA next, for God's sake.'

'So I know that, whatever they asked, you answered in the negative.'

'Oh, don't be so evasive, Professor Fryerne,' said Andrew. 'They asked if I knew anything about a dead owl. I said yes, someone had told me about it. They asked if I had seen anything on the drive home last night. I said that I had seen no other cars or any unusual activity that might suggest poachers or anyone else was prowling about. Then one of them said to me, 'You want to get that chip on your windscreen ground out, sir. It might shatter while you are driving.' I said I would call the glass people, and then they left.'

Andrew's answers were not outright untruths.

159

They were literal and, as far as they went, accurate. It was just that he hadn't told them what he knew. I began to wish I hadn't got myself involved in all this. I had become part of a lie: someone else's lie, but a lie nevertheless. It was all very complicated.

'Look, Andrew,' I told him. 'You're asking me what I can do to help you communicate with your voters. All my professional life I have found that there is a distrust of professional communicators such as myself and a huge distrust of those who use their services. Senior politicians are contaminated by this lack of trust, this feeling the public have that they are being spun to.'

'Which they are,' said Andrew.

'Which they are. My response, and my guiding principle through my career, has always been to tell the truth. By that I mean, giving the public the unedited truth rather than presenting them with a menu of items that might be truthful but don't really give you a proper or complete idea of who the candidate is. The hard part is to avoid boring the audience while giving them both the bad news and the good news. If you can achieve that, you have a winning formula.'

Andrew yawned. For a moment it was as if the mask had slipped. Instead of the youngish, energetic politician of a moment ago I saw lines of fatigue, a face portraying utter exhaustion.

'Sorry, that police visit has scrambled my brains a bit,' he said. 'Did I mention we've got Matt Dilcombe joining us for dinner?'

'Matt Dilcombe!'

Matt Dilcombe was one of a new breed of

adviser, a kind of gun for hire who was tasked with mapping out tactics during a political campaign. He had achieved fame, or maybe notoriety, by turning around an electoral campaign in New Zealand and snatching victory from the jaws of defeat — or whatever cliché the newspapers had reached for at the time. He certainly had an impressive record.

'I didn't realise he was on your team,' I said to Andrew.

'He isn't yet. He might be. I wanted the two of you to meet. You would do the big-picture stuff and he would be responsible for execution. He's coming up by train and John's picking him up at Carlisle in about an hour.'

'It's a long way to come for dinner,' I said flippantly.

'Matt Dilcombe would go to Timbuktu for dinner if he thought it would give him an edge. He's a very driven man. If I can get him — and you — in harness, then my campaign to become party leader stands a very good chance of succeeding. Now, I need to catch up with the newspapers, so let's pick up again over a drink when Matt arrives.'

I was — politely but firmly — dismissed and left to my own resources for a while.

For Andrew, reading the papers was not, as it was for others, a pleasant interlude; it was a religion. I had already spotted all the Saturday papers laid out on a coffee table, including the *Financial Times* and the *Wall Street Journal*, together with the *Spectator* and *Prospect*. Andrew would go through these with scissors

161

and yellow highlighters, cutting articles out or highlighting things that interested him. He made an unholy mess, which John and Mary had to tidy up afterwards, although I never heard them complain. Then he would sit at his laptop and scroll through the news sites and political blogs.

I admired his application even though I thought it was a complete waste of time. He claimed it kept him 'in the loop'.

That was another thing I was going to have to get Andrew to unlearn. He believed that all information had value, no matter how tiny, and you couldn't afford to miss that last scrap of gold dust. I believed that most of what you read in the papers was rubbish, and that other people's opinions were a distraction. You had to sort out what you believed first.

★ ★ ★

I met Caroline in the hall.

'Christ, this is a boring weekend,' she said, as she struggled out of her Wellington boots. I hushed her — she either didn't know she could be overheard or didn't care — and followed her up to our room. She sat on the bed, and continued her complaint.

'Helen can't really be doing 'household accounts' this afternoon, can she? That's what people like Helen employ accountants to do. Either she's sleeping or' — a thought struck her — 'maybe she's a secret drinker and she's sitting in her little room boozing. That would certainly make life more interesting!'

'Surely not?'

'Well, what else are you expected to do here? Either you have to go for a walk in this tedious bit of country, or else you might as well go to sleep yourself.'

'It's no more boring than being at home,' I said, before I could stop myself.

Caroline stared at me for a moment. Then she said, 'Thanks, buddy. Thanks very much for that. That certainly makes me feel a whole lot better.'

She burst into tears. I came and sat beside her, and put an arm around her. She shrugged me off and lay flat on the bed with her face in the pillows. I couldn't tell whether she was still sobbing, but reached a hand out towards her, across the crumpled sea of the bed cover. 'I'm sorry. You know I didn't mean that, darling. I'm just as bored as you are and it's put me in a bad mood. That was an unforgivable thing to say.'

Caroline ignored me. Eventually she sat up and said, in a peremptory manner, 'I have a very bad feeling about that owl. I think Andrew has done something terrible, and doesn't realise it. You have no idea what he is capable of.'

'But it was just an accident. What's one dead bird to anyone?'

She took my hand, looking at me mournfully. 'Sometimes I really wonder whether you understand anything about how the world works at all.'

Then she turned away from me, curling up on the other side of the bed. In the unflattering grey light of late afternoon, we lay on the bed waiting for an angel to come and rescue our marriage.

3

Matt Dilcombe arrived at about six. Half an hour later we joined him on the garden terrace. It was a mild evening for the time of year and the garden door had been flung open. John had brought out a table and chairs so we sat outside with our drinks. Matt was a small man, with tight dark curls covering his head, and sharp brown eyes. He crackled with energy, and had a direct gaze that could make the recipient uncomfortable.

He took my hand when we were introduced, as would someone who has been offered a dead fish to hold, and dropped it immediately. I told myself it was just his manner. He gave me an interrogative stare when Andrew told him what I did.

'I Googled you,' he told me. 'Strategic Communications, huh? We could use some of that around here.'

That sounded like a criticism, and I was about to say something when Andrew handed us our drinks.

'You can see the Roman Wall from here,' said Andrew. 'Beyond Minniver Wood.'

'Minniver Wood?' I asked.

He pointed up at the long planting of spruce that bordered the pasture beyond the garden. An evening breeze stirred the tops of the trees, and for a moment they seemed to bend apart, as if the forest were opening up. I stared at them, but could see only shadow beyond.

At that moment there was a distant screech and as we watched a large white bird detached itself from the trees and began skimming and quartering the ground. An owl, hunting for shrews and voles. Helen flinched as the bird came closer. Then with another cry it turned away and flew back into the wood.

No one said a word. Caroline took a large gulp of her drink, and brushed a loose strand of hair away from her forehead.

'Let's go inside,' said Andrew abruptly, standing up. 'I'm being bitten. Aren't you, Matt?'

'Can't say I am, but we'll go inside if you like.' He glanced round the table at us all, frozen like statues, and chuckled. 'You lot look like you've seen a ghost.'

★ ★ ★

At dinner our visitor was scathing about the present state of party politics.

'Nobody is in charge in a coalition,' he said, 'certainly not in this new one. All the headline policies are about rubbish collection, carbon trading, a tax on goodness knows what. Nobody has anything to say about what our policies are on defence, on energy, on Europe — they're too frightened of being held hostage by the other side. It's pathetic. The first person who can answer the really hard questions is the one who deserves to win the confidence of the party and the electorate.'

165

'Charles always says that telling the unvarnished truth is the only option when faced with a cynical electorate,' Andrew told him.

'Then we shall get on,' said Matt firmly. 'That's exactly what is needed.'

'What about Maldwyn?' asked Andrew. 'How much should I worry about him?'

'Maldwyn is a dead duck. He just doesn't know it.'

I was fascinated.

'Why is Maldwyn a dead duck?'

'Yes, why?' asked Caroline. 'I know he's your rival, Andrew, but all the same I'm fond of Maldwyn, and they say he has heaps of friends on the back benches.'

'I'm fond of him too,' agreed Andrew. 'We were at college together and he's one of the few, apart from Charles here, that I've kept up with.'

'Maldwyn's got some good ideas,' said Matt, 'and we can use them when he withdraws from the leadership contest. I like his ideas on asymmetrical demobilisation.'

'What on earth's that?' I asked.

'Hang on a minute,' said Andrew. 'What on earth makes you think that Maldwyn will withdraw from the leadership contest?'

There was a pause while Matt glanced around the table, trying to gauge the impact his words might have. Then he continued, 'Because in about a fortnight's time one of the weekend nationals will do an op-ed piece on the fact that Maldwyn is gay. The headline will be along the lines of 'Can you remember the last time a gay man led the party?''

166

There was a silence and then an explosion of indignation from Caroline and Helen.

'You can't do that to Maldwyn, that would be vile,' said Caroline. Helen's face had the lustrous glow of someone who has had too much to drink. She hadn't overdone it at dinner, as far as I could see. Maybe Caroline was right and she was a secret drinker.

Helen said, 'Yes, poor cuddly Maldwyn. We all love him.'

'All the women do,' said Matt. 'The story has been out there for a while but nobody has picked it up yet. But they will. If we take charge of the way it comes out then at least it will be done sensitively. We'll praise him as a man and as a politician. But we'll ask the question: will the grassroots members vote for a gay man to become party leader? Will the voters choose him as the next prime minister? And the answer we will get is no. Sorry, everybody, but the country isn't ready for that yet.'

Maldwyn had never made a particular secret of his sexuality, but we had rarely discussed it together, and I found it hard to gauge how he would react to such a public outing.

'Who will stick the dagger in?' I asked.

Matt named a well-known columnist.

'He likes Maldwyn. He really wants to save him from the scurrilous reporting that the tabloids will put him through — if they don't get to the story first.'

I felt blank. I couldn't be part of this, could I? The political assassination of an old friend was a depth to which I had not thought to sink.

167

Maldwyn might never speak to me again. But Matt talked as if the whole process was inexorable: a few hundred words of newsprint that would effectively destroy Maldwyn's political career before it had really taken off. It would either be written by someone well-disposed to Maldwyn, or by someone hostile who would write something poisonous. I shook my head. Where was the choice? There was none.

'Aren't you going to say something, Charles?' asked Caroline in indignation. But Matt held up his hand.

'Listen. Back home I've run more than one successful election campaign using what I call the flat possum strategy.'

Caroline nearly spat out her drink. 'A flat possum?' said Andrew, frowning.

'Very common roadkill where I come from, I'm afraid. They dash out from the bush and pick a fight with a truck or trailer that they're never going to win. But I'm talking about winning arguments here. Maldwyn is a strong candidate with a loyal following. The more he shores up his base, the less good the picture looks for you. So I recommend you slap him in the face with a flat possum, so to speak.'

We all looked at each other. Did Matt know something about the previous night's events? No one had said a word to him, as far as I knew. 'What I mean is that if you really slapped Maldwyn in the face with a flat possum, everyone would be appalled and shocked. What a disgusting thing to do to someone. So what? They would be so busy moaning and wailing

168

about the squashed possum, they would no longer be talking about his strengths as a candidate. And while your main opponent and the commentariat are distracted with debates about his sexuality, even the rights and wrongs of revealing it, you will have a window to present your alternative vision as leader.'

There was a long silence while John poured out more wine. I took a very long draught. I had no idea this weekend was going to be so packed with flattened animals.

Andrew was the first to speak.

'We have to do this. Matt, can I assume you are happy to work for my campaign, together with Charles?'

'Assuming the terms are the same as we discussed last week, then yes.' He extended his hand across the table and I took the proffered hand-shake. 'And I'm happy to work with Charles.'

This time his grip was firm.

'Charles?' asked Andrew.

'I'm in, but I don't want there to be any briefing against Maldwyn by any of our team.'

'Good God, no,' said Matt. 'That would kill us. Our line will be distress that this subject should be taboo for so many people in the second decade of the twenty-first century, and our hope that we shall see Maldwyn on the front bench soon despite the prejudice of some sections of society.'

And so we agreed, if not comfortably, to what amounted to the psychological murder of one of our friends and colleagues who just happened to be a rival.

Matt and I arranged to meet in London the following week.

★ ★ ★

It was over coffee that the next difficult conversation occurred. Matt heaped three spoonfuls of sugar into his cup and stirred the resulting syrup with vigour. Confident he had our attention he said, 'And now, it's skeleton time.'

'It's what?' asked Helen, in an amused voice, as if Matt had just proposed a game of charades. But Matt was not joking.

'Skeleton time is when we 'fess up to our own dark secrets. Has anyone been convicted of anything that I don't know about? Has anyone borrowed a large sum of money they're unable to repay? Has anyone sold any shares in a public company of which they are a director, and if so, how much did they earn and when?'

'Oh dear,' said Helen. 'That doesn't sound much fun at all. Can't we discuss this tomorrow morning?'

'I've got to leave around 6:30 so that John can get me to the station on time.'

'Well, let's get on with it,' said Andrew. 'Do the girls have to sit in on this?'

'They're your wives. They are part of it. Let's start right there. Was there any acrimony when you and Caroline split up, Andrew?'

For a moment, a look flickered across Andrew's face, then he assumed a politician's fixed grin once more, as we all reassured Matt

170

there had been no serious tension. Our words sounded brittle and unconvincing, but the truth was there had been no explicit falling out, more of a falling away. In fact, as we recounted the events of the past fifteen years, it became tedious to see what blameless lives we had been leading. We talked about tax; driving offences; we didn't quite get round to disclosing overdue books at the local library. I wondered if Andrew was going to mention that story I had once heard about him and a punting pole at Oxford, but either it was just a rumour or he considered the episode sufficiently buried not to merit a mention. I was relieved, because the stream of mundane confession was exhausting enough and it must have been close to midnight when Matt gave up writing notes.

'Is that all?' he said.

I looked at Andrew, and he caught my glance and nodded hesitantly. He knew that if he didn't bring the subject up, I would.

'There is one thing. It's a silly thing, really,' he said with visible reluctance.

'Tell me,' said Matt.

So then the whole story came out: the owl flying into the windscreen; its impromptu killing; the meeting with the neighbour and the visit from the police.

'Sounds like they're on to you,' said Matt. 'That wasn't just a random visit. How many cars go up and down this lane every day? Not many. And you said there was a chip in your windscreen?'

'That could have been a stone hitting it.'

171

'Mmm,' said Matt. 'Maybe. You seem to have dug yourself into a bit of a hole. Leave it to Charles and me and we'll try to come up with something if the police decide to interview you again.'

'Let's go to bed,' said Helen, yawning. We all stood up and Andrew stretched himself.

'I thought we might spend some of this evening talking about what we might do for the country if we win the leadership. How we might take the party into the next general election. Instead, we've ended up discussing owls.'

'Thanks to your Committee's recommendations, it is now a notifiable offence to kill one, even if by accident.' Matt reminded him.

There was a strange taste in my mouth, and I felt a sense of creeping unease. We shouldn't have been discussing owls at all. Andrew was a potential future prime minister. And yet here we were.

John suddenly appeared in the doorway behind us, as if by magic, and cleared away the coffee things while we went to bed.

4

When I drew the curtains the morning was dour and grey. Caroline awoke as the daylight touched her face and stretched.

'Let's get out of here,' she said, 'straight after breakfast.'

'We're supposed to stay for lunch,' I reminded her.

'They'll be as glad to be rid of us as we will be to go.'

This proved to be the case. Andrew accepted my weak excuse of needing to clear my desk before I took on his work with the merest formality of a protest.

'Mary will be so disappointed — she loves to show off her English roast, it's really very good,' said Helen. 'But of course you must go. Only try to make it a longer stay next time?'

They waved us off from the doorstep: Andrew in bright yellow corduroys and a blue sleeveless cardigan, Helen in a tweed skirt and cashmere top — the very image of the perfect English couple dressed for the countryside.

As John drove us away in the Range Rover Caroline said, 'What a weekend that was! Never again.'

I pointed to John and to my ears to indicate the need for discretion, but Caroline pressed on regardless.

'She's a soak, by the way.'

'What do you want to do about lunch now we're not getting any at Gilcaster Head?' I said by way of distraction.

'I could smell it on her breath before dinner. She was fried even before we sat down.'

John had gone very quiet in the front. He had an unnerving habit of constantly glancing at his phone while he was driving. I thought he would have learned the way to the station by now. Caroline was oblivious.

'And that weird little guy, Matt Dilcombe! Actually, I kinda liked him.'

I leaned forward and said to our driver, 'Since my wife is determined to talk me through our whole weekend, would you mind turning on your radio so you can't overhear everything?'

John smiled, and with a slight shrug of his shoulders, put away his iPhone and turned on the radio. Caroline glanced at me angrily and subsided.

★ ★ ★

When we got back to Newcastle she started again, banging around the kitchen with pots and pans in an effort to produce something for lunch.

'What did you think of Helen?' she asked, 'Apart from the eye-candy aspect.'

'I think she could be very tough if she didn't get her way. Andrew had better deliver the goods.'

'Mmm. Yes. I don't think Gilcaster Head will survive. She'll be on at him to sell up and get a

174

place in the Home Counties where all the smart people live.'

Some kind of lunch emerged from the Aga and I poured us both a gin and tonic. We both felt like children who had been let out of school early.

'That was a bizarre weekend,' said Caroline.

'Do you think Andrew has changed much?' I asked. We had rarely talked about the period when Caroline had been Andrew's girlfriend. She glanced at me.

'Hard to say.'

'What did you mean when you said something about his 'psychopath side'?'

'Oh, that,' said Caroline. 'He didn't beat me, or yell at me, if that's what you're thinking. But he was super-intense. He hated not being in control of whatever was going on. Sometimes it came out in small things, like deliberately not tipping a waiter who had pissed him off.'

'That just sounds mean, not psycho.'

'Mean is a good word. He had a mean side to him.'

'He wasn't just mean to that owl. He battered it to death. We could have saved that bird. As far as I could tell, it had only broken its wing.'

'Then you should have said so.'

'I know,' I admitted. 'It all happened too quickly.'

We finished our drinks and ate lunch, a dish which included a lot of pasta and not much else. Caroline was not a good cook, which had surprised me when I first found out. She said that taking pots in and out of ovens all day at the studio was enough for her and she didn't much care for doing it in the evenings as well.

'Andrew was very intense,' Caroline continued, 'and very self-absorbed. He was generous with gifts but I always felt that when he gave me one of those little blue boxes with something wonderful inside, he was really telling me that he had the money to do what he liked. There was nothing the least bit romantic about it. You would be amazed at how much jewellery I acquired during the three years we were together. I sent it all back, of course, when I left him.'

'But you never saw him in a rage before?'

'Oh yes,' said Caroline. 'He would go very quiet and then completely pale. He wouldn't speak to me — or anybody — until he had sorted the problem out. It was usually something to do with his work.'

'He never got angry with you?'

'Of course he did, sometimes.'

Caroline reflected for a moment.

'It was chilling. He would sit me down and say something like, 'You need to understand my red lines, Caroline. If you cross them, our relationship is something we will have to review together.' I mean he talked to me as if I were some subordinate at his bank.'

I laughed.

'You must have found that hard to take?'

'Very. I told him not to talk such crap. He would just give a little laugh and say, 'Don't ever make the mistake of thinking I don't mean what I say.' That usually shut me up.'

176

'And what were his red lines?' I asked.

'Andrew objected to people who didn't take him seriously. He would fly into a rage and I really believe that when he was like that he could have killed somebody, maybe even me. But it's all history now, anyway. We're talking about over a decade ago.'

I saw no point in pursuing the matter. Andrew Landford was an unusual, possibly great, man. Everything he had set out to do — playing the piano, rifle shooting, doing deals with the first generation of Russian oligarchs — he had done not well, but extremely well. Somebody I knew who had heard Andrew giving a private recital said that he could have been a concert pianist if he had chosen to.

My own views about Andrew were mixed. I had to admit his talents. His other qualities were less clear. Did he have the warmth to bond with his party? Could he enthuse the backbenchers and the grassroots party activists enough to support him?

The policies he was going to promote at the forthcoming party conference were, of course, set in stone long ago. As was the agenda. There would be no actual leadership challenge. There would be no real debate apart from the possibility of hecklers from the extreme right of the party. But the conference would be alert to a possible challenge sometime in the near future. The incumbent was a dead man walking — his failure to win an outright majority in the recent general election had seen to that. But no clear challenger had emerged. Nor would they at this conference. There might be mutterings off-stage. Glances would be cast towards Maldwyn and Andrew. Maybe a journo or two would try their luck with an off-the-cuff question: 'Will you be putting yourself forward for election, Mr Christie?' And they would receive the standard reply: 'There is no leadership contest that I know of. I'm just getting on with my job.' In 1990 the challenge hadn't come until November, well after the end of the conference season, when Mrs Thatcher had withdrawn after failing to get enough votes. She had lost not only because of splits over Europe; there were real questions about her ability to govern. People doubted her ability to work with her own Cabinet.

I wondered if that was the issue with Andrew. Would people think that he was too aloof, too self-assured? He was a talented only child who — so far — had never been given any convincing reason to believe he could ever be wrong about anything. He'd made his millions and didn't need to work. This feeling that I had whenever I met Andrew, that he was intellectually my superior, would affect other people in different ways. I tolerated it: but why? Because I had known him a long time, because I knew he had meant to be kind when he first asked me to 'look after Caroline' while he was away in Moscow, because he had not kicked up a fuss when I ended up taking Caroline away from him and marrying her. Other people would not be aware of Andrew's more human side, as I was. How would they react to him?

In the middle of the night, something strange happened. At first I thought I was having a nightmare, but I wasn't. I was awake, Caroline clutching at my arm. Her hand felt cold.

'Listen,' was all she said.

Trying to clear my head, I heard a violent noise coming from the windows. A storm rattling the frames, banging a branch against the glass. There was a yew branch overshadowing one wall of the house. It must have grown more than I had imagined this summer. I had earmarked it for cutting back next year but the job might have to be done sooner than I had thought. I started to get up to see what it was, but Caroline grabbed my arm again, pulling me closer.

'Just listen!'

For a brief moment, it sounded as if some monstrous creature was trying to get in, so violently was it scratching the window. I tried to rationalise the sound away. A branch from a tree had snapped off in the storm, and perhaps become trapped against the window. Or was it just a neighbourhood cat, clamouring to get in? I had just woken up and the room was pitch-black. In such moments quite innocuous noises can seem distorted and louder than they really are.

We lay there, saying nothing, just willing the noise to go away. Then, all of a sudden, the wind dropped, and the scratching subsided. In the long silence that followed, some distance away, I heard a solitary hoot, echoing through the empty streets.

'You see darling,' I whispered, 'it was just an owl. We've got owls on the brain, that's all it is.' I put my arm around her and pulled her against me. After a while she stopped shaking. We both slept, wrapped tight around each other, the first time we had done so in a long while. By the time morning arrived, any memory of alarm had faded with the night. The innocent yew branch that I thought had woken me was far too short to reach the windows. We went around the house closing all the windows that hadn't already been rendered unusable by the last lot of careless painters. But subsequent events would recall this as the moment when it all began.

5

I decided I needed to see Andrew with his supporters. I needed to see him work a crowd. That was one of the main topics over lunch when I met Matt Dilcombe in London the following week. We met in a small Italian restaurant on one of those anonymous streets north of the British Museum. The taxi driver had some trouble finding it and I arrived a few minutes late. There was only one table occupied in the gloomy little room. With Matt was a woman I did not recognise.

'Hello, Charles. This is Jane Everett. She has kindly agreed to be Andrew's campaign manager, if we get a shot at the top job.'

'I'm sorry I'm late,' I said, as we shook hands. 'Had some difficulty finding the place.'

We sat down.

'It has the advantage of being quiet, so you are unlikely to be overheard, or meet anyone you know. I didn't choose it for the food, as you'll discover,' said Matt. A depressed-looking waiter arrived and took orders for drinks and handed out menus.

Jane Everett was an MP for a Home Counties constituency. She was, I guessed, in her forties and was bright with an easy charm.

'At this stage I'm here to listen and I can't stay too long as I need to get up to Birmingham this afternoon. Conference starts this weekend but I have to be up a day or two early. I want to hear what people are saying about our leader, and what they're saying about Andrew and Maldwyn.'

'Are there any other names in the frame that you know of?' asked Matt.

'Not so far.'

The waiter arrived with drinks and we studied the menu. Once we'd ordered, Matt said, 'You know about the story that's going to break on Sunday, don't you?'

Jane said, with visible distaste, 'Yes. I wish it didn't have to happen this way. You do realise it could backfire on our candidate.'

'I don't see why,' said Matt. 'We didn't leak the story. It's been out there for ages and a journalist — someone who likes Maldwyn, by the way — has decided to do an op-ed. After all, he's only asking the question: is the party ready for a gay leader? For all I know, the answer might be a resounding yes.'

'It won't be, though, will it?' I asked.

'Of course not. But the story will do three things. It will imply very clearly that there *will* be a leadership challenge, and soon. It will beg the question of whether Maldwyn is a suitable candidate. And for those who don't think Maldwyn is the right person, it will get them thinking about who is right. That's where you come in, Jane.'

'Yes, I understand. You want me to work the conference, and some of the fringe meetings, to take soundings for Andrew. When Parliament is recalled, you want me to work the tea rooms, and start having one to ones with some of the key people.'

'Including the chairman of the 1922 Committee.'

'Yes. Him. He might be difficult.'

'It's all difficult,' said Matt. 'But we want Andrew to win. We need a no-confidence letter with fifty signatures or thereabouts to get the ball rolling. Andrew mustn't start promoting himself at this conference. And it's better that you don't attend, Charles. We don't want our campaign team to be visible just yet.'

'I haven't been invited, as it happens,' I admitted. As an adviser for hire, I tried to keep my private beliefs and my professional life separate, even when they intersected, and had never been a paid-up member of any political party.

'What do you think about our timing?' asked Jane.

'I'm thinking mid-November. Later than that and we'll struggle to get press coverage coming into the Christmas period. If we try sooner, it doesn't give us enough time. Later than Christmas and we'll risk losing momentum and the whole thing will have to be pushed back. And that might allow too much time for another candidate to emerge.'

'Or another story,' said Jane. 'I mean, I like and respect Andrew but I don't feel I really know him. I take it there will be no surprises on his side. No skeletons in the cupboard?'

'No skeletons,' said Matt. The food arrived, providing a useful distraction. Matt had committed us. The owl incident would remain hidden. 'But if you don't feel you know Andrew, it's time you did. He's at conference and I'll arrange for you two to meet again, as long as it's discreet.'

'Oh, I know him well enough to feel he's the best possible candidate right now. And I know we can't go on with the present leader. But I don't have a sense of Andrew as a person. That's what's missing.'

When Jane had left to catch her train, Matt said, 'So how are you going to portray Andrew?'

'To whom?'

'I'll take care of that. We just need a storyboard to work with. A profile of Andrew that we can place somewhere high-profile or give to a journalist to make their own. About two thousand words ought to do it. What's your take going to be?'

I tried to collect my thoughts. 'Well, we tell it like it is. Only child, a loner, a self-made, driven man. Doesn't have to be in politics but wants to be, has a strong sense of civic duty — all the old-fashioned virtues. Passionate about whatever he does, a happily married man with one child, so understands about family issues.'

Matt grimaced.

'You make him sound like some rich banker who has time to kill and has gone into politics to stop himself dying from boredom.'

I laughed.

'Could be. But if you don't put the basic facts about Andrew out there, people will unearth them and reconstruct them in different and possibly less favourable ways.'

184

'It could be tough to get people to like him,' said Matt.

'Maybe people don't want someone they like. Maybe we don't want matey-down-the-road to be our next prime minister. I think we're telling people that our man is supremely competent at whatever he does. He'll get the job done. He's worked in places like Moscow where they play hardball, and he's come out on top. He's survived and prospered in the real world. He's someone you'd want on your side in any argument. Think of Mrs Thatcher. Not everybody liked her, but a lot of people respected her because they knew she worked harder than most, was master of her brief, and unafraid to be unpopular as long as she was right.'

Matt was thoughtful.

'That's a good analogy,' he said after a while. 'I can see where you're going. We'll tell it like it is.'

'It's the only way,' I told him.

★ ★ ★

Conference came and went. I watched some of the coverage at home, making notes for the profile of Andrew I was writing for Matt. What I saw was boring, as it was bound to be after such a disappointing election. Everyone spoke as if they were attending the memorial service of a not particularly well-beloved colleague. In a way, they were. The triumphant music playing over the loudspeakers as the present leader took his seat jarred. Maybe the PR company that had organised the staging had overlooked the fact

185

that they had just lost an election, not won it. The leader seemed physically diminished: he sat, a tired grey man in a grey suit that suddenly seemed too large for him, presiding over what even he must have realised were the declining days of his power. The other Cabinet ministers seemed equally deflated and uncertain of their message. A year ago they had been towering and victorious, more than mortal men; now they were shrunken, almost invisible. Unelectable, one might even say.

All that changed when Andrew came on to the podium as the warm-up for the leader's main speech. I had to admit he looked good: almost presidential. He was taller than the leader and better dressed. His command of his brief — which was really only to act as cheerleader — was nevertheless absolute. In the two or three minutes when he had the conference's attention he appeared — and sounded — to be everything we could have asked for in a candidate. He said not one single word he shouldn't have. By neither gesture nor omission did he detract from the praise he had heaped on the leader. But at the end of his short slot I doubted there was anyone at conference who, if they hadn't already been wondering about Andrew Landford's potential to go further, wasn't thinking about it now. It was impressive.

★ ★ ★

Conference ended on a Wednesday. The phone call came the following day. I was in my office in

Newcastle and Caroline was working in her studio in London (I had tried and so far failed to persuade her to move her kilns and gases and other equipment north). It was from Andrew.

'Are you free this afternoon?' he asked abruptly.

'No, I'm not free,' I said rather testily. 'I do have other work to do here.' The article on Andrew was taking up more time than I had allowed, and my Head of School was beginning to grumble about my repeated absences.

'You need to come to the police station in Carlisle.'

For a moment everything disconnected. Then I said, 'Not that owl thing?'

'Yes, that 'owl thing',' replied Andrew flatly.

'What do they want?'

'They've had information lodged with them that claims I was responsible for the death of that stupid owl. They want to interview me under caution. In fact they want to interview all four of us, but I explained that the girls were in London and couldn't get up until the weekend.'

I felt a little out of breath.

'Hang on,' I said. 'Information lodged with them. Do you mean your neighbour?'

'They aren't saying. But I wouldn't be surprised if it was him. Tom's just the type. He's never quite forgiven me for not letting him dig up my land to poke around for some old temple or other. Or maybe the local police have it in for me. I did vote for the latest round of cuts, after all.'

I hadn't noticed before how adept Andrew was

at acquiring enemies. In many ways, of course, it was an essential quality in a potential leader; someone who wasn't afraid to speak their mind, regardless of the consequences. But at this rate we were going to need to find him some more vocal allies.

'Bloody hell,' I said, not very helpfully.

'What are we going to do, Charles? What shall I tell them?'

'The truth. What else? We don't know what they know and what they don't know.'

'And how will I explain the fact,' asked Andrew, 'that this story will be different from the last one I told them?' Andrew sounded rather acerbic, as if it were my fault he'd been caught out telling a lie.

'Say you were in the middle of an important meeting and you just wanted the police, and the problem, to go away.'

'So if the press ever get hold of this, we will just have to hope they decide the matter is as trivial as you're making out,' said Andrew. 'I'm on the Wildlife and Countryside Committee. We've just updated the legislation protecting threatened species. These fucking barn owls are a threatened species. What will the press say when they hear about that? They'll think it's Christmas and Easter come together. They'll dance upon my grave.'

'Andrew, I don't know what the press will do. The first thing is the police. Let me give you some thoughts.'

Andrew began to calm down, and the slightly hysterical note that had crept into his voice

188

disappeared. We agreed I would leave my car in Brampton and he would drive us together into Carlisle. On the way across from Newcastle to Brampton I rang Matt and brought him up to speed. He listened in silence. When I had finished relaying the exchanges between Andrew and myself he said:

'Mmm. Not good. I'll tell Jane.'

'Does she have to know?'

'In fairness, yes. If she wants to leave the ship, now's the time, before she becomes part of the story.'

'When you say, 'not good', are you referring to Andrew's reaction, or the whole thing?'

'The whole thing. It's all down to Andrew in the end. He wants to be leader. He'll have to fix this somehow. We've got a potential leadership challenge — and both of the candidates are damaged. It will be a complete and unmitigated disaster for the party if there isn't a credible contest.'

'What do we do?'

'Call me after the interview and meanwhile I'll see if I can catch any whispers of this out in the jungle.'

* * *

Andrew picked me up from the station car park in Brampton and we drove into Carlisle, to the regional police headquarters. We sat in a waiting room until a large officer came to meet us. He didn't mean to be intimidating, but he was. Andrew glanced at me nervously as we followed

189

the officer down to the check-in desk where we gave our personal details. To our great surprise, Andrew was then arrested and fingerprinted and read his rights. By this stage Andrew was in shock. Nobody had told him what to expect, and he obviously hadn't known.

'I'm a Member of Parliament,' he kept saying.

'Yes sir, we're well aware of who you are.'

'They can't do this to me,' he kept saying to me until I told him to be quiet.

'They can, and they are, and they will,' I told him. 'Meanwhile, least said, soonest mended.'

My mind was racing as I tried to think of a way out of this mess. And the selfish part of my brain was thinking 'if I get a criminal record through my association with Andrew, how will that affect my job?'

Andrew was taken into an interview suite, a small windowless room with twin tape decks set into the wall, beside which was a table surrounded by four chairs. Then the officer from the Wildlife Crimes Unit, the intimidating man who had greeted us at the entrance, closed the door behind him. As he did, he scowled at me.

When he opened the door again, just twenty minutes later, his voice was mild. 'Thank you, Mr Landford,' he said. 'You are free to go now.'

'Is that it?' asked Andrew as he walked out, as if he had been expecting to be chained up and thrown into a dungeon.

'I will pass this report on to my superiors who will decide whether we wish to take any further action following your statement. I will be in touch in due course. Please make sure you are available and don't leave the country until you have heard from us again.'

'How long might that be?' I asked.

'I can't say. It could be days, or months, depending on the case load.'

'And until then the information will remain confidential?' I asked. The interviewing officer almost growled.

'That goes without saying, sir.'

I had the sense to keep my mouth shut until we were back in the car.

'I thought that went OK,' said Andrew as we drove away. He sounded as if he had just emerged from a successful job interview.

'It was a very short interrogation. What did you tell them?'

He glanced at me.

'Exactly what we agreed. That over a month ago, I was driving my Range Rover when an owl flew into the windscreen.'

'Did they ask about the chip in the glass?'

'Yes. I fudged that, saying it was dark, and could have been caused by anything.'

Andrew relayed the rest of the conversation, which seemed reassuringly perfunctory. He had described to them very briefly how he had 'tried to put the owl out of its misery' and then the interview was over.

'You did the right thing by telling the truth. Unfortunately, you had no choice as somebody else out there has been in touch with the police.'

Andrew said, 'Well, we're all going to have to wait and see what the police decide to do.'

I looked at him in surprise.

'They'll send the file to the Crown Prosecution Service, of course. The CPS will decide whether they have enough evidence to prosecute. Did you hit the bird? Yes. Did you pick it up and kill it? Yes. It sounds rather like you've admitted to both those charges.'

'True, but in my defence I can say that I clearly didn't intend to hit it. After that, killing it was the right thing to do.'

I winced. 'The right thing to do' was one of my least favourite political clichés.

'The most humane thing to do, perhaps?'

'That's it. 'Humane', that's a good word.'

I couldn't understand Andrew's mood. It was almost euphoric. Perhaps now that he had finally told the truth, he felt as if a burden had been lifted from his shoulders.

'Andrew, you do realise the trouble we're in, don't you?'

'Oh, I expect a few silly headlines will emerge at some point. And I'm going to have to explain my actions to the Committee.'

'What will you say?'

'Oh, I think we were all agreed that the owl had to be put out of its misery. That's what I'll say. And I'll apologise for not telling them before I was called in by the police. That should mend any broken fences, I think.'

Maybe that's the quality all successful politicians need to possess. To come up with some version of the truth that suits them, oblivious of how it might appear to other people. That's what Andrew was doing. He had his story. It wasn't the truth. The truth was that he hadn't told the truth until the police cornered him.

I had to try to get his feet on the ground.

'Do you want to go on with the leadership campaign?' I asked.

Andrew looked at me as if I were mad.

'Of course. I shall be talking about political crises to come: the debt mountain, and how to solve it without endless decades of austerity. You're talking about a trivial incident with a dead owl. Who on earth is going to worry about me knocking a wounded bird on the head? It's a diary piece, not an editorial. A bit of amusing gossip that I shall have to endure and which you will help me to play down. We're talking about the leadership of the party, and then probably the leadership of the country. In two or three years' time I expect to be prime minister, Charles.'

I shook my head and muttered, 'Men, not measures.'

'What's that?'

'Oh, just something that a Victorian novelist once wrote: that in the end people vote for the man, not the policy.'

'I'm afraid I don't have the time to read novels these days, and if I did, I don't think I'd bother with one that was over a hundred years out of date.'

We drove on in silence until we approached Brampton.

'I'll tell you what I think privately.'

'What do you privately think, Andrew?'

'The police and the CPS will sit on this. They

know I'm an ally of the Wildlife Crimes Unit. They know I've been fighting for their corner and campaigning for more resources to help police wildlife crime. The last thing they will want to do is weaken my position.'

'You think so?'

'I do think so.'

I didn't reply. If Andrew wanted to delude himself then there was nothing I could do to stop him. Maybe he would come to his senses in a while. Or maybe he was right?

Maybe commitment was more important than the truth?

'There's another thing,' said Andrew. 'Are the police and the CPS going to consider the political impact of prosecuting me? I mean, even the Director of Public Prosecutions might have to weigh up the fact that I might be the next prime minister.'

'Andrew, this isn't Moscow. They don't bend the rules here. They don't do favours.'

He looked hurt, and gave me a wounded expression as he dropped me off at my car.

'You'll see,' was all he said.

6

I drove back alongside the Roman Wall as the sun dropped behind the horizon, looking at all the backpackers hurrying to finish their day's march before the light went. There was very little cloud, and the evening sky felt electric. The stars above this dark stretch of land would be spectacular tonight. I envied the hikers, especially the solitary ones, often having huge stretches of countryside to themselves at a time. It was quite safe, of course, and there were plenty of hostels and pubs one could turn to for shelter if the weather took an unexpected turn for the worse. There had been a time, of course, when any lone wanderer might have encountered a marauding reiver on their horse or, even further back, a Roman patrol armed with spears and shields.

Quite without warning a large shadow passed across my windscreen, blocking my view for a moment, and I had to brake sharply, only just avoiding a young family who were crossing the road to reach a car park on the other side. The car behind me honked loudly. I looked at myself in the mirror. I had gone quite pale.

What was I doing, daydreaming about reivers and Romans? I had to focus on the matter in hand. I had to ring Matt. What could I tell him? That Andrew thought the incident wasn't a problem any more? That he had said he reckoned the whole thing would just blow over, with no more impact on his leadership campaign than a fieldful of thistledown.

And maybe Andrew was right. Maybe the concoction of half-truths he had come up with would suffice. The great British public might buy into the 'humane killing' argument. Which of us has not killed a sparrow or run over a hedgehog whilst driving our car? Perhaps the story would even work in Andrew's favour: to err is human.

I rang Matt.

'I don't see what else he could have done or said,' he remarked when I'd gone through the gist of Andrew's conversation with the police.

'Do you think he will get away with it?'

'It depends what you mean by that. If you mean, do I think the whole thing will remain buried, the answer is no. But if you're asking me how much it matters when the story — a story — leaks out, the answer is less obvious. I think Andrew may have muddied the water so much that it won't matter. It won't be a fatal blow to the leadership campaign, although it won't help.'

I drove on in a state of some confusion. It seemed that, after all, I lived in a world where telling the truth wasn't that important. Telling half-truths, changing the truth until the distinction between truth and lies became less important: that was the way to prosper in today's world.

I was in a grim mood when I arrived back home.

★ ★ ★

On Friday afternoon when Caroline came up from London, we immediately had a disagreement about something. We didn't have the energy to have a full-blown row. We were both tired and inclined to be grumpy. Caroline had a show on in London, which I hadn't been to see yet because spending the day with Andrew had meant postponing my trip to London. It wasn't selling very well and had not been favoured with many reviews. The reviews she did get were relatively kind: 'Woodchester has recaptured some of her earlier visionary talent' was the sort of line they were taking, as if suggesting the best was now in the past. Maybe it was?

I was in a bad mood because I was beginning to regret my whole involvement with Andrew Landford. Why had I agreed to support him? Did I really think that, from behind the walls of academia, I could reach out into the real world without fear of corruption, and guide a man as hungry for power as he was towards some greater good? I was astonished to discover that despite years of experience, of witnessing firsthand evidence to the contrary, some of my beliefs were as naive and as unchanged as when I had first arrived at Oxford. In my head I had never stopped being an outsider observing the British system of power, with its incestuous oligarchies and slavish adherence to the status quo. And yet here I was, acting as an establishment insider. I had fantasised about being able to exert some form of benign, restraining hand on power, from behind the throne, but I had not restrained Andrew

197

Landford. At worst, I had merely accommodated him, in order to satisfy my own desires. The whole business was a terrible mess and Andrew was retreating from reality at great speed.

★ ★ ★

It was a cold and unfriendly weekend. Grey and windy skies overhead. Inside the house, draughts made doors slam unexpectedly and window casings rattle, so that it seemed as if an army of unseen people was walking about the house. Caroline was sitting in the kitchen, watching television and drinking coffee when I walked in to see what she was doing. She switched off the TV and immediately began to tell me that splitting her time between London and Newcastle was damaging her concentration and her work. The quality of her glazes, her instinct for form, had all declined since she had begun commuting. Maybe it would be better if she just lived in the London flat and came north for the occasional weekend. This sounded like the precursor to a more dramatic decision, and I fought back, arguing she should spend all of her time in the north. Caroline countered by saying that all her customers were in the south.

'Then find new buyers up here,' I suggested. 'There's a growing market for ceramics in Newcastle.' This was true, but she wouldn't accept it. She was already working on a new show, but for the first time in our marriage, she wouldn't tell me anything about it. Laptops were slammed shut as I came into the room, drawings shoved hurriedly out of sight under piles of catalogues and periodicals, enquiries left hanging in the air. All I knew was that her work was taking her away from me more and more, and I wondered if the reveal would be worth the secrecy.

We went to bed early on Saturday night, conversation at a stalemate, spirits low.

★ ★ ★

One week later, everything changed. The following Sunday morning I got up and went straight over to the newsagent on the corner, to buy a copy of every paper he stocked. I went into the kitchen and covered the kitchen table with them. I soon found the piece on Maldwyn. The article began by speculating about a forthcoming leadership election:

> For the first time in his party's history, Maldwyn Christie looks set to be a candidate in what everyone now believes to be inevitable: a leadership contest sometime this autumn. So far nobody has put his hat in the ring and the official line is that the leader is just 'getting on with his job'. But we are reliably informed that a letter of no confidence, with the requisite number of signatures, will soon be produced and may even already be in circulation. In this case, Maldwyn Christie would put his name forward as candidate, and maybe others too, including Andrew Landford.

Having set the scene, with a few more rounded phrases, the writer moved on to the question of how suitable a candidate Maldwyn might be.

Maldwyn Christie is an engaging, highly articulate individual who has certainly captured the loyalty and often enthusiastic support of wide sections of the party. He scores high on recognition amongst the grassroots activists so treasured by pollsters and other commentators. But are they in possession of all of the facts? It is perhaps not widely known outside his intimate circle that Mr Christie will be the first gay politician, if he prevails, to lead the party and therefore be a candidate to become our next prime minister. Mr Christie has not made any secret of his sexual preferences, but neither has he openly proclaimed himself as gay.

The question we now face, after all the divisions within the party, and the country, over gay marriage is: are we ready for a gay leader? And are we confident that voters will accept Mr Christie for what he is; namely a fine, instinctive politician who commands wide respect? Will that respect survive the inevitable debate about his sexuality? Will the party grandees support what must inevitably be seen as a risky candidacy? Above all, will voters be open-minded enough to accept that in the twenty-first century, such issues should no longer be relevant in judging a person's suitability to run for the top job.

What the party needs right now is a candidate who can bring the party, whose loyalties have been sorely tested, back together again. Unfortunately Mr Christie's campaign promises to be divisive. Had he chosen to bring this issue before the public himself at an earlier stage, maybe we would not have had the uncomfortable duty of bringing it to the public's attention at this juncture, before the formal processes of a leadership challenge have begun . . .

And so on, and so on.

The story was reproduced in different form in a couple of other broadsheets. One tabloid had got in on the act, somehow snatching the story out of the air. The headline ran:

PINK OR BLUE? WHAT'S YOUR FANCY?

I couldn't read the rest of the article. My head spinning with the complexity of the web we now found ourselves tangled up in, I pushed aside the rest of the papers. I summoned enough focus to boil a half-decent egg and butter some toast. Caroline came downstairs in her dressing gown and made herself a mug of tea.

The phone rang.

I could have ignored it but I knew it would just go on ringing, so I picked up.

It was Maldwyn.

'Did you know about this piece?' he asked me, without saying hello.

I didn't know how much he knew about my involvement with Andrew.

'I had heard some rumours on the grapevine . . . but you have to believe me, Maldwyn, it was a totally independent article. I really don't think there was anything we could have done to stop it.'

Maldwyn gave a weary sigh.

'Even if you'd wanted to, which I suspect you didn't. You could have given me a heads-up on this, Charlie. I mean, we have known each other for twenty years or so.'

'You know as well as I do that that could have backfired, and done you more harm than good. I really think it will blow over by tomorrow.'

'Oh well, what are friends for,' said Maldwyn, 'if not to dump on you from a great height. I'll do the same for you, Charlie, when your turn comes.'

He rang off. Strike one old friend from my Christmas card list.

'Who was that?' asked Caroline. I handed her the newspaper folded open at the article about Maldwyn. She read it carefully.

'Well, it could have been a lot worse.'

'I suppose that's true,' I said, somewhat surprised. 'The publicity generated by the conference will all be consumed by this, rather than by our failure to win a majority.'

'I meant,' said Caroline, 'that it wasn't too mean to Maldwyn. Now everyone who has a gay friend or relative will be asking themselves the question: should you be condemned to stay out of civic life? Would you vote for a gay prime minister? I think it's a thoughtful piece. It's a pity they didn't ask you to write it. Why didn't they?'

'Somebody else had the story and was determined to write it. It's lucky for us that he chose a neutral stance.'

The phone rang again.

I picked it up as if it were a snake about to bite me. It was Matt.

'I thought the tone was about right, didn't you?' he asked. Without waiting for my reply he went on, 'Nobody can accuse our team of hitting below the belt.'

'I've never asked you, Matt, but who actually leaked that story?'

'You don't want to know,' he told me.

I couldn't bring myself to reply. Matt smoothed his way on, quite unruffled.

'Charlie, politics is not a clean game. Not always. I know your pitch is that you always tell the truth, but truth is a strange commodity. It's one thing to me and another thing to you. It's never an absolute. It's sometimes a point of view. Do bear that in mind, because otherwise you might start to feel very uncomfortable. Meanwhile, if the press call you — I think it's unlikely, your connection to Andrew is not widely known — then you are to keep schtum. Don't know, never heard of him, and so on.'

'Point noted,' I said. Matt hung up.

The phone rang.

'Jesus,' said Caroline, 'is this going to go on all day?'

'Probably.'

It was Andrew. I put the phone on to speaker.

'Caroline's in the room,' I said.

The two exchanged a cautious good-morning. 'Well, that wasn't too bad after all,' he said cheerfully.

'I suppose not.'

'Quite funny, really.'

'That's not the word I would have chosen,' I said. If Andrew was going to start gloating, I would hang up on him. I was surprised at his choice of words.

'Well, when you consider what the coverage might have been. I was bracing myself for something a lot more savage than what we got.'

An awful doubt was beginning to emerge in my mind.

'Andrew, what are we talking about here?'

'The owl thing, of course.'

'I thought you were talking about the article on Maldwyn?'

'Oh, that,' he said.

'Oh, that?'

My incredulity finally reached Andrew.

'Yes, I'm very pleased that the article wasn't too personal. But that's not what I'm ringing you about. Diary on page thirteen of the *Daily Mail*.'

'Hang on a moment,' I said, struggling with the heaps of newsprint in front of me. 'Got it.'

The piece was written in typical style.

A BIT OF AN 'OWLER?

We hear that Andrew Landford ran over an owl the other night. Couldn't have happened to a nicer guy, as they say, except

— hang on, isn't he on the parliamentary Committee that amended the new Wildlife and Countryside Act? Doesn't it say something in there about running over owls? What a hoot, as they say.

'What do you think?' said Andrew, rather as if he had just handed in an essay and was expecting praise.

'You think that's the end of the owl thing?'

'Well, no, they might run a follow-up, but I don't expect that to be too troublesome.'

I wondered if I was becoming paranoid.

'Let's hope you're right.'

We returned back to the question of the Maldwyn Christie piece. Andrew sounded bored by the topic.

'Kid-glove stuff,' he said.

'Would you mind if it was you?'

'If you can't stand the heat, as a famous predecessor at Number 10 said, get out of the kitchen.'

His arrogance staggered me. I wanted to shout at him. But all I said was, 'You think your campaign is in the bag, then?'

'You can never say that. To quote the Lady again, never say never. Was she the one who first said that?'

'I think it was Julius Caesar.'

Caroline had been half-listening to this. When I had finished, the phone mercifully remained silent for a while.

'Why do you work for that guy?' she asked.

It was fast becoming an increasingly difficult

question to answer.

'I wish I knew. I said I'd do it, though. So now I'm stuck with a candidate who I think is dead in the water. In his own mind, he's already won.'

'You can pull out. I would,' said Caroline.

'I can't. I still believe I can make a difference here. I'm committed.'

'Is that what you say to yourself when you think about our marriage?'

I rocked on my heels as if I'd taken a punch. In a way, it was true. I pushed the papers away from me, then put out my hand to take hers but coolly she withdrew it.

'Come on, Charlie, you're a grown up. This is no time for sentiment. We're talking about our marriage, not a love affair. How are we going to get by? Are we going to get by?'

She stood up. She had no make-up on yet, and in the morning light her skin looked grey. Had I done this to her, I wondered? What had happened to the girl from the Fryerne Arms all those years ago? Or to me, for that matter. It was hard to tell whether it was the years of marriage that had changed us, or whether we had been changed by external forces beyond our control, pulled in different directions, only appearing now as distorted reflections of the people we had once fallen in love with. I would have done anything to return us to some semblance of our former selves, but I had no idea how.

'I'm going to take a bath and get dressed,' she said, stretching. 'And then, because I never got around to any shopping, you're going to take me somewhere nice to have Sunday lunch. And I don't mean soggy Yorkshire pudding and floury roast potatoes, either. Let's get a bit of glamour back into our lives, buster.'

As she closed the bathroom door the phone rang again. It was Matt.

'They've shoe-horned Maldwyn into the *Sunday Politics* show.'

'Today? This morning? Who's his media guy? That's very quick work.'

'I think it's smart of Maldwyn to get on it. He'll have national attention by tonight. How did your conversation with Andrew go?'

'Like talking to someone in outer space.'

Matt sounded amused.

'Andrew's been asked to appear on a Radio 4 documentary about politics and the environment. It's a set-up, of course. He's been asked to talk about the effects of pollution on UK wildlife. Halfway through owls will get to the top of the agenda. I've told him not to accept. He wants to do it but it's all risk and not much reward. We have a grid and I want him to stick to it. When's your own piece coming out and what are you going to say?'

'I'll have it by Tuesday. I don't know what I'm going to say yet. I'll send you a draft on Monday night.'

7

I found a restaurant with a view of the Tyne and an elaborate menu. We sat and gazed at the river below, with its many bridges, and the spire of St Nicholas's Cathedral. There was a flood tide and the river was full, the flow upstream meeting a headwind so that white caps broke the surface of the water. For a while we were both absorbed in the view, our silence punctuated by the padding of waiters' feet; the leather-bound menus and wine list were handed round so reverently they could have been illuminated fourteenth-century missals.

When the necessary business of ordering food and drink was complete, I asked Caroline, 'So what did you mean when you asked me this morning, 'are we going to get by?''

Caroline gave me a tired smile. Weary as it was, it recaptured for me many of the reasons why we were still together. She still fascinated me. Her intelligence was livelier than mine; her ability to cut to the chase, no matter what the circumstances. There was a dimple beside the curve of her mouth that had always entranced me.

'Well, we're just going through the motions, aren't we? You don't even make love to me. Even our arguments aren't any fun.'

'Fun?'

'Well, you know what I mean.'

I did know. In the old days we had enjoyed

some fiery rows, which Caroline seemed to relish more than I. My response was, inevitably, to retreat into silence, fleeing the slamming doors for a solitary walk along the river. It was true though that whilst I found these micro-dramas intensely discomfiting, they were also cathartic, and our relationship often felt on a more even keel afterwards.

'I know what you mean.'

Some indescribable mixture in a shot glass with a tiny spoon was placed in front of us.

'What the hell is this?' asked Caroline. Without flinching, the waiter gave us a brief description.

When he had gone I asked, 'But are you telling me you want us to separate?'

'We are already separate,' said Caroline. 'We lead separate lives and most of the time we live in separate places. You don't even pretend to be excited by my work and as for yours — I am still trying to get my head around what it is that you actually do.'

'Oh, come on. We've just spent most of a weekend doing it.'

'You used to tell me that 'truth speaks to power'. But in the last few weeks your version of the truth has become elastic. The closer you've got to real power — meaning Andrew and Matt — the more you've changed. Andrew's been covering his tracks on the owl story as fast as he can. Don't think I haven't noticed. 'We decided to put the owl out of its misery', not 'I decided'. He's made you — and me — an accessory to whatever breaches of the law that entails. Doesn't that bother you? Apparently not. Then there's the story that was leaked about Maldwyn. I heard you tell Maldwyn, when you were on the phone to him this morning, that you knew something was in the wind. That was double-talk, buddy. And don't give me that innocent look. You knew all about it.'

The food arrived at that moment, and the wine, and four waiters to lift the silver covers from our plates. A candle was lit and the sommelier looked thoughtfully at the colour of the rather indifferent wine I had ordered, and pronounced it fit for consumption. At last we were able to speak again.

'Are you saying I'm telling lies?'

'No. But you're close.'

'What's this got to do with us?'

'All I know is you're a different person to the one I married.'

The food looked delicious, and for a while we were caught up in that religious peace that settles over a room where people are gathered for a really good lunch.

'Mmm. This is delicious,' said Caroline.

'I was thinking about our wedding earlier,' I said.

'Oh yeah. We had that colossal row about whether we should ask any of your so-called family.'

'But we had to ask Uncle Brad, and that rather let the cat out of the bag.'

Caroline smiled at the memory.

'Andrew sent flowers, didn't he?' I asked.

'A sinister-looking bunch of lilies,' agreed Caroline.

I remembered that bunch of lilies, like a cold finger laid upon my hand; a reminder: she was mine before she was yours. The gesture was typical of Andrew. He needed to exert his will over us even when there was no longer any point. For in those days Caroline was mine. Whatever relationship she had with Andrew had disintegrated.

'Must we separate?' I asked Caroline. 'Is there no hope for us?'

'You're hurting me,' she replied, and I realised I was clutching her hand.

'I'm sorry, I didn't mean to.'

She didn't speak for a moment, just softly massaged her fingers where I had gripped her.

'It will just happen, Charlie, won't it? I'm not seeing anybody else and I haven't the strength to even think about what life would be like without you. But we're drifting apart. There's no commitment any more. And I'm not sure I can spend much more time in that house, not after dark.'

'The house? What do you mean?'

She didn't reply. She didn't need to. I knew perfectly well what she was referring to. The scratching at the glass that now woke us most nights. The faint solitary hoot that had now become a chorus of hoots, haunting our dreams. I didn't want to talk about it. I couldn't. It felt irrational and absurd even to acknowledge it. I had to focus on Andrew's campaign.

Down below the wind had dropped, or else the tide had turned, and the surface of the river was like glass, dark and implacable.

* * *

211

Checking my phone afterwards I found a stack of calls waiting for me on my voicemail. There were two press calls, which was worrying. Nobody was supposed to know of my connection with Andrew. I ignored them. There was also another call from Andrew himself, so I returned that first.

'Very funny,' he said.

'What was?'

'Maldwyn's interview on the *Sunday Politics* show.'

'I don't understand . . . '

'Oh, you know what he's like,' said Andrew. 'Instead of moaning on about smear tactics and character assassination he was actually quite funny about it. It's no good me trying to imitate him, you must watch it on iPlayer or something. Can you do that?'

'I think so,' I told him.

'Watch it and tell me what you think.'

I turned on the TV and scrolled forward until I saw Maldwyn appear on the screen.

'What are we to make of these disclosures in the newspapers today?' asked the presenter.

'The disclosure that I might be seeking to run against the leader of my party for his job is embarrassing but inevitable after an election like the one we've just had. We all have to shrug our shoulders and just get on with our day job. We'd like to talk about our policies; the media want to talk about personalities.'

'In your case there is an allegation about your private life as well.'

Maldwyn smiled. He seemed quite at ease.

'I don't know where that story came from — I assume you are referring to the question about whether I am gay or not — but I do know why it was published, which was as a distraction from the real issues: the need to bring down our borrowing, to reduce the cost of the state and to create more space for the private sector to grow . . . '

'Are you gay?' asked the interviewer.

'Anybody who knows me knows that yes, of course I am. It's not a secret. I'm gay, middle-aged, white and I support Chelsea. That's all there is to know about me, really.'

'Do you think these revelations will harm your candidacy?'

'I'm not a candidate for anything, but if I were, I imagine I might have alienated a few Arsenal or Man U supporters. I hope not.'

The presenter laughed. That was Maldwyn's secret. He put you at ease. He made you laugh despite yourself. The interviewer began again, 'But . . . '

'I'm not avoiding the question,' said Maldwyn. 'You want to know whether, if I were to become a candidate — which I repeat, is not my present position — voters would desert me because I am gay. The answer is, I don't know. I'd like to think that my constituents and any other supporters I may have would be rather offended if you asked them that question. I think they'd ask you to go away and come back with a question about my political preferences, not my sexual orientation. Haven't we all got past that stage of the debate?'

As Maldwyn spoke the camera moved to focus in on him. He was wearing an old tweed jacket over rather grubby corduroy trousers, a checked shirt and a paisley tie knotted somewhere under his left ear. His horn-rimmed spectacles lent him a perpetual air of mild surprise. He was the despair of every PR man in the business who had ever tried to tidy him up. Now he ran his hand through receding, curly hair and waited for a reply.

As I watched the discussion I saw an extraordinary thing: the BBC, or more correctly the mainstream voice of middle England that the presenter was speaking for, went on the defensive. It was as if the interviewer had intruded not only on Maldwyn's private life, but on all our private lives, on our right to be who we were without fear of censure. I heard myself say out loud, 'Well done, Maldwyn!' It was almost a cheer. When the interview concluded a few minutes later I felt a sense of elation that was quite at odds with my job. My job was to ensure Andrew ran as the main candidate and won. The last ten minutes or so had changed everything. I didn't think it had much altered people's view of Maldwyn's suitability as a future prime minister; but it had altered the terms of the debate.

We weren't talking any more about Maldwyn as a gay MP. We were talking about Maldwyn as a human being, someone you could imagine sitting at your kitchen table and discussing politics or football with you. Whether I could position Andrew against him as a 'man who got things done' and whether that would be enough to counter Andrew's lack of warmth, that was the challenge now.

★ ★ ★

Later that week I happened to be in London for a conference, still trying to juggle my academic day job with the increasing demands of Andrew's campaign. I agreed to meet Matt for a drink afterwards. Yet again he chose an unassuming venue, a Victorian pub just off Tottenham Court Road, packed with builders still in their work clothes and local shop workers. We sat in a gloomy wooden corner, his eyes darting nervously around the crowd. He wanted to know what I thought of Maldwyn's TV appearance.

'If I'm honest, Matt, I'm worried that we might come out of it looking rather grubby.'

'We weren't the ones who started this. The article was going to be written whatever we did. I must admit I did think it might shut Maldwyn's campaign down. Now it's not so obvious. Our line, by the way, is that 'we respect Maldwyn's right to a private life and we don't think it has any bearing on his eligibility as a leadership candidate or any other position he might be interested in.''

I nodded, but it was a fraught conversation, and I was relieved when Matt didn't accept my offer of a second round, allowing me to catch an earlier train back to Newcastle.

On the way back I tried to call Andrew but his line was busy so I left a message. It was probably for the best — I was rather fed up with the whole business. When I got home, the door was on the latch but the house was unlit. Surprisingly — given the previous weekend's conversation — Caroline had come up from London earlier than usual. I found her lying on the bed in the spare room. It was a small room with only one high window which faced a wall. She wasn't asleep, but lay with her eyes wide open, staring at the ceiling.

'I might sleep in here tonight,' she said. 'Do you mind?'

I couldn't see that anything would be gained by insisting otherwise.

'Of course,' I said. 'Is there anything I can get you?'

She looked at me in surprise.

'Yes. You could get rid of them. I don't care what you do, or how you do it, just make them leave us alone.'

I glanced up at the window. There was nothing there, apart from a single long scratch down the middle of the pane, which I couldn't recall having seen there before.

$$\star\ \star\ \star$$

That night I decided to write my piece on Andrew, which would be shaped and no doubt reshaped by Matt and our other media advisers. I hoped that what emerged in the newspapers and elsewhere would bear some resemblance to my original document.

It was a hard piece to write, made more difficult by Andrew's current mood which

216

seemed to me to be curiously detached from what should have been one of the most important weeks of his life. He believed he had dealt with the twin challenges of Maldwyn and the owl incident, which I felt was still out there but which Andrew had decided was nothing more than a joke for the diary columns. And hovering like a warning over every phrase I wrote were Caroline's words. She was right. I had always prided myself on telling the truth — to those in power, to the public, to whoever cared to hear it. It was the basis for my whole career. But what did I really know about Andrew, other than a few spare facts? Moscow, or Westminster, or a toxic combination of the two experiences had altered him, and his true self remained a mystery to me, wrapped in smoke. I believed in his ability to lead, to be decisive, but I struggled to expand that obvious gift into anything approaching a philosophy. Once or twice I picked up the phone half-inclined to talk to the man himself, but I couldn't bring myself to do it.

It was late when I finished the article but I reread it before I went to bed. I had downloaded a photo of Andrew from a press library. It had been taken when he was still with his bank in Moscow and showed a gaunt-looking figure, his face thinner than it was now, with intense, brooding eyes. Behind him was a brick wall unrelieved by door or window. Snow lay on the ground. My text started from that point:

Andrew Landford is a driven man. He learned his trade in Moscow in the 1990s (see picture above) which was not a place or a time for the faint-hearted. Nevertheless, great things were achieved, and fortunes were made and lost. Much that was accomplished in those chaotic days has been overlaid and replaced as successive governments came and went, and the era of Putin began. Whatever one's views about Putin, there is now a desire to invest in Russia and some of the battles that had to be fought to assist the progress of democracy and the rule of law were fought by Andrew.

It is that same drive to succeed, that same stubborn intensity that makes Andrew Landford the most eligible person to emerge so far in the race for a future party leader. At home, he is a different person. His wife, Helen, is a former corporate lawyer. She well knows the world that Andrew once worked in and is equally at home in political circles . . .

I read through this and more of the same, before starting the weary process of editing. Eventually I had had enough and closed up my laptop for the night. When I went upstairs I looked around the door of the spare room. Caroline appeared to be fast asleep, but her face was flushed. She murmured something into her pillow as I stood there. I waited a moment and then gently pushed the door to.

I went to bed alone, which I was used to, but never before when Caroline had actually been at home with me. It felt odd: a little alien. The

218

windows rattled, as they always did on windy nights. As I fell asleep I heard a familiar noise, like the whistle of a passing train. But that was long ago, I told myself sleepily, they don't make trains like that any more. The next second, it seemed, I was woken by a drumming of rain on the windows; or was it the scraping of twigs? The noise was slow, deliberate and insistent.

I sat up in bed, feeling Caroline's absence immediately.

'Hello?' I said, stupidly.

The drumming turned into a hammering, which turned into such a thunder of force against the glass that I thought it would smash. I wanted to get out of bed and snatch the curtain away, so that I could see it was nothing but a stupid trick of the mind. I couldn't. An unknowable fear pinned me where I sat.

The hammering became a cacophony of wing and claw, accompanied by harsh shrieks.

This time there was no mistaking it.

The owls were trying to get in.

8

The following week, the war began.

It started, as all wars do, with hints of mobilisation underway, of divisions being manoeuvred into position. In the lobbies and in the bars and tea rooms the talk was all about Maldwyn and Andrew. Jane and Matt, who seemed to have access to everyone and everything, kept me up to date. My piece on Andrew was handed in, quarrelled over and edited. Various forms of it began to appear in the broadsheets. The *Daily Telegraph* gave it a page. The gaunt black and white picture of Andrew was shown alongside a picture of Maldwyn looking no less tousled than usual in a pinstriped suit that didn't quite fit him.

The comment in the left-of-centre dailies and weeklies was more or less hostile. They portrayed Andrew as a banker on the make, but through the sometimes contemptuous commentary, one sensed fear. They thought Andrew might win the leadership election, and they feared his hard-nosed approach might do real damage in a general election. He wouldn't pull his punches.

The interviews began, and more in-depth pieces appeared featuring both candidates. In all of these, Andrew scored highly. He spoke of Maldwyn, if he spoke of him at all, as 'a really nice guy — someone I knew at university but sadly lost touch with while I was working in

Russia'. The implication, never spoken but left hanging in the air, was that while Andrew had been working his guts out, Maldwyn had been playing around. 'Lightweight' was the adjective Andrew was indirectly trying to attach to Maldwyn, although it was probably Matt's idea.

Nobody said anything, or asked anything, about owls.

★ ★ ★

The decision came as no surprise when it arrived. Under Tory Party rules, the leadership could be changed only if the current leader resigned or a letter of no confidence collected a sufficient number of signatures. In the event, the leader decided to pre-empt the no-confidence process. It was clear he no longer had the backing of his party so he decided to move on before he was pushed. Still carrying himself like a wounded man, he popped up on television to repeat his willingness to do his duty for his party and his country, but asked the chairman of the 1922 Committee to accept his resignation. This was duly written and accepted. To the leader's credit he did not hang around and let uncertainty damage his party any further than the current level of speculation already had. On the other hand, the casual way in which his party — and even his friends — had turned their backs on him was quite something to behold.

In the second week after the appearance of the letter, the first round of voting began. Andrew now openly lobbied his cause in the tea rooms

221

and bars. It did me good to see this: he was not too proud to work his cause. He and Maldwyn met one night in the Strangers' Bar. I was with Andrew that evening, watching him at work and trying to get a feel of how the debate was running. With us was a Yorkshire MP and his wife. The man from Yorkshire had piggy eyes and was as hard as nails. He was pro-Andrew, pro-anybody who would speak out for Good Honest Party Principles, as he saw them. Maldwyn had just come into the bar with another MP and was buying drinks.

'Hello, Andrew,' he said — we were only a few feet apart — 'I'd offer to buy you a drink but I expect that would count as bribery. How are you?'

'I'm very well, Maldwyn. And I couldn't drink another thing. I've had enough cups of tea to sink a battleship.'

'It's hard work, this electioneering business. So, you think you are going to win?'

There was some laughter from around us.

'Go, Maldwyn!' somebody said.

'Who can say?' Andrew replied. 'It's in the lap of the gods.'

'Or in the hands of the bookmakers,' said Maldwyn. 'Or even a certain wise goddess.' He turned away with a laugh as if he'd just made a joke. If he had, it was a very obscure one and left his companion looking as baffled as everyone else.

Andrew turned quite white for a second. 'What did he mean by that?' he said quietly to me. 'I'm going to ask him.' I looked across to where Maldwyn was now standing at the centre

222

of a group of people, exerting his customary charm. I put a restraining hand on Andrew's elbow.

'Don't even think about it,' I said.

A certain wise goddess. The only one who immediately sprang to mind was Minerva, the goddess of wisdom, and by long association . . . owls. But to imagine that Maldwyn was making a deliberate allusion to the bird incident was surely ridiculous. To me the exchange had an almost random quality to it, as if Maldwyn had scarcely known what he was saying. The whole thing was odd; very odd.

On a normal day it would have been something to follow up on but this was not a normal day. When the votes were counted at the end of the first ballot several names that one expected to see on the list appeared with predictable results. However, most of the attention was focused on Andrew and Maldwyn. The surprise was that there was no outright winner. Andrew had a lead, but it was not decisive. Under party rules, the candidate with the lowest number of votes dropped out, but as several MPs had put their names forward, the ballots would continue until there were only two candidates left, at which point the contest would be thrown open to the whole party via a postal vote.

★ ★ ★

The following week I was in London again to see Caroline's current exhibition, having missed the private view, thanks to Andrew and his police interview. It was the least I could do. She greeted my arrival at the flat with her face half-averted so that a kiss aimed at her lips was deflected to her cheek. I told myself it was not an outright rejection.

'Shall we go out to dinner after the show?' I asked.

'I suppose so. Let's see who's there.'

Ignoring the implication that my company wasn't enough, I spruced up after my train journey and we took a taxi to the gallery.

'It's not my most exciting work ever. Do say if you can't stand it and we'll leave,' said Caroline anxiously. In fact the work was better than I had expected from her remarks. There were a decent number of red spots. There was a ceramic toad prince that I rather liked and would have bought if somebody hadn't got there first.

'I love this,' I told her.

'It's just a lightweight thing. A joke.'

We wandered along the rows of sculptures. Straightening up after bending to look at a white Ophelia in a pool of ceramic lilies with a graphite glaze I bumped into someone.

'I'm sorry,' I said, without looking round.

'And so you should be,' said Maldwyn sharply. 'I cut you off like a dead hand and now I gather you never even noticed. I clearly need to work on my technique.'

'I wasn't sure you wanted to speak to me,' I said. 'The article doesn't seem to have done you any harm. You've been extremely good at turning the situation around.'

'Now you listen to me, young feller me lad,' said Maldwyn. 'If you think I went into politics for a pile of sloppily written pieces chuntering on about how many nice gay friends people have, and what a good cook and conversationalist I must be . . . '

'Don't be so cynical Maldwyn,' said Caroline, trying to leaven the mood. 'It doesn't suit you.'

He punched her lightly on the arm. 'Oh don't you worry. I'll let you know when I'm being cynical. There's no fun in it otherwise.' He paused, then said, 'Look here, what are you two ne'er-do-wells doing later on?'

'Having supper, I suppose.'

'I rather fancy we all need a proper chinwag, don't you, Mr Fryerne?' He eyeballed me in that Maldwyn way which suggested there was only one answer to the question. I shrugged. 'It'll be just like old times, only we'll be talking about grown-up things, like who should run the country. There's a rather nice little place round the corner. I wouldn't touch the food if I were you but the cellar's not bad . . . '

My face must have given me away.

'Don't worry, old fruit, I'm not asking you to betray Andrew. Much as it pains me to admit it, I might actually have an olive branch stuffed up my sleeve.'

'Why don't you talk to Andrew himself?'

'And end up all over the front pages of tomorrow's newspapers, thanks to that Kiwi terrier who's always scuttling along behind him? I'm rather over negotiation via the press, if you don't mind. Forgive me for being terribly old-fashioned, but I like the expression 'smoke-filled backroom deal' and that's exactly what I intend to do.'

I left the two of them and went and looked out of the window. This felt like a set-up of some sort. But was there more to it than that?

There was only one way to find out.

'OK,' I said, turning back. 'No photos, no tape recordings, no leaks of this meeting at all. Is that understood?'

'Yes, yes, I'll stand MI5 down,' said Maldwyn, and stepped outside to make a call.

'Well done, darling,' said Caroline.

'Were you in on this?' I asked her.

'Well, he did ring me about an hour before you arrived,' she said. 'I thought it was time you two sorted things out.'

We hung around the gallery for a while in case anyone important came in, then shut up shop and went outside. We walked down Kensington Church Street. The three of us were dressed in drab grey coats and looked like a bunch of conspirators heading for a putsch. Perhaps we were. It was still quite early but the street lamps were on, haloed in a soft drizzle. Maldwyn dived down a side street until we came to the dimly lit entrance to a restaurant. We let ourselves in and found a dark, comfortable area with cane chairs and glass-topped tables, which I suppose was the bar. A waiter came and took our coats and our drinks order. Maldwyn said nothing until his whisky and water arrived.

'Well, how does my fine friend think he's

doing?' he asked abruptly, before taking a large swig.

'He's content,' I said.

'Content . . . an interesting choice of word.'

'What did you want to talk about, Maldwyn?'

'Oh, I rather fancied a bit of a heart to heart with you. Maybe even do a deal. But let's order first. I'm so much more relaxed once I'm certain of proper browsing and sluicing.'

So the waiter was summoned and we ordered and then Maldwyn leaned back in his chair until it creaked dangerously and said, 'I'm at a turning point. I've had all the nice little 'the only gay in the village' pieces I'm going to get. It's becoming rather thin gruel. Next week the wheel will turn, and out will come the backlashers, as they always do, dragging their chains behind them. Is a man like me going to be strong enough in times of crisis? Are Mr and Mrs Middle England sitting in their conservatory in Nuneaton ready for such a revolution? And will it be fair to the other person in my life who will no doubt be named and whose whole past will be given a forensic going-over, as if he were a common criminal.' Quite unexpectedly for Maldwyn, he flushed, and there was a crack to his voice. 'I can see all the ghastliness coming and I just don't think I can face it.'

'The tide went out and now it's coming back in,' I nodded sympathetically.

'Maybe so, King Canute,' said Maldwyn. 'Meanwhile, I'm busy in my Exchequer counting up the votes I think I can guarantee for the final round. I might have picked up a few riders from fallen horses, but equally a few of my own have tumbled into the ditch. When I tot it all up what it comes down to is this — I don't think I can win.'

We'd already thought about this and were coming to the same conclusions: a dull, attritional campaign, which was the last thing any political party needed and might even tempt the interim leader to put himself forward as a compromise candidate. That would be the worst sort of intervention.

Caroline looked at me. Maldwyn looked at me. Did I get it? Had I understood the meaning of this plot?

Our dinner arrived and with it my light-bulb moment.

'You want to offer yourself as deputy leader and Andrew as leader. Then everybody's happy. We march on in step and win the next election.'

'By jove, I think he's finally twigged,' murmured Maldwyn, dry as a nut.

Between Andrew and Maldwyn they could command enough votes to shut out any rival candidates. It was a 'dream ticket': Andrew's hard-edged style would appeal to some in the party; others would look to Maldwyn to be a softening and more humanising influence, likely to smooth the ragged edges in Andrew's persona and make him more electable when the day for the real election came: the one that counted. The next general election.

I could see everything that was to be gained by saying yes. I couldn't — I didn't see — what reasons there might be for saying no. I didn't see what was out there.

I realised everyone was waiting for me to say something.

'I'll take it to Matt and Andrew.'

'And?' asked Maldwyn and Caroline simultaneously.

'I'll say I think we should go for it. Matt might be a little disconcerted he wasn't consulted first.'

'Let me get on the blower to my own people first before you send the cavalry dashing in with Andrew,' said Maldwyn. 'Best we pitch it as my genius invention, roping you in as a go-between for old times' sake. Don't you think?'

After that the evening became just another dinner. It was like the good old Oxford days, sitting around a table with Maldwyn, who in his usual unassuming way was the centre of our conversation. They were his jokes we laughed at; his gossip that was the freshest and the most revealing. Before we left, I had the chance to ask him a question unobserved while Caroline was collecting her coat.

'Maldwyn, the other day when you met Andrew, do you remember that you asked him if he thought he would win?'

'Vaguely.'

'You did. And he answered that it was in the lap of the gods.'

'Fair enough,' replied Maldwyn.

'But you then said: or in the lap of a certain goddess. What did you mean by that?'

'Did I? I really can't remember, my dear,' answered Maldwyn. 'Does it matter? It's precisely the sort of inane remark one makes on such occasions, the kind I pray any considerate biographer will strike from the record.'

And that was how the matter was left that evening.

9

The following morning I rang Andrew and told him we needed to talk about a proposition from Maldwyn. We agreed we should meet, and I went to his office in St Stephen's Buildings. He summoned me into his inner sanctum with a nod and shoved a cup of black coffee across the table without asking me what I wanted. He was drinking a glass of water and looked tired. There was a rawness to his features I had not seen before. He must have seen me staring, and batted away my unasked question. 'I've not been sleeping well. It's . . . nothing.' He drummed his fingers on the table. The nails were bitten to shreds. 'So, you've been having secret meetings with the competition, have you?'

He was in a sour mood, which I tried to temper.

'It's not quite how it looks. I only agreed to the meeting because I thought we should hear what he had to say.'

'You could have called me first. Or maybe it might have been nice to invite Matt. At a stretch you could even have asked your boss — that's me, by the way — whether contact of this sort was appropriate at this stage of the campaign.'

I decided I could be equally bad-tempered.

'Andrew, that's just not the way it happened. One minute Maldwyn arrived in the gallery, and fifteen minutes later we were sitting down with him. After all, he is an old friend. He said he wanted to talk and then told me his idea. I felt there was a deal to be done — subject to your approval — and that deal was either going to be done now or we could just continue on with the current process and go into yet more rounds of voting. You know what I think about the risks of that.'

'What you think doesn't matter. Matt is in charge of tactics.'

We both went silent. Then Andrew caved in.

'Tell me what the fucking deal is then.'

I told him.

The problem for Andrew was that the deal was irresistible. It gave him a lock on the leadership and an almost guaranteed run for prime minister at the next general election. Even Andrew had to concede that Maldwyn's presence as deputy would be a terrific plus. It would demonstrate as clearly as possible that the party rejected any prejudice and indeed it embraced the strengths that Maldwyn could bring as leader. Andrew thought about it for a long time while I sat opposite him, drinking his bitter coffee. In the end he tried to look stern, failed and allowed a thin smile.

'Well, you rat,' he said. 'I guess you think you've got it all sewn up, don't you?'

'The decision rests with you, Andrew. You need to tell him yes or no. That's how I left it. When you've spoken to Maldwyn, he'll call Matt and apologise for not bringing him into the loop before now.'

'I need to know what Maldwyn's view of a

deputy leader's duties are before I can sign up to this.'

'Quite right. You need to ask him that.'

We talked for a while longer and then Andrew stood up. 'I'll speak to Matt and then Maldwyn. Your role in this business is over now. Please don't have any more contact with Maldwyn until it is all put to bed. I don't want any crossed lines.'

'But you're going to say yes?'

'I'm going to say yes.'

At that moment everything appeared to be within our power. The doubts and anxieties that had been clouding the horizon over the past weeks suddenly lifted, and I felt the bright, dazzling surge of light one always receives from a new Jerusalem. My mind was already bent on our campaign for the next general election.

I got up to go, but Andrew stayed me with a hand on my arm. 'Oh, by the way, Charles, I should probably mention the police at Carlisle have asked to speak to me again about this wretched owl business. This evening. They assure me it's still routine, but I'm going to take my lawyer with me this time. Just to be sure.'

I nodded.

'How tiresome. Will you let me know what they say?'

'Of course.'

He beamed and we grasped each other's hands in a sort of valedictory handshake.

When I left Andrew's office it was with the self-conscious step of an operator, someone who got things done, who made kings out of princes.

I felt so buoyed up that I only just noticed the flap of broad wings, soaring overhead from one rooftop to another, as I strode off down the street,

★　★　★

That weekend the media awoke to the possibility of a Landford/Christie ticket sweeping away all before them. I hadn't been asked to do any press releases or articles so I assumed that Matt had organised all that. If so, he had done it very well. There wasn't a single negative comment in the press at all; nothing but praise for 'a carefully crafted deal that none of us could see was staring us in the face until Landford and Christie had the courage to shake hands on it'.

Other headlines followed:

LANDFORD AND CHRISTIE: COULD THIS BE THE WINNING TEAM?

read one.

STRONG DOUBLE TICKET THREATENS TO SHORTEN ODDS AT GENERAL ELECTION

read another.

The ballots had now reduced the field to Maldwyn and Andrew. So when Maldwyn formally withdrew from the contest that week, Andrew became the new leader of the Conservative Party and the postal vote was no longer necessary. The flurry of commentary and analysis after the announcement came to the conclusion that the double ticket deal had indeed given Andrew the deciding edge. Maldwyn may have been honest and humorous about his outing, but in the final analysis he paled as a weaker figure alongside his square-jawed rival. This perception was nothing, commentators were at pains to underline, to do with his sexuality, but rather it was the downside of his mild and self-effacing public demeanour. He would therefore, all agreed, make an outstanding deputy.

Standing in front of Conservative Central Office, the short victory speech the new leader gave, which was covered live online and across all the news channels, was Andrew Landford at his most unforgettable. I watched from hundreds of miles away, on Caroline's ancient, juddering kitchen TV, and still felt the hairs rise on the back of my neck. The backdrop of weathered pillars and a cluster of bright young men and women, stern-faced with their hands clasped, set the mood. Helen swayed gently in front of them, flushed with colour, a distant look in her eyes. Maldwyn stood to the side, shrewd and pensive. Someone had helpfully erected a lectern for Andrew, a prominent Union Jack emblazoned on the front, with the name of the party in smaller letters underneath. The general election to come almost seemed an irrelevant detail, as Andrew strode out, looked the cameras in the eye, and began to speak.

'It is a very great honour and privilege to have

been given the opportunity to lead your party at this difficult time for the country. Let me say now, I will do it with every fibre of my being, and I will not rest until the job is done. Nothing will distract me from the task in hand.'

Perhaps it was my imagination, but he seemed to glance up at the sky when he said this. He went on to thank Maldwyn and the other candidates and to commend their campaigns as decent and well fought, praising Maldwyn for his honesty, 'which has set an example to us all. No longer can a person's sexuality be a barrier to public service, even at the very highest levels.'

Andrew looked forward to 'gathering the many and diverse talents of the party under one roof. Then together, we will fix that roof and make it a stronger one for all of Britain. A roof to last in all weathers, in the good times and the bad.'

Then he stopped looking down at his notes and relaxed his shoulders, giving a half-smile.

'I have to say, whoever you voted for, I am sure you are all glad that I have been elected leader of the Conservative Party, and not President of the RAC. Suffice to say, I will, from now on, be making full use of the driver that comes with the job.'

There was a ripple of polite laughter, although Maldwyn frowned. As the scrolling subtitles below the picture hurried to try and explain the reference, Andrew knitted his brows, and returned to his serious tone.

'I shall use that time in the back of the car, as I shall be using all my time now, to think deeply about the problems that face us as a nation. How

236

we can learn to pay our way in the world. How we can continue to be valued partners to our allies, yet always defend our own interests. How we can once more make this country a place we want our children to grow up in.'

He went on to list his now familiar policy shopping list: achieving sustainable economic growth, public service reform, eradicating the Westminster bubble, promoting renewable energy and, of course, protecting the wildlife that helps make this country great.

The words began not just to scroll along the bottom of the screen, but to drift into my head and dissolve into a blur of 'trust . . . values . . . responsibility . . . principle . . . challenge and change'.

Some changes are easier and quicker to make than others. I was at first surprised, then hurt, to find that my post-victory phone calls, texts and emails to Andrew went unanswered. As the wall of silence built, with no communication from even Matt or Jane, it became clear I had been shut out from the inner circle.

Too much initiative was a dangerous thing to have, it appeared. I had played a part in the deal with Maldwyn that had unlocked power for Andrew, but now Andrew had to protect that power. His main rival was now his deputy; a threat contained but also given a potentially dangerous advantage. I suspected that Andrew thought if he removed intermediaries such as myself, Maldwyn would be further isolated from the real seat of power.

This suspicion was confirmed when two days

later there was finally a text:

'Please accept this note as termination of your contract of employment with Andrew Landford. An email confirmation will follow, on which your signature will be required.'

It came as Caroline and I were sitting down to supper together in our house in Newcastle. We seemed to have arrived at something of an uneasy truce. She had spent, as ever, the week in London working on her mysterious new show, but had returned home without comment. I wondered if it was a temporary reprieve, and whether this news might help the situation. I handed her my mobile so that she could read the text.

'Bastards,' she said. 'I wonder what Maldwyn will think about that?'

The answer came the following week.

10

The casual observer might have passed over it at
first — only a paragraph or two in a satirical
magazine. The piece ran:

> Andrew Landford likes to have his cake and
> eat it. First of all he cuddled up to Maldwyn
> Christie to ensure his leadership election
> chances rose from something less than 50%
> to something close to 100%. Now he's
> trying to bury the affair of the dead owl to
> ensure that doesn't get in the way of his
> general election chances.
>
> The affair of the dead owl began a couple
> of months ago when a car containing
> Andrew Landford, his profiler Charles
> Fryerne and his wife, and Helen Landford,
> collided with an owl. The owl, according to
> an independent source, sustained only a
> broken wing. What killed it were multiple
> injuries to its head. Landford claims this
> was done on the advice of his passengers. In
> one version it was his passenger Charles
> Fryerne who killed the bird. These are
> murky waters.
>
> What is not murky is that the owl was
> found by a passer-by and handed in to the
> police. In their efforts to trace witnesses,
> police interviewed Landford informally and
> he denied any knowledge of the incident.

Then when interviewed under caution on a later occasion he accepted he *had* been present when the owl was killed. We don't seem to be able to get a straight answer as to why or how the owl was killed, or why Landford simply didn't call the incident in when it happened. Could it be he was embarrassed by serving on the parliamentary Committee which recently amended the Wildlife and Countryside Act to give further protection to certain endangered species, including barn owls?

I didn't know for sure, but I would have put money on the fact that Maldwyn had spied this growing scandal from afar as he sat making his plans. I felt a flush of shame, recalling his description of his treatment in the press, his fear of what might yet come of it. He wasn't a natural at revenge, but this little jab in the ribs had his mischievous touch all over it. The casual remark in the House of Commons bar, and now this. Perhaps he and his advisers had realised that you can't kick a man's feet from underneath him when they are floating two feet above the ground. But you can start to bring him down to earth.

I just wished that they hadn't chosen this particular story to take the shine off Andrew's halo. A minor accident months ago was now in danger of being blown out of all proportion. The Tory Party had always been an unofficial coalition of those on the right, centre and left of Conservative political thought. It was natural that having settled for deputy, Maldwyn would want to consolidate his position and prevent Andrew from becoming an unassailable fixture. But he was playing around with some very explosive material. I was tempted to tell him so, except that would have meant accusing him of the leak to the magazine, which he would have furiously denied.

The article prompted me to cast my mind back over the owl incident. What had made Andrew completely lose himself like that? It would surely have been possible for him to cradle the bird, to handle it gently until we could find a vet. But he had grabbed at it and then, when it had understandably pecked him back, he had smashed the poor bird's skull to bits. Was it because he thought it might have damaged his new car? Or was it because he hated not being in control?

* * *

The following days were bad ones for me. Not only had I been kicked out of Andrew's team for no good reason — in fact for helping Andrew get what he wanted — but I could see a danger that this random encounter on a northern road could mutate into a much bigger story. One that risked engulfing us all.

My fears proved to be quite right when the following Monday it was my turn to be summoned by the police in Carlisle for a little chat. 'Just to gather further evidence after our conversations with Mr Landford, sir,' said the voice on the phone. They gave me next to no notice, and despite repeated attempts to contact Andrew so we could coordinate our stories, that line of communication appeared to be permanently down.

The same interviewing officer as before ushered me into the tiny interview room, along with another policeman, the one who had come to the door at Gilcaster Head. There was a brief preamble, while they set the tapes going, before he launched in with — 'Mr Fryerne, did you see or hear anything on the Friday night in question that could help us identify how this owl died and who was responsible for its death?'

The tone threw me, and the hairs prickled on the back of my neck in warning. They knew who had killed the owl. I'd been with Andrew when he came to this very station and confessed. But something had changed, and I didn't know what. I began to babble.

'Andrew had no chance at all, officer,' I said. 'The owl flew out of nowhere. It must have been dazzled by the headlights — '

'I'm not talking about what Mr Landford did or saw, sir,' the officer broke in. 'I'm talking about you. What you did and said. Or rather, didn't say.'

I took a deep breath and tried to tell the story of the evening in my own words, as calmly and truthfully as I could. Yes, we were driving slowly because we were on a narrow single-track road. No, there had been no time at all to avoid the bird. It was flying fast and had come straight at us. I added that I had advised we look for a vet to get the bird's broken wing pinned. I accepted this might have been impractical given the bird's demeanour but I also noted that Andrew had picked up the bird and killed it before any discussion could take place. Then I said, 'The bird was badly injured, you see. Mr Landford couldn't bear to see it suffer so he killed it as efficiently as possible.'

'Mr Landford certainly used plenty of force,' said the other policeman. 'He crushed the bird's skull.'

I winced. 'We didn't want there to be any possibility of the bird dying a lingering death. We couldn't think of what else to do.'

'We couldn't think of what else to do? So you're saying he killed the bird under your instruction?'

This I furiously denied, but the police just scratched their heads and kept asking me if I was sure, that I was being interviewed under caution, and so on. One of them even asked if I had been driving the car. 'Mr Landford cannot recall whether you were in fact driving at the time.'

'Of course I wasn't,' I replied sharply. 'I hope his memory has improved because I cannot agree with his statement that I advised him to kill the owl.'

'But the fact remains that both of you decided not to report the incident.'

'No,' I said firmly. 'We were just anxious to get home. I suppose we thought it was something we could worry about in the morning, as the bird was obviously dead.'

'And did you?' asked the interviewing officer.

243

I stared at him blankly.

'Did we what?'

'Worry about it in the morning?'

'Yes. We went for a walk but before we got to the place where the incident had taken place we met a neighbour who said he'd found the bird and had handed it in at the police station in Brampton.'

'So did you tell him you were responsible for the owl's death?'

'No, I did not,' I said indignantly. 'Because I wasn't.'

'Did you contact the police at Brampton to notify them that a protected species had been killed, accidentally or not?'

'No, I didn't. It was just an accident. I wasn't even driving the car!'

I felt events unravelling between my fingers.

'Just trying to find out if there is any evidence of criminality,' said my interviewer. 'As you know, your former employer, Mr Landford, was on the parliamentary Committee which recently made an amendment to the Wildlife and Countryside Act, so you both must have been aware of your obligation under the new Act to report the death of a protected species as soon as possible. He is doing fine work there, if I may say so, sir. It encourages me and my colleagues to see Parliament giving some time to conservation issues.'

I looked at him in complete astonishment.

'And you were working for him in the capacity of a . . . ' The man looked down at his notes. ' . . . Communications Adviser?'

'Yes, but — '

'So you would have been familiar with his work as an MP? In order to promote and communicate the value of that work to his constituents?'

'Up to a point, of course.'

'In which case he would surely have explained to you that the death of an owl in such circumstances is a notifiable event.'

'Perhaps he did, but I'm not sure how — '

'So you should have, in compliance with the strict letter of the law, notified us, Mr Fryerne.'

I slammed my hands down on the desk. 'I don't know why you're asking me these questions! I wasn't driving the car. I didn't run the bloody bird over. It wasn't my idea to wring its neck.'

The officer raised his eyebrows, and slid a sheaf of typed pages across to me. They were the transcript of a conversation: Andrew's last interview with the police.

'That's not what Mr Landford says, sir.'

* * *

In due course I was allowed to go. Somebody at Carlisle must have been swift to get hold of the new twist and call Andrew about it because the next thing I heard was an interview on the radio the following morning.

'Andrew Landford, you're the newly elected leader of the Opposition. You could one day be our prime minister. So why did you lie about butchering an innocent owl?' demanded the presenter, jumping in with both feet, as usual.

Andrew tried to laugh it off. 'I didn't butcher anything . . . it was the most awful and unfortunate accident, and the immediate advice I was given was to do the humane thing, which was to put the wretched creature out of its misery. As I've said before, this whole story is a huge distraction from the real issues — '

'You say 'immediate advice' . . . Did you decide to kill the owl, or were you told to by one of your advisers? There are stories in the papers this morning which say that your communications manager, Charles Fryerne, who was travelling with you has now been interviewed under caution as well?'

'Look, you'll have to ask Charles about that — '

'It sounds like you're saying you killed the owl on his advice, which he's denying — is one of you not telling the truth?'

'The difficulty I have,' said Andrew, 'is that Charlie is by trade a professional storyteller. He has been a very valued colleague but at the same time he has made his living — and a very good one too — by writing articles that are invariably spun in one direction or another. But let me be clear about one thing. The time has come for politicians to stand alone, and speak for themselves. The public is tired of spin. They want to hear the truth, direct from our own mouths, and that's something I'm determined to do. Not just about personal matters such as this, but on the issues that really matter to real people. I will speak out loud and clear, for myself, about Europe, the NHS, the economy . . . '

I turned off the radio. It had obviously been a last-minute piece, a phone call to Andrew based on the piece in the magazine and that morning's papers. I didn't like being called a storyteller, especially when criminal charges might be involved. But what I liked least of all was what was happening to Andrew. It was as if a familiar but relatively harmless beast was sloughing off its skin to reveal something more sinister beneath. He sounded almost mad to me. His behaviour ever since the owl incident had been unbalanced and now it seemed that what he believed had supplanted the facts he actually knew.

★   ★   ★

It was Caroline, who had unexpectedly decided to stay up in Newcastle for the week, who brought me the next instalment in the saga. She had gone downstairs to make a mug of tea and came back with the newspaper folded open at a particular page.

'News for you, lover boy,' she said in a laconic voice.

It was news.

The gist of the article was that the Crown Prosecution Service was considering filing charges against Andrew Landford for obstructing the course of justice. The matter in question was his failure to report the death of an owl, as required by the newly updated Wildlife and Countryside Act. There was a bit more about

247

Andrew's membership of the Committee reviewing penalties under the Act. Clearly, despite his attempt to fling as much mud at me as he could scoop up, none of it had stuck. The police had not been convinced by his story, and nothing I said had given them reason to change that opinion.

I took the paper off to the bathroom, whistling.

At breakfast, Caroline asked me why I was so cheerful.

'Because, don't you see — '

Then I stopped. Part of me felt vindicated after the way he'd treated me. Yet there was also a part that felt sad because despite his obvious flaws, and our differences, I had once truly believed he would make a good leader for the country.

'I see that it's a mess all right,' said Caroline. 'I could see him getting ready to fire you a mile off. You crossed one of his precious red lines, and that's never a smart move. Now he's trying to pass the buck over for that poor bird too.'

This was followed by the long silence that now fell upon us whenever the owl was mentioned.

★ ★ ★

My life with Caroline seemed to be hovering on the edge of a precipice as she spent increasing amounts of time browsing through property websites. She could afford to buy, and passed hours every day comparing places, but as far as I knew, she rarely viewed anywhere. Perhaps she thought the birds would follow her wherever she went.

She also seemed to be waiting for something to change in me; but I didn't know what it was, what part of my moral landscape needed to be changed or abolished. I didn't like to ask. We continued to sleep in separate rooms and now I had begun to ache with the absence of her at nights: the drowsy press of warm flesh, her scent.

My inability to ask her a simple question or two that might have resolved the whole matter was partly due to the fear that the question itself would dynamite what was left of our relationship. It was also partly because of what I would call the Fryerne tradition. The Fryerne of Fryerne Court was supposed to remain true to an imagined Englishness: to the stiff upper lip, a communal wall of silence erected by a disjointed and perhaps dysfunctional family whose only common ground was a legend. We could not even be sure if this legend had any basis in reality. Perhaps if I gave up some of my time to researching our mythology, I could liberate my own life. A search for the truth. I didn't know what I'd do with it when I'd got it.

But life doesn't often proceed according to plan. The next thing to happen was an article in one of the tabloids entitled 'The Owls Have It'.

New Tory leader Andrew Landford is blaming the press for exaggerating the scandal that is threatening to derail his political career.

The former member of the Wildlife and

Countryside Committee is facing more and more questions about the incident that took place on a road near his luxury country mansion two months ago, when he ran over a protected barn owl in his state-of-the-art Range Rover.

In a bold attempt to deflect attention, he accused the newspapers and media of focusing on a 'minor car accident, when they should be focusing on the real issues which matter to party members — Europe, the NHS and the economy'.

Despite the slightly frivolous title the piece didn't pull any punches. When the tabloids started to sharpen their knives for a new Tory leader, the outlook was not good. My heart sank further when I read the next line.

'Landford appeared to suggest that his advisers were as much at fault as he was, for suggesting that he kill a wounded bird rather than take it to a vet.'

What had begun as a shadowy insinuation was taking on the lurid hue of a full-blown lie.

There was also a full-page leader in one of the broadsheets. This contained nothing new but recited the facts of the owl affair in an orderly and senatorial way that could not be ignored. Indeed it was a delight to read, with sonorous phrases such as 'had Mr Landford had more regard for his new role as Her Majesty's Leader of the Opposition — a position he now seems unlikely to occupy for long — his cavalier treatment of the truth would not seem so reprehensible'.

The point being made was that Andrew had — allegedly — obstructed the course of justice by repeatedly changing his evidence. He had also used his position as a member of the relevant Committee to blow smoke over the story. He was in trouble and it looked like he wanted to try and drag us all, or more specifically me, down with him.

* * *

Caroline and I had a conference over the breakfast table, the newspaper sitting between us.

'It says that Andrew could face criminal charges,' she said.

'Don't worry, darling,' I said.

'But I do,' she said. Unexpectedly, she leaned over the table and took my hand. 'Your whole life has been built on people placing trust in you. Whatever else may have gone wrong between us, you've always been the straight guy, Mr Plain Talker, the person who tells the truth. That's what I first liked about you. From the moment we met, and you wouldn't come upstairs with me. You stayed put to hear your dad's speech. Now you're the head of the family, and you seem to come out in hives just thinking about it. Maybe this whole Fryerne thing is one big private joke between you and me, but I bet the others take it more seriously, and deep inside, you do too. If you're hurt, they are. If your reputation suffers, they suffer too.'

251

'You don't really believe that, do you?'

I felt appalled by what she had said yet at the same time I knew it was true. Being able to claim kinship to Charles Fryerne of Fryerne Court was the reason some of them got out of bed in the morning. If the present incumbent threw away his reputation, and their trust in him, what was left for them? Of course it might just mean they could ignore all future family gatherings, possibly with some relief. But I suspected not.

'With what's been going on here, I could believe anything,' Caroline said. Her face was pale, and she looked exhausted. I felt the same. She didn't need to explain what she meant. We both heard the sounds at night, the tapping, the gentle but persistent scratching, as if something was trying to get in. I had thought of contacting the council, but the thought of being ridiculed as well as slandered was too much.

A tiny brush with a single bird on a deserted country road was quickly transforming into a full-scale political scandal. Above and beyond all of that, I cared about Caroline and what this was doing to her. To us. Whether we were imagining the owls that haunted our house at night or not, she was suffering as much as I was. She had expected Andrew to behave in the way he had. But now my failure to stand up to him had placed our marriage at risk.

One man had started this, and only he could end it. He might be Leader of the Opposition, protected by powerful gatekeepers, but it didn't matter.

I had to see Andrew, before he destroyed everything.

3

MINNIVER WOOD

1

Eventually, after numerous phone calls to assistants and badgering emails, I tracked Andrew down. He seemed curiously subdued. 'I'm still not sleeping at all well,' he admitted. It was heartening to hear that Caroline and I were not the only ones.

I suppose, given all that had occurred since my last visit to Gilcaster Head, I should have been more surprised that after I put my case, he warily agreed to meet me at Gilcaster Head that Friday night. Perhaps I was meant to feel flattered. In fact I felt anything but as I took the train to Carlisle on a blustery winter evening, gazing out of the window at black branches twisting in the wind. I felt restless, unable to concentrate on a book or even a newspaper.

On previous visits, Andrew had been content to let me take a taxi from the station or send John in his car. But now I found him pacing up and down the platform, a dark tweed coat wrapped around him, like the villain of some Victorian melodrama. When he saw me he did not smile, but reached out both arms to grasp my hands. 'So good to see you,' he said, moving from the darkness into the light.

I stepped back in shock. His eyes were red from exhaustion, and there were scratches on his face that looked inflamed.

'You've got some explaining to do,' I said.

'Some,' he said. 'Let's go.' He picked up my case, a gesture of hospitality he had never made before, and we left.

He said nothing on the journey back. His profile in the dying light looked gaunt, and hard, like it had all those years ago when he arrived back from Moscow. The sky was almost black as we turned up the lane that led to Gilcaster Head. Beyond the house loomed a dark cloud that might have been Minniver Wood. The security lights snapped on and then we were inside. My case and coat were taken and a whisky and water handed to me by the ever-efficient John, then I was seated in an armchair. The damask was grubbier than I remembered, and some of the blue piping had been ripped away from the sides, as if a cat had got its claws into it.

For a while we talked of this and that, like old friends who hadn't seen each other in some time. This with a man who had just sacked me, then gone on the radio to drag me further into the mess he had created. With anyone else, you could hardly warrant it, but Andrew had this ability — as he had when I began my relationship with Caroline — to effortlessly march on from the past as if it had never occurred. Perhaps that was what he was trying to do with the owl as well.

Stiffly at first, but with growing ease, we raked over the economy, and what the big new ideas were from various think tanks and central banks. None of them seemed that big or that new on closer inspection, but Andrew had a forensic grasp of detail which meant he was able to dissect the science of each one with a ruthless precision, getting straight to the heart of the matter while I was left grappling with the broader implications.

John slid silently in and topped up our drinks, as we moved on to the various members of the government Andrew would have to face at the next election. He knew their record backwards, admired virtue where he found it, and seemed acquainted with skeletons in closets not yet open for general viewing. Then, like he was skinning the day's quarry, he peeled back their skin to reveal the tender, weak spot that he would savage through counter-policy, rhetoric and ruthless, targeted mockery.

At length, he drew breath, and I remembered why I was actually here.

'You said you could explain things,' I ventured.

'Yes.' Andrew stood in front of the fire, looking down at his drink. 'The truth is, Charles, I've behaved rather badly towards you.'

It wasn't just out of character for Andrew to apologise; it was out of character for him even to admit a failing. I was so taken aback I nearly spilt my scotch.

'This whole business with Maldwyn . . . I was foolish to be cross about it. I mean, obviously, I still don't like the fact you went behind my back — but you were only trying to help. I see that now.'

I murmured something about it being unimportant, which was perhaps true, given recent developments. The announcement of the

257

CPS pressing charges had only been made that week, and already I had observed Andrew's character and judgement increasingly being called into question by commentators. He had only just won the leadership contest. It was not a great start.

'Also they keep telling me that I still need you, so I've given in just to shut them up.' He gave a disconcerting grin.

'They? You mean Matt and Jane?'

Andrew waved my question away. Instead, he focused his gaze on a hole in the rug between us that I didn't recall being there on my last visit. Clearly there was now a pet resident in Gilcaster Head. Perhaps Matt and Jane had told him to acquire a puppy, no doubt secreted away, in case there were any animal-friendly photo opportunities. But Andrew's thoughts were elsewhere.

'Do you know why I wanted to become leader, Charles?'

I shrugged. 'Well, of course. We talked about it for your profile. You want to move the party back towards the centre ground, reform the membership, get more women in — '

'No, I don't mean all that. Of course it's true, but I can assure you that reforming our party membership rules is not what drives me.'

'It was the chance to have a shot at the big job.'

He nodded. 'Yes. And the fact is, however much of an old friend he may be to both of us, we both know I'll do a better job than Maldwyn. I'm more likely to be invited by the country to do it too.'

I had come to Gilcaster Head in one of my rare pugnacious moods. Helpfully, the second large scotch on an empty stomach had loosened my tongue.

'You really think so? Why? Because you're facing criminal charges?'

A branch banged against the window — although that struck me as odd, because the nearest trees were at the end of the field. Andrew glanced sharply in the direction of the noise, then strode past me, and opened the sitting room door. I turned to see him checking the corridor, before closing the door again, firmly. Andrew dragged his chair over the torn rug nearer to mine, and spoke softly.

'I've never told anyone this before, Charles, and if you repeat a word of it outside this room, I'll send every lawyer in London after you with enough writs to sink the *Titanic* three times over — '

'Oh, come on, Andrew, if you can't trust me, who can you trust?'

His eyes caught the glow from the fire.

'What you've got to understand is that from a young age, I just knew I wanted to be prime minister. It's hard to explain to anyone who's never felt that way. I'm not just talking about ambition or vision, it's more than that. It's like it's in my DNA.'

'Well, if you still think I can help you articulate that to the electorate — ' I began.

'Charles. Come on.' He cut me off. 'With all your nous, all your experience — you must know we're beyond the realms of articulation and spin

259

now. One stupid mistake by a bird has been thrown out of all proportion and now I'm damaged goods.' Andrew bit his lip and scowled, as if the act of apology caused him physical pain. 'And I'm sorry for dragging you into it without warning the way I did — that was wrong too. At least . . . it was wrong not to have discussed it with you first.'

There was that sound at the window again. Andrew flinched, but didn't turn towards the noise.

'So why did you drag me into it?'

'Isn't it obvious?'

'I'm obviously being rather dim.' Although I felt far from dim — patronised and irritated perhaps; and wondering how soon I could make my escape from this increasingly oppressive drawing room. The heat from the fire seemed to be getting more intense, and I ran a finger around the inside of my collar. Andrew didn't seem to notice.

'We need actions now, not words. Focus on my ability to act. That's how you can help me. Show how decisive I could be as prime minister — reclaim the narrative.'

I thought back to the think tank, the investment bank in Russia, to Caroline and to my recent abrupt dismissal, now apparently rescinded. Andrew was certainly decisive when it came to jettisoning projects or people, so I proceeded with caution.

'Yes. That is one definite advantage you have over your opponents.'

He leaned over and slapped my thigh, in an

attempt to be either jovial or affectionate. It felt like neither, more like a physical warning.

'That's the idea, Charles. Now I need you to act with me, perhaps even act for me . . . But first, let's have something to eat.'

★   ★   ★

We sat at opposite ends of the polished table in the dining room, where a wood-burning stove was casting yet more heat into the room. I wondered if Andrew would think it eccentric if I removed my shirt. Sweat beaded my brow, and I dabbed at it continually with my damask napkin. Every flat surface — a mantelpiece, deep stone window sills, an eighteenth-century sideboard — was covered with framed photos of Andrew. Winning a charity rowing event for a global bank. Accompanying a trade delegation to China with the Mayor of London. Speaking at the last party conference. I was straining to see if I could spot a blurred Maldwyn in the corner of the latter when Mary bustled in and set down a steaming dish of pheasant casserole.

At least, I hoped it was pheasant. It was bony enough to be one of any number of birds, although I didn't dwell on the possibilities.

Andrew took a mouthful, then continued. 'So. You wouldn't believe me if I told you what's been going on . . . '

'I've read the papers.'

'It's not what's in the papers that's getting me down,' said Andrew, and with a gesture he raised the palms of both hands outwards as if dismissing the entire political world.

'So what is?'

He leaned back in his chair and glowered at me. I noticed that the scratches on his face seemed to have reddened by the fire, and a horrible thought occurred to me. 'It's the owls, isn't it? They're attacking you as well.'

He simply stared at me, the flicker of the candles on the table lending his eyes a hellish hue. As he held up his hand to silence any further conversation, it was not entirely clear what or who he was listening to. For the first time in our long acquaintance I began to doubt how secure his grip on sanity actually was.

'Have I ever told you about the history of this house?'

I shook my head. A dim memory floated into my mind of something Andrew had mentioned on our first fateful visit here. How his parents had sold up their family business, and bought this farm out in the middle of nowhere. But of the history of the house, I knew no more than what I could see around me: an overheated Cumbrian farmhouse bedecked in silk and tassels.

'I never told anyone at Oxford much about my past,' he said. 'I heard some people thought my parents owned a gold mine. I didn't start the rumour but I saw no harm in letting it go round either.' He picked up his fork and jabbed at his food savagely, as if it were to blame for the accident of his birth. 'Don't get me wrong, we were well-off enough but the only gold mine in my background was the one my parents spent on renovating this place.'

Andrew grinned at me. It was like his greeting at the station, an attempted display of warmth that ended up looking wolfish and vaguely alarming. 'Don't worry, I'm not about to tell you some sob story. If I had one of those, I would have given it to you for the campaign. Perhaps we should make one up for the election? I'd like to see the other side knock that.'

As if in echo of his words, there was another rap at the window, and we both started, the grin vanishing from his face.

'Probably just the wind,' I said.

'Yes, probably the wind . . . ' he said bitterly, staring at the darkened glass. 'This place was nothing when my parents bought it, just a crude farmhouse with a couple of outbuildings. They sold their company for a very good price and spent a packet turning some peasant hovels into the grand building you see today. That facade as you come up the drive, the gabling, Georgian windows and porch — they were all lifted straight from the pages of a country magazine. And the land that came with the property was as wild as the moors we drove though just now. The wood beyond these windows used to come right up to the property, but my parents stripped it all back. A few of the locals got a bit upset, saying the wood was of historical importance, something to do with an ancient Roman settlement, but my father employed a very modern lawyer and that was the end of the matter.'

Andrew took a large gulp of his wine, his face flushed. He had never opened up to me in this way before, and I supposed I was meant to feel flattered. But there was an unsteady quality to his voice and movements, which were not so much those of a drunk man, more one trying to navigate the deck of a ship in troubled waters.

'By the time they'd finished, hardly a stone of the old outhouse was left, and the wood was reduced to the copse you see now. Of course, I gather there have been people farming this land in one way or another for centuries. This stone wall was built by so and so, that barn used to belong to Old Whatsisname, Farmer X once kept his flock in that field over there. All that. But you can thank my parents for the introduction of the telephone line, central heating and the refrigerator. Even the name is a post-war invention. I think it was called something like Little Gill when they bought it, but my father thought Gilcaster Head sounded more respectable.'

I had a brief vision of my long-dead genealogist uncle, Roland. Andrew emptied his glass and set it down on the table, his movements deliberate and wooden. 'They are as ungrateful as the electorate. We came here, we cleared the weeds, we landscaped the wood. We made changes so it was a better place to live. Then you make one tiny slip, and they go for you.'

'The locals or the owls?'

If Andrew heard my question, it didn't seem to register. Maybe, to someone like him, in this wind-blasted corner of remote countryside, they amounted to the same thing. 'They won't stop me. I have done nothing wrong. A bird flew into

264

my windscreen and I did the humane thing. The right thing. They can flap all they like, it doesn't make any difference. Now I'm leader of the party I'll probably be spending most of my time in London. No danger of wretched owls there.'

It was the first time I had heard an owl referred to as a threat.

The conversation paused as Mary brought in a daunting pudding, which sank straight to the bottom of my stomach, and John poured out glasses of something treacly and viscous. The conversation now turned closer to home and to family. Andrew even summoned the grace to ask about Caroline. The mask of the political operator vanished for a moment, and he seemed to be genuinely curious as he enquired about her health and her work. Indeed his tone was verging on the wistful, which given his reputation as a man of decisive action made me nervous, so I steered us back to Helen. The enthusiasm faded from his face, and he gave closed, peremptory answers about her abandoned legal career and their child.

It occurred to me that this was the longest and most intimate conversation we had ever shared. John and Mary appeared to have retreated to some inner sanctum. Remarkably, given the media storm blowing a gale in London, Andrew kept his phone switched off so I had his full and undivided attention. Yet I was also aware that when the rich and powerful remove their mask, it often comes with a large price tag attached.

On some invisible signal, Mary returned to clear the dishes. Andrew produced a cigar from somewhere and offered me one, which I declined.

'I didn't know you smoked,' I said.

'This isn't smoking,' he said, puffing away, before examining the cigar. 'Filthy habit, I know. One of those things you more or less had to do after dinner with bankers in Russia. It's been a temptation ever since.'

Woody fumes filled the room. I was feeling drunk, hot, liverish and had the beginnings of a migraine.

'Can I ask you a leading question, Charles?' he said.

I nodded.

'Do you think I deserve this?'

'What — becoming prime minister or the criminal charges?'

'Don't be facetious, it doesn't suit you. I mean it, do you think I deserve this?' He blew another green cloud into the air. 'Do you think I'm good enough?'

'Why does that matter?'

'Because unless you do, why did you back me?' Andrew stood up and began to pace around the small dining room. For some reason I entertained anxious visions as he strode behind my chair, that at any moment, like a psychotic Groucho Marx, he might lean over and poke his burning cigar into my eye.

'I mentioned dreams earlier. It won't surprise you to learn that I've been having some very bad ones. This owl thing has really gone to my head, clearly. So many of them, circling and swooping, crying out. At times, I couldn't tell whether I was sleeping or waking or somewhere in between. In one they flew into my room and ripped apart my most expensive suits. And in another, you came in and cleared them away. Sometimes, it hasn't just been a dream, either. There are things happening, things I don't understand. Damage to the outside of the house, and inside too, for God's sake. One of the damn things must have got in through an open window or door. I gave John hell for that. But I've even been attacked in my own garden.'

He stopped pacing and stood at the table, cigar poised, staring at me. I could see the scratches and marks down one side of his face clearly now.

'It was just a dream, Andrew,' I muttered. 'These events are just unfortunate coincidences, unconnected . . .'

'No, they aren't,' he said. 'I know you can do it for me, Charles. You can make this . . . owl problem disappear. You're the most trustworthy person I know, you always have been.'

Either the bird we had just consumed hadn't been cooked properly, or wasn't a bird fit for human consumption. I tried not to think about it, but it was hard not to. My stomach pitched and billowed with nausea. The dining room felt hotter than a ship's boiler room, the air as thick and smoky. I wished, too late, that I hadn't complicated matters further with the steamed pudding and dessert wine.

I stood up, unsteadily, clutching my chair.

'Well, Charles? Will you do it?'

'I'm sorry,' I mumbled. 'I must have picked

267

something up in London, I'm not feeling terribly well . . . '

'Fine. Just answer me this one thing before you go,' Andrew said, without a shred of sympathy, stubbing his cigar out in the dregs of the wine. 'I know you believe in me. You are perceptive, you saw the same thing in me that I have known for years. The ability to put my mind to almost any activity and succeed. God knows I have failings in other areas, Charles, just ask Caroline or Helen. But succeeding has never been an issue for me. I have turned a boutique New York investment bank into a global giant. I can do the same for our great country, but not if the opportunity is denied to me because of some ridiculous misunderstanding over a bird of prey. You have been constant and loyal ever since we met. People who may not trust me will believe you. So will you do it for me, Charles? Will you make that sacrifice?'

He was beginning to rant, which did nothing for my nausea. Waving away the cigar smoke, I gingerly made my way towards the door. As I brushed past the heavy curtains, I noticed that the hems were completely shredded. With another heave of my stomach, I realised that no puppy or kitten could have caused such savage damage.

'If not for me, at least for the country,' Andrew called after me.

'Yes,' I turned. The migraine and nausea were so intense I could barely speak. 'Yes, Andrew, I'll do whatever it is you want. Don't worry, we'll get you out of this mess, I'm sure.'

He lifted his arms in silent triumph. I bolted for the ground floor lavatory, and was still throwing up when I heard him mount the stairs for bed.

★ ★ ★

The next morning I awoke with a ferocious hangover, and a vague sense of having agreed to do something I shouldn't have. I had received an apology of sorts, but as for assurances as to what would happen in the future, they felt very thin on the ground.

For a moment, I lay in bed, dry mouthed and immobile, as memories replayed themselves with a feverish intensity. Andrew in his Gothic coat at the station, his scratched face, then the flames leaping up the chimney, noises at the window, my host wielding his cigar like a lethal weapon.

With a great effort I got myself up and dressed. Drawing back the curtains, I sat on the bed and stared blankly out of the window. The bleak landscape of russets and greys stared blankly back. Except . . . I stood up, and pressed my face to the glass.

Something had changed.

Below my room lay an acre or so of patchy lawn, crudely bisected by a weed-strewn path. A peeling summer house and algae-filled pond completed the view. But beyond the ha-ha which bordered this idyll, the land looked different.

I could have sworn that before, there was at least another acre of rough pasture between the garden and the wood. That was the memory from my last visit. So either the spruces had matured and grown since then, which seemed unlikely, or Minniver Wood had moved closer to the house.

My exhausted and fevered mind was doubtless confusing things. The last time I had seen the wood was at dusk, and we were drinking. Either way, the darkening aisles between them were gloomier than ever, even in the fresh light of day. The forest appeared to hover above the field, like a shadow of some far older place, a primeval echo. A movement caught my eye, and I started, but it was just the flap of a bird as it left a branch. Probably a wood pigeon.

I thought I would ask Andrew about this unusual phenomenon over breakfast, but when I came down, he was nowhere to be seen. Sitting alone in the farmhouse kitchen, while Mary busied herself behind me at the Aga, I poked at a boiled egg and studied the morning papers.

The furore over the owl was beginning to dominate the headlines. There was more commentary and opinion on the inside pages. Wildlife charities did battle with the motoring lobby over the ethics of what to do with roadkill, while legal experts explained the relevant Act in painstaking detail. The story was already being called Owlgate, which made my heart sink. I had agreed to do something with all this, but what?

The answer came, perhaps appropriately, by way of a text, pinging on to the phone next to my plate. 'I had to leave early to make an urgent shadow Cabinet meeting,' it read. 'Thank you again for being a true ally. Matt will be in touch re next steps.'

Again I felt a sense of unease about what I was being thanked for. I finished my breakfast, made my farewell to the ever silent Mary, grabbed my bag, and let John drive me to the station. I thought I would feel relieved to be out of the oppressive atmosphere of Gilcaster Head and to an extent, I was. But the echoes of my hangover were soon replaced by a far more troubling sensation.

It was slight and flickering, but persistent all the same. The very distinctive feeling that someone, or something, was following me.

2

We sped off towards the station in Andrew's car, with John at the wheel. I noticed that the windscreen had been repaired; all physical trace of the infamous collision was now gone. Sitting on the passenger seat with my overnight case perched on my lap, I wondered whether I should make some attempt at conversation. John and Mary had been nothing but courteous to Caroline and me when we had stayed, but I couldn't recall exchanging more than three words with them in as many months. Their English, as far as it went, seemed flawless, but I did not know how much further it went. And I knew nothing of their former lives, or how they had come to be working for the Landfords.

We approached a tight corner and John put his foot to the floor. We barrelled round, narrowly avoiding a collision with an agricultural digger, its great claw raised in alarm. A phone and some loose change tumbled out of the dashboard compartment on to the floor. My heart leapt into my mouth, but my driver seemed unconcerned, merely reaching down to retrieve his mobile.

I felt I should say something.

'I understand from Andrew that you were . . . in the Gurkhas.'

John gave a broad smile, shaking his wrinkled head. 'Oh yes.'

'What was that like, if you don't mind me asking?'

His smile vanished. 'It was difficult, but nothing compared to how tough life was before. I was a farmer, you see. Life was tough. We made very little money, yet we worked hard. Sometimes in one week we would earn less than . . . four pence?'

I nodded, slightly thrown by the detail and fullness of his answer.

'So I joined the Gurkhas. It was incredible training, only for the fittest. But it was hard, so many people dropped out. Then, I was in Borneo in the Sixties, with the Paras. That was unbelievable. Every day on your feet, in the jungle. We marched through swamps . . . climbed mountains . . . and our packs were heavy. You never knew when you would come under fire. I lost many friends.'

'That must have been awful,' I said dumbly. I hadn't quite realised how old he was.

'The most awful things you ever saw. Some of the nights were so long, I thought I would never see my family again. But all of that is nothing compared to what we face now. My wife and I have no money. We are in our seventies and we have to work like slaves every day of our life just to stay alive. So you ask was I in the Gurkhas? Sure I was. Yet now I can hardly believe that I ever fought for this country.'

I didn't know how to respond. My mind, still sluggish after the hallucinatory events of the previous night, grasped for something to fill the void. Unbidden, an image of something sharp

273

flashed into my mind. I was determined not to make it an owl claw.

'Do you still have your kukri?'

John raised his eyebrows, as if I had asked him if he and his wife enjoyed Scottish dancing in the nude.

'Yes, but now I only use the knife for cooking.'

He shook his head, gnawing his lip, and we were both spared further communication by my phone vibrating in my pocket.

It was Matt Dilcombe. 'Charles, good to hear your voice. Now, where are you?'

'I'm in Gilcaster. I've just left Andrew and I'm on my way back to Newcastle — '

'Can you change your plans? We need you in London. Urgently.'

I tensed with irritation. Even when I was no longer in his employ, Andrew and his team treated me as if I was at their beck and call. What it must be like for the man sitting next to me in the car didn't bear thinking about.

'Can't it wait till tomorrow?'

'I've spoken to Andrew. We are all very grateful Charles, but I think the sooner we resolve this, the better. My PA has looked up some trains . . . there's a direct service to Euston leaving in half an hour. Shall I see you at my office at 6?'

He hung up before I could reply. Minutes later, John's car skidded into the station forecourt and he deposited me and my holdall on the pavement with a wide smile and a wave. The car screeched off before I could mutter a word of thanks. As it was, my mind was now preoccupied with how I was going to explain my delayed return to Caroline, and with something Matt had said. He was grateful, and it was unlike Matt to be grateful for anything. I was curious, so I took the train to London.

★ ★ ★

Matt's office was a small glass box stuffed into the corner of Andrew's open plan estate in St Stephen's Buildings. Most of it was occupied by a large circular wooden table, around which were squeezed Matt and a man in a dark suit wedged between two younger women, none of whom I recognised. The table was scattered with piles of documents, and plastic cups of coffee going cold. Owing to some quirk of the air conditioning, the room managed to be stifling hot and draughty at the same time. I manoeuvred myself into a seat with my back pressed against an internal window.

Matt pressed the door shut, which had the effect of creating an airlock.

'Thank you for coming at such short notice, Charles,' he said without any preamble. 'These guys are Andrew's lawyers.'

I felt constrained as it was, hardly able to move my arms and legs, but I felt my chest tighten even more at the mention of their profession. The man in the dark suit offered a heavy hand across the table.

'Keith Jackman,' he said. 'From Wuk, and these are my colleagues Joanna and Felicity, who will be drafting the paperwork.'

Law was not my field, but I knew 'Wuk' (spelt

WK), or at least, I had found it hard to escape their expensive rebranding, the new name sprayed in luminous green over blue billboards wherever one looked. Previously Witheridge and Knight, a firm of solicitors which sounded like it might occupy a dusty Victorian parlour on a provincial high street, it was in fact now one of the largest law firms in the city, occupying a steel monolith in Canary Wharf. Jeremy and I had worked for them once or twice in the Nineties. I had heard the name mentioned again recently, but where exactly I couldn't recall. Loose ends at some dinner party, no doubt. I did recollect that their clients ranged from petroleum multinationals to tech companies, hedge funds to foreign governments, but had only the vaguest idea why three of their highly paid representatives might be sitting in Matt's office waiting to talk to me.

I presumed it must have something to do with Andrew taking me on board again.

'I didn't know Wuk had an employment law department,' I said as breezily as I could manage.

Everyone stared at me.

'Charles,' said Matt, spreading his hands on the table, 'Keith isn't from employment law. He's on their criminal side.'

'Mr Fryerne,' said Keith Jackman, measuring his words, 'we represent Mr Landford in the matter of Regina v Andrew Landford.' He opened a glossy corporate folder in front of him, and smoothed the white pages down with a hairy hand.

I then realised where I had heard the name of

276

WK more recently than my brush with them in the Nineties. Helen had worked for them. Before Andrew had scooped her up, transforming her into the million-pound haircut wife he had once envisaged Caroline being. He had insisted she give up her job in order to raise the one Landford child that no one ever saw. The last time I saw her, she had been drinking heavily, her breath sweet sour with Chardonnay.

Keith Jackman turned for a moment to Joanna, who whispered in his ear, and thumbed through the sheaf of documents, before laying a densely typed and highlighted page before him. Something about it seemed familiar, but I couldn't divine what. He glanced down at it, before continuing. He had sleepy eyes, which combined with the airless room, and his incantatory tone, left me feeling very drowsy.

'The Crown is preparing to drop the charges against Mr Landford.'

'Finally. About time, too.'

'But they are instead preparing a case against you.'

If I hadn't been so wedged in I would have leapt out of my seat.

'That's absurd. I had nothing to do with it.'

'That is what Mr Landford feels as well . . . it's just unfortunate that the CPS has been handed evidence at a late stage which has persuaded them to take another view. Which is why we need to have your testimony on record, before matters proceed.'

Felicity produced a small digital voice recorder, which she slid across the table towards me. I looked at Matt, my face flushed with bewilderment.

'We're all very grateful, Charles,' he said. 'Andrew is so grateful. He spoke so highly of your honesty and commitment. When all of this is over, you can be sure of a seat at the high table after the next election.'

So this was what I had agreed to, unsettled and drunk, over a dinner table in Cumbria. This was the decisive action Andrew had spoken of. I had moved from communicating the message to in effect being the message. A message of deflection. Suddenly all I wanted was to be very far away from this stifling room. Keith Jackman continued in his soporific drawl.

'The Crown is satisfied that Mr Landford killed the owl at your direction, and is preparing charges on that basis.'

A shot of real anger pulsed through me.

'On what bloody basis? The owl flew into the windscreen, and Andrew was furious that some bird had chipped his precious motor, so he clashed its brains to a pulp. I was a bystander, nothing more.'

Jackman peered down his nose at the page in front of him, and I realised why the blur of names and words seemed familiar.

'But on the 16 October, you were interviewed under caution at Carlisle police station, and said, 'We couldn't think of what else to do.''

'So? I was trying to assist Andrew in a very difficult situation. I was going to be one of his advisers, which meant — '

'Andrew would take your advice on how to

278

behave in such a critical situation?'

I could see where this was going.

'I don't think I'd like to say any more on this without my own lawyer present, if you don't mind.'

Keith's baggy face broke into its first smile of the afternoon.

'But Mr Fryerne, we are your lawyers now too. That's why we're here. Mr Landford has asked us to represent you. He's paying.'

* * *

By the time the meeting was over, it was past ten in the evening and the last train back to Newcastle had departed. Matt had offered to pay for a hotel, but I didn't want a penny more of Andrew Landford's money that day, if ever. I refused their offer of food and drink as well. I needed to think.

Under the guise of welcoming me back into the fold, oozing flattery over my ability to communicate his message, Andrew had laid a giant trap for me which I had leapt straight into. Keith Jackman had also offered me a very large amount of money, quite possibly a life-changing amount of money, to put myself in line for the criminal charges facing our future prime minister.

'The evidence is circumstantial,' he had drawled, 'but highly persuasive. In exchange for a guilty plea, the sentence may be very light, and if you're lucky, non-custodial. But it's a test case for Andrew's new law, so they're likely to want to set an example.'

'And if I refuse?'

'Then this conversation never happened.'

'How about if I accept?'

'Then this conversation still never happened, but please take this with Mr Landford's sincerest thanks for your trouble.' He pushed a thick cream envelope across the table. I knew what was inside, but I didn't even touch it.

They did not allow me to leave without signing several documents in triplicate, witnessed by Matt. If I didn't sign them, Andrew would sue me for breach of confidence over the Maldwyn deal. If I did sign, I wouldn't be able to tell anyone about the attempted bribe, whether I agreed to face the charges or not. If I signed them and changed my mind, they would sue me. In the end — whatever I did — Andrew would (unless the polls changed dramatically) fulfil his dream of running the country.

I wondered whether I should just obediently lie down and accept my role in the grander narrative. Did I believe a word of what I had written about Andrew for my profile of him? If I did, then I felt bound to support his political project, and play my part in its successful completion. My whole family history was predicated on a Fryerne lending critical aid to a usurper king at his time of need. True, he had not been obliged to sign a non-disclosure agreement amongst the corpses and gore of Bosworth Field, but perhaps as a backdrop, they were of a similarly persuasive nature. On the other hand, if I didn't believe a word of what I had written, then what little integrity I still possessed evaporated in a single weak puff before my eyes.

★ ★ ★

I was no Fryerne knight. But I was not prepared to accept my fate without a battle, either. My thoughts ablaze with feelings of betrayal and injustice, I hoped a walk would offer some relief. Winter was drawing in, the streets around Andrew's offices in Euston were blank and unlit. The trade union officials and civil engineering consultants who occupied the anonymous towers by day had long since departed for the shires or the pub, and only the odd rough sleeper remained, huddled under cardboard boxes and sleeping bags. Everything reeked of abandonment. Car parks, warehouses, a library. I hurried down avenues of garage shutters, security gates and blank walls. They seemed to be closing in on me, and at times I felt short of breath.

At the end of the street, a shadow soared in and out of the street lamp's arc. It could have been a large city crow or some less friendly bird.

I quickly turned the corner, and found myself wandering through a grid of grubby Edwardian terraces towards Mornington Crescent, where Caroline kept her basement studio. At a certain time of day sunlight flooded down through the railings and she could often be found on the greening steps, wrapped in a Persian shawl and sucking meditatively on a cigarette.

My hand rested for a moment on the flaking iron gate at the top of the steps. We had not spoken since I went to visit Andrew. We were only just speaking before I left. I felt that he was coming between us in a way he never had when she was actually living with him. All things considered, it had been a very bad idea for us to reconnect with him after all that time. Right from the moment he had collected us from the station on that night in his polished Range Rover, he had begun to cloud the very air we breathed.

The gate squeaked open, and I paused on the front step, looking behind me. Parked cars lined both sides of the road, and here and there were lighted front rooms. Further up the road I could hear a couple laughing as they walked along. I was being ridiculous. There were no angry owls in Mornington Crescent.

I hurried down the steps, and peered in, through a clay-smeared window, at the dimly lit silhouettes of Caroline's new sculptures, some still resting under cloth, ready to be fired and glazed. This must be for her new show, the one she had so obsessively kept secret from me.

It was Saturday and I knew she was back in Newcastle. But after the trap Andrew had laid the previous night, and the grim ambush of this afternoon, I needed to feel close to her in some way. I had a key. The door opened slowly, against a pile of junk mail. There was a musty smell about the place that I did not remember being there before. I wondered if Caroline had left something to rot in the small fridge she kept in the kitchen. It was unlikely, as normally the only thing to be found in there was a bottle of white burgundy.

I headed on into the studio, and as I did, I felt something under foot.

Something soft and brittle at the same time.

A draught from nowhere sucked the door shut behind me with a slam. When I looked down I saw that the floor was covered with feathers. The nausea I had been feeling over the last two days now threatened to overpower me completely, and fumbling for a light switch in the dark, I stumbled into one of the new statues arranged on the bench.

It was smooth and cold to the touch. As I stepped back, I saw with horror what it was.

An enormous owl, carved out of black stone, its wings raised, its eyes fixed in a furious glare. The work to make it must have been back-breaking. And, I saw now, all the new sculptures were of a similar turn. Owls. Sitting on a bench in a row and staring at me. I could see why Caroline had kept this new work hidden from me. For a moment, it was as if I had stumbled into an ancient temple. Hook-winged, beak-nosed, cold-eyed, they were a line of implacable judges, designed to sit in judgement for eternity.

By design or not, Andrew's single act of violence had now penetrated every corner of our lives. The birds demanded justice and would not be appeased until it was done.

3

The next day, I sat on the train to Newcastle checking my phone again and again for any news stories that might suggest it was I who had advised Andrew to kill the owl. It wouldn't be long before Matt Dilcombe made sure that the briefing was falling on to every editor's desk. Yet there was nothing. As I scrolled through various news sites by way of distraction, I came across other headlines. 'WHY ANDREW LANDFORD ISN'T FIT TO LEAD THE COUNTRY' turned out to be a disconnected series of mini-rants about Andrew's political beliefs and background. There was no coherent articulation of either his or Maldwyn's actual positions, and no mention of the dead owl, but there was, to my surprise, a mention of Merlin's.

'Landford was a member of the elite Oxbridge supper club Merlin's, which regularly caused thousands of pounds worth of damage to local businesses.'

I recalled that certainly being true of Merlin's, at least in the past, but as I had never seen Andrew at any of the dinners, blaming him for that behaviour seemed unfair. Merlin's had never held any real power in Oxford, and Andrew Landford's rise to the top was entirely of his own making. Blaming or giving credit for that rise to a self-important dining club seemed to be obscuring the issue. Maldwyn had never been a member. Andrew had joined purely for show but almost never attended. The source of their power lay quite outside its gilded halls, and refusing to acknowledge that seemed blinkered to me.

The more interesting story that I had once heard about Andrew and an accident with a punting pole seemed to have been swallowed up by history. Or erased from public view with clinical precision. I wondered if I was heading the same way.

Caroline opened the door to me in stockinged feet, a cigarette dangling from her hand. I kissed her, but found her stiff and unresponsive.

Without another word, she turned, and I followed her into the house, my bag trailing behind me.

Even by her standards, the house was a tip. Piles of plates, unwashed glasses, overflowing ashtrays and heaps of clothes lay everywhere. There was a smell in the air, an unlikeable combination of clay and cigarette smoke, as in her basement studio. No owl feathers covered the floor, at least, but I could not help noticing the sharp scratches down several of the tall windows.

She led me into the kitchen, where she sat and rested her feet on the table, still smoking. I dropped on to a small wooden chair opposite her and we regarded one another through the haze.

'Well, buddy?' she asked, finally.

I shrugged.

'Did you clear your name? Did you clear our name? Did you finally tell that bastard where to go?'

I didn't need to reply. I could barely look my own wife in the eye. She sighed.

'I thought as much. Because the owls sure as hell haven't stopped.' She flicked a bit of ash in the direction of the scarred window. 'You know, I'm beginning to wonder whether you're capable of standing up for anything.'

'It's not that simple. It's hard when you don't know what to believe.'

Caroline snorted. 'What to believe? It's not very hard. He ran over an owl and bashed its brains out on a wall.'

'Well, firstly, that's not quite true . . . the owl flew into the windscreen first, he didn't run it over . . . but regardless of that, it's not what I believe about the owl. It's what I believe about Andrew.'

What I still believed, couldn't help believing, despite the way he had treated me. There was no denying that he was a master communicator, popular with the party, with a vision for the country that resonated with the electorate. That was the problem with being someone who had a reputation for telling the truth. Even when it wounded me directly, I could always see his strengths. I was baffled by self-delusion. I was turning into my father, who continued to believe in the institutions that had left him out to fester. Caroline gave an angry laugh.

'That he's a controlling, psychopathic monster who will stop at nothing to get into power?'

I shook my head. Caroline's analysis of Andrew was surely skewed by her personal history with him.

'Maybe he is controlling. But what if he actually is also a good thing for the country? Plenty of leaders are sociopaths to a degree. Look at Thatcher. Perhaps she needed to be. Andrew is strong. You've seen him work a crowd, work a room — the man has something. We have wave after wave of dull jobbing politicians who turn the voters off, and then someone comes along with that electrifying presence, the ability to project charisma and vision, to bring about change . . . and you think we should trash him for the sake of a single bird? Is it worth throwing away that bigger truth for a smaller one?' I could scarcely believe my own words, yet out they tumbled. 'They're going to claim I killed the owl. I know what you're going to say, but listen to me, it's one small sacrifice for a grander aim — '

She cut me off with a wave of her arm, stubbed out her cigarette and got up. 'I want to give up on you, Charlie boy. I want to give up on you so bad. But the thing is I just can't . . . ' Her voice faltered and she left the room.

★   ★   ★

I seemed to spend the next week sitting at the same kitchen table, in a state of near-paralysis. I did leave the house, several times, never for a good reason, but my memory is of unseasonably strong November sunshine flooding through the tall windows, the nicotine-stained kitchen reeking of stale smoke, my head itching with sweat as my phone hopped about angrily on the

287

table, buzzing like an oversized beetle bruising for a fight.

Matt and his team planted the seeds of my destruction carefully. First, it was reported as rumour, radio reports promising 'that we will learn later today', then the rumour was confirmed through a press conference during which Andrew dropped me in it with very little ceremony — although with no personal acrimony, at least — and finally the story broadcast far and wide. As far as the world was concerned, I was responsible for all the savagery formerly attributed to Andrew. It was nothing short of a miracle that they hadn't also suggested I arrange for the owl to fly into the windscreen in the first place.

Anything resembling the facts of the case had receded so far into the distance that it was impossible even to make out their outline. Facts had been replaced by something far more tempting and palatable. A plausible lie that people would want to swallow.

And swallow it they did, with relish.

I received so much abuse from assorted party loyalists and owl lovers, both electronically and physically, that I had to close various email accounts. I even felt the wrath of the distant Fryernes. A crumpled postcard in a stained envelope arrived from Alan Fryerne-Smith, the strange individual I had encountered at my father's funeral. He accused me in a spindly hand of 'bringing the Fryerne name into disrepute', and threatened to snub the next Fryerne gathering, which of all the many threats

I received that week, was probably the most welcome.

Maldwyn, in typical low-key fashion, declined to exploit the revelations to his own advantage, merely issuing a statement alongside Andrew's that flatlined with non-judgemental disappointment. He didn't ring or email, and I didn't contact him. His non-statement said everything.

After a few days, Caroline and I stopped opening the post and let it pile up by the front door. This shoal of envelopes grew and grew, like a drift of autumn leaves, making it almost impossible to get out of the house.

Leaving the building was further complicated by the group of journalists and photographers now camped on the steps, who even if I went out to buy a pint of milk from the corner shop, flashed light bulbs and shouted questions in my face.

'Did you really kill the owl, Mr. Fryerne? Or are you covering for Landford?'

'Are you going to admit it in court, Charlie?'

'Is Landford paying you?'

In the early days of the story, they tailed me to our local police station, where I endured a day-long interview, going over the same ground so many times that I began to wonder whether the whole incident had been a dream. The Newcastle police were far more organised than their colleagues in Carlisle. Now they produced enlarged photographs of the stretch of road in question, snaps of the long-dead owl next to a tape measure. They also temporarily relieved me of my mobile phone and laptop, which was probably just as well — given the torrent of abuse flooding into them.

Andrew had a sudden change of heart over paying my legal fees, no doubt seeking to put as much legal and professional distance between us as possible. I learned this from Keith Jackson and his sharp-suited colleagues at Wuk via a very terse one-line email. So I faced the police officer's barrage of questioning with an amiable but clueless family solicitor by my side, recommended by a friend of Caroline. His main contribution to proceedings was to repeatedly offer me a fruit pastille and ask if I was feeling all right. Then Mr Barraclough of Barraclough's would sit with me in the breaks and rub a hand over his drooping features, and talk about how new all this Internet stuff was.

I returned to our house under another barrage of flash bulbs, but soon began to wonder if they might be preferable to the punishing silence I endured from Caroline indoors. She had chosen not to return to London, worried that the press hounding there would be even worse.

The only other time I left the house for any considerable amount of time during this purgatory was for a short but decisive meeting at the university, where a self-important panel of managers showered me with platitudes about dutiful service and appreciation before suspending me on full pay with immediate effect.

I took my cue and wrote a letter of regretful resignation to the Vice Chancellor, apologising for any damage I had caused the institution. It was an act of faith, implying that one day, I might not only want my job back but be in a position to take it.

★ ★ ★

In this alternative universe, it was not the strong and decisive leader of the Conservative Party who had mindlessly smashed out the brains of a defenceless owl. It was his 'so-called' communications adviser — which was in fact a title Andrew had invested me with only after the weekend in question, but now hung like a dunce's placard around my neck. My up and down employment record with Andrew only contributed to the impression that I was inflating my own importance. That notwithstanding, the same commentators who decried my level of importance in 'the Landford circle' never once doubted my ability to fatally influence him at a critical moment, when he held the life of a protected species in his hands.

In addition to contending with the plodding but insistent police investigation, and along with the shrill daily attacks from the wildlife lobby, the commentariat and the government, Andrew himself flung several flaming bolts at my head. He sweet-talked his neighbour Tom Gazelee into a tabloid 'Exclusive' in which Gazelee confirmed I had denied all knowledge of the accident at our chance meeting the following day. Apparently 'my silence spoke volumes'. Andrew's more vocal denials at the time were not mentioned. I also happened to notice in the same edition of the paper, buried in the back pages, a piece about the campaign Tom was organising to have a local Roman temple site properly excavated.

★ ★ ★

While this onslaught continued, Caroline finally decamped to London. Our muttered farewell in the hate-mail-strewn hallway was the only meaningful conversation we'd had for days. Despite the pressure, she looked more bright-eyed than she had in months. Perhaps it was the prospect of uninterrupted work in her London studio. Or being without me. Or both.

She gave a sad laugh, shaking her head.

'I've still got faith in you, believe it or not. I've got faith that one day you will finally understand what standing up for the truth actually involves.'

Then she was gone, dragging her bag down the steps to the click-clack chorus of cameras.

That evening I hauled myself into bed, pale-faced and twitchy from too much screen gazing. It was hard to resist when your own invented past and projected future was the subject of the drama. Pressure was mounting fast on the CPS to bring matters to a head. Senior party figures argued that it would be impossible to conduct a fair general election with any kind of cloud hanging over Andrew.

I lay back on my pillow and stared at the ceiling. Outside, the camera crews had packed up for the night and retreated to a nearby pub. Raindrops began to patter gently against the windows, the street lights casting them into a Morse code of dot and dash shadows over the

292

floor. Wind rattled the crumbling sash frame. And then came another sound. Faint at first — it might have been a distant siren, or perhaps a passing drunk — but then the unmistakeable sound of hooting began to echo through the room.

Perhaps I was asleep, or having a waking dream. Perhaps my over-stimulated brain was suffering a hallucination. Either way, the effect was the same. I had grown used to beaks and claws scraping at the windows and the hooting in the night. But this time it was different. In my mind the birds seemed to be calling to me. They cried and screeched until I pulled the covers tight over my head, and somehow drifted off into a restless sleep.

★   ★   ★

The next morning, I awoke with new thoughts that formed slowly and inexorably in my head. The owls knocked, they called, but they never did me any harm, or even much lasting damage to the windows. They were not coming after me or Caroline.

There were other players in the drama who knew the truth after all, who had the most passionate cause to defend it. Perhaps, I thought, the owls were offering their help.

4

How exactly any form of assistance from my winged allies might materialise was less clear. But some form of aid was urgently required and I would take it from any quarter. The fevered media and political speculation was rising to a crescendo.

So it was not entirely a surprise when, a few days later, a sombre-suited Director of Public Prosecutions announced to a bouquet of microphones that after due consideration, there was 'ample and compelling evidence' that I should be tried on the new charge of 'inciting another to commit an offence against the Wildlife and Countryside Act'.

Perhaps I should have felt a sense of relief that the waiting was over. But in truth, I felt nothing. As is the modern way, I discovered the news via the public statement on television. The summons arrived later in the day by courier. I accepted without comment and withdrew into the house. The questions from the press mob on the doorstep no longer alarmed me, or seemed in any way unusual. They had become part of my daily routine, as the owls had made the night time their own.

I did what was required of me. I called Mr Barraclough who murmured his professional sympathies over the phone, and advised me not to book any holidays, before walking me through the court appearance that was to follow, and asking me for information which seemed both irrelevant and unlikely to change anything. I waited in vain for a call from the people who still mattered in my life. Caroline. Andrew. Maldwyn. But none came.

I discovered Andrew's view, of course, quite easily. He told the 'World at One' that 'it was a sad day for British politics and in particular, political advisers'. He also used the opportunity to call for reform to the system which provided advisers and vetted them, a system of which I was not previously aware. Batting away questions about his own culpability, I could almost hear him brandishing a rolled Wildlife and Countryside Act over the radio. The interview was followed by a short report on how this reversal of fortunes was gaining him traction amongst the undecided voters in the country, claiming that 'even those who disliked him on initial acquaintance will have changed their minds following Andrew Landford's superb handling of these ridiculous and unfounded allegations'.

★   ★   ★

Late one evening, as I was scraping the pallid remains of some ready meal into the bin, my phone rang. But it wasn't Caroline. It was Brad.

'Charles, how you holding up?' He was much older now, and thousands of miles away across the Atlantic, but his gravelly, soft voice purred out of the speaker as if we were sitting opposite each other in leather club armchairs, each clutching our scotch and soda. He didn't wait for my reply. 'Terrible business, if you ask me. We're all behind you, Charles, the whole clan. This thing stinks to high heaven. Is there anything I can do?'

'That's very kind of you Brad, but not really — '

'Leave it to me, Charlie. I'll make a few calls. Help out where I can. And look on the bright side — you won't be the first Fryerne this has happened too.'

This was news. 'Really?'

'Ha! I knew you'd never read all of Uncle Roland's book. Well some of us have had more than a couple of transatlantic flights to fill over the years. You should perhaps read up on the first Charles Fryerne.'

My fragmented mind wasn't really up for a history tutorial, but somehow summoned up the founding images of the Fryerne clan. Bosworth Field. Henry Tudor.

'Yes . . . I remember now. There was a story about him helping the king on the battlefield or something. That's how our ancestors got the house and the name in the first place.'

Or at least, that's how I'd understood it. Like all such stories, I couldn't ever say whether I'd believed it or not. Uncle Roland's laboriously produced piece of private genealogy, full of generalised assertions backed up by highly selective interpretations of rolls and church registers, had never convinced on the facts.

'Well, to cut a long story short, I hired

someone over here to look into the whole thing a while back.'

'In God's name, why?'

'No real reason. I guess I was curious. Too much time and too much money, Charles. Story of my life, you could say.'

'Who?'

'I can't remember now. Some old eagle from Harvard got me one of his brightest and best sophomores digging around . . . Anyhow, you'll never guess what they found.'

I trusted that my silence spoke volumes. Brad ploughed on.

'There was a Fryerne at Bosworth Field. He was recognised by the new king with a grant of land after the battle. But he didn't start the day fighting for Henry Tudor. He was with the other guy, the hunchback.'

'Richard III?'

'Exactly. Except he stabbed him in the ribs when he saw which way the wind was blowing. Which is what I'm trying to tell you, Charlie. Loyalty and truth are fine, but they only get you so far in this game. Your old man would have approved of the way you're playing this. Hell, I approve. But you want to win in this game, you need to play dirty. I've got the number of a lawyer for you to call . . .'

Brad continued to talk but my mind was elsewhere, slipping off into the deep Atlantic waters. I had finished with lawyers, of any kind. I was playing what Brad described as a game the only way I knew how, and losing badly. His suggestion was not the answer, but he was right

297

that I could not possibly win on my own. I made my excuses and hung up.

I tried Caroline a couple of times, at her studio and on the mobile, but got no answer. She had disappeared from my life with the same consummate grace and ease with which she had first entered it. Realising that made me miss her even more. I briefly considered an impulsive dash to London, but the thought faded before it had even begun. Perhaps she was working, or like me, festering in a trough of inaction. Wherever she was, I knew she would be waiting for me to find a way to redeem myself and rescue my name. My first court appearance was the following day, and somehow I didn't think redemption was amongst the likely outcomes.

The afternoon shadows behind me lengthened, and I could hear the edgeless noise of a radio from the flat next door. I contemplated calling Andrew once or twice, but thought better of it. He would either ignore me or box clever, and I was in no form to retaliate.

I realised that what I actually felt was an earnest and heartfelt desire *not* to communicate. I had done little else for the last twenty years but investigate, articulate and communicate the views of others. Motivations had been laid bare, ambitions projected, visions encapsulated, arguments distilled. Suddenly, all I really wanted was peace.

The peace and stillness of the owl wood.

I pressed myself flat against the kitchen wall, and peered sideways out of the window, at the press pack camped outside, waiting to capture the moment of my downfall. But their flashlights and satellite dishes faded into a distant blur, and I was in another room — one that felt a world away. I was sitting amongst the polished oak chairs and tables of the Fryerne Arms, squinting through the bay window, across the car park at the row of drab post-war detached houses where Fryerne Court had once stood. My father was searching for his notes and getting to his feet. Caroline was standing, and beckoning me upstairs.

But I ignored them all. I dismissed my mother, reaching out for me. I even left Caroline standing at the bottom of the stairs. Instead, I walked out into the car park, under the sagging carvery banner and the blinking coloured bulbs. I looked across the road at the manicured asphalt drives and the neat pitched roofs where the house had once stood. There was not a trace of it left. Uncle Roland's book had been mostly conjecture. My parents now existed only in my memory. I was the last Fryerne of Fryerne Court.

It meant nothing, and yet I felt more committed to it now than ever before. There was, perhaps, some way to give the role meaning.

I could not rebuild the house, but I could at least do something worthy of the trust the family had placed in me.

I could start by telling the truth.

5

The magistrate's court in Newcastle was a monumental lump of grey and forbidding stone. A north-eastern December morning at its bleakest did nothing to favour the architecture.

I approached the building on foot, having asked the minicab driver to drop me a few streets away, as I wanted to get some air before being plunged into the chilly embrace of the justice system.

Air I certainly got, as I approached my every step was dogged by cameras and recording devices thrust into my face. 'Are you sorry for what you've done, Mr Fryerne?' 'Do you think you've wrecked Andrew Landford's election chances?' 'Do you like being cruel to animals, Charlie?'

I stretched out my hands in front of my eyes, like a man trying to shield himself from a distant explosion, and marched on. A young constable in a high-visibility jacket did his best to intervene, but his presence did little to mollify the press and the general hounding continued unabated.

Yet despite the cacophony, for the first time in weeks, I felt calm inside. I had no faith in trial by media, and only limited faith in trial by magistrate. But I had faith in something else. What exactly, I was struggling to comprehend. I only knew it had something to do with the winged creatures who had been haunting my dreams.

Then a different voice, which sounded out of key with the rest of the pack, said 'Do you regret betraying the family name, Charles?' It could have been my father, or my mother. Or Uncle Roland. Even Brad. I put down my hands and looked up, but there was only the same cameraman in a fleece I had seen everywhere, adjusting his focus, and the reporter who seemed barely out of school, adjusting his tie and asking me questions about animal rights.

★ ★ ★

The sheet taped to the peeling wall announced that my hearing was in just over an hour. Waiting in the vestibule, sitting on cheap furniture I stared at the wall, while Mr Barraclough wobbled his jowls through the depressing state of play. 'Not looking good I'm afraid . . . rather formidable witness statement by Mr Landford . . . highly respected politician, of course . . . his neighbour is none too keen on you and it rather looks like the local constabulary have now taken their MP's side as well . . . the RSPB is sending an expert witness . . . something of an owl crusader, it seems . . . in short, unless you have any rabbits in hats . . .'

I thought for a brief moment of mentioning my quasi-vision of the other night, but one look at Barraclough reminded me that he was not the sort of man who would regard hallucinations favourably. Shaking my head, I took a sip of coffee out of a thin plastic cup. 'What are we looking at, do you think — a fine or some kind of community sentence?'

I had, of course, tried to discuss this with him before over several fruit pastilles. But Mr Barraclough had fudged and fussed, endlessly deferring the matter, and now my optimistic fantasy of helping a team of young offenders to rescue baby owls was swept away by his first straight answer.

'Oh dear, Charles, I thought we'd . . . It's just that you're being charged with incitement, you see . . . Unfortunately that's rather more serious than if Landford had just run the thing over . . . In the eyes of the law — and this area is very much not my expertise, as you know — you inciting him to do it is as serious an offence as organising a dog fight. Then there's perverting the course of justice when you lied to the police. And this is something of a test case . . . '

The litany of punishment about to be brought down upon me rolled on and on.

★ ★ ★

I glanced around the echoing corridors and stairways of the court building for any sign of owls poised to fly to my aid, but there wasn't even a pigeon pecking on a window ledge. The only solution was to pretend that what happened today didn't matter, it was only the first step of many down a deep and winding staircase. There might be appeals. While I sat and contemplated my fate, my phone buzzed in my pocket. I

302

glanced at the screen and saw I had several missed calls from an unidentified caller, and a voicemail from a Cumbria number I suspected might be the local police station. As I tried to check the message, my solicitor put his pink hand on my arm. 'They'll ask you to turn that off, I'm afraid. Not allowed.'

I obliged him, and shortly after, the main group of witnesses filed past us towards a waiting room. Then it was Andrew's turn. As he swept into the court building backlit by the same flashing lights as me, Andrew had never looked more presidential. He was surrounded by an entourage of advisers, including Matt Dilcombe, and wheeled past me towards the waiting room in a blur of pinstripe. I kept my head down, staring at the cooling coffee in my cup. Then, halfway down the corridor, Andrew stopped. Breaking free of his scrum, he came back and stood before me.

'I don't think I should be talking to you,' I said.

'No,' said Andrew. 'But I just wanted to let you know that I'm very grateful. We all are. For everything you've done.'

'Well. We'll see,' I muttered.

'I'm sorry we haven't had much of a chance to chat before now . . . but as you can imagine, it's been non-stop.'

I glanced up at him. Immersed in trying to shape my own impending future, I had almost forgotten about the political image I had once been hired to help manage. Andrew's hair was immaculate, his tie perfectly knotted, his suit pristine, but there was something in his face that alarmed me. He, or someone close to him, had tried to conceal them with makeup, but the scratches were still there. And there were more of them. He was about to return to his pack, but I called out after him.

'May I ask you one thing?'

He shrugged.

'They attacked you, didn't they? You know they will never rest until they get what they want.'

His eyes had never looked more cold. There was only the tiniest twitch at the edge of his mouth that let me know the truth.

'I'm afraid I don't know what you're talking about.'

Then he was gone, disappearing into a side room. Others followed. Helen, who tottered past with barely a frosty nod in my direction, leaving the very faintest scent of brandy in the air behind her. Tom Gazelee, wearing filthy farm boots, treading mud all over the place. The policemen from Cumbria. A wild-haired woman in a cable-knit jumper stomped past, who Barra-clough revealed to me was the expert witness from the RSPB. There was also a motoring expert, whom we had summoned as a defence witness, and then . . . She was the last to arrive.

The doors to the outside world slid open one final time and my heart skipped a beat as Caroline stepped in, removing a large hat and looking around, stamping her wet shoes on the entrance mat. She spoke briefly to the receptionist who pointed her in our direction. I looked over and waved, and her expression was one of such injury that I thought it was unlikely I would see or hear anything that pained me more over the next few hours, whatever was said in the courtroom.

Moments later, she stood before me, her winter coat fringed with drops of bright rain. There were bags under her eyes, and she had lost weight. Catching sight of my expression, she broke into a grimace.

'You aren't exactly an oil painting, yourself, Charlie.'

'I've missed you so much,' I said.

She nodded, eyeing the people drifting across the hallway.

'You're still seeing those damn birds, huh?'

'Andrew is too, but he won't admit it.'

'So what are you going to do in there that will make any of it stop?'

'I'm going to tell the truth.'

The words felt limp in my mouth, as I was no longer quite sure what telling the truth actually meant. Caroline clasped my hands. It wasn't so much a loving gesture as an act of desperation. 'Me too, Charlie. So make sure you do.'

I wanted to talk to her about so much suddenly — about her work, where she'd been staying, even the wretched owls — but she had already released me.

'You understand I can't . . . not till this is over,' she said, looking down at her boots. 'I want to be there for you. I am there for you. But I miss the old Charlie. The guy who said right out what he thought.'

'Yes, well . . . that seems to have got me into this mess in the first place.'

'And it can get you out of it,' she said, then she pecked me on the cheek before disappearing to wait with the other witnesses.

★ ★ ★

The waiting continued. 10 a.m., the allotted time for my appearance, came and went. Officials emerged from the courtroom, some stopping to have whispered conversations with Barraclough that he chose not to share with me. Landford dispatched a couple of earnest-faced young men from his encampment to find out what was going on, but they had no more luck than us. I looked meaningfully at Barraclough, who shrugged. 'I think there's some kind of delay,' he mouthed helpfully, before popping another sweet down his throat.

It didn't matter. I had made up my mind. Or rather, Caroline, the sight of her, the sound of her voice, her scent, had brought me to my senses.

'Mr Barraclough,' I began. 'I've changed my mind. In regards to the plea . . .'

But before I could make my grand declaration, the clerk of the court marched out from his lair, and summoned Barraclough into a huddle with the prosecuting solicitor. Mr Barraclough seemed to inflate majestically to twice his size, like a pinstriped barrage balloon, as he addressed them. Phrases drifted over towards me . . . 'New evidence . . . come to light . . . quite impossible . . .'

Something had happened, but I had no idea what.

Photographers began to hammer on the doors of the courthouse, held back by police, even jumping up and down trying to get a shot.

Barraclough sat down with a contented sigh, loosening his tie in satisfaction. 'Don't count your horses,' he beamed, 'but we might be looking at postponing till next week, to give us a chance to review the new evidence.'

I was about to ask him to explain further when, amid an explosion of protesting voices, Andrew shot out of the door further down the corridor and strode past us, the huddle of his praetorian guard marching alongside him. He didn't give me or Mr Barraclough a second glance, but headed straight for the exit, brushing aside the attempts of court officials and police to stop him.

As he vanished into the scrum outside, I heard a brief cry of 'Are you going to resign, Mr Landford?' Inside the court building, there was only shocked silence as the court staff gaped at one another in astonishment.

'Where does he think he's going?' my solicitor wheezed. 'He's a major witness!'

I didn't care whether it was allowed or not. I fired up my phone and skipped down some concrete steps to the gents, where standing on the seat in a cubicle and holding the device aloft, I managed to find a bar of signal.

The BBC website was tinted in garish blues and purples. But not so much that I couldn't see exactly what was going on. There was the now all

307

too familiar scrum of microphones and cameras outside a building, which I soon recognised as the Cumbria police station where Andrew and I had given our interview. The scrum seemed to be swallowing two people, but eventually they were allowed to pass, their hands raised for protection. And there, blinking in the flashlights, were two people I had not given a moment's thought to since I last saw them.

John and Mary, the housekeepers at Gilcaster Head.

They had — as the rolling banner across the bottom of the screen, the texts and emails now swarming into my mobile all repeatedly informed me — sold their version of the story.

A version that could not be more different to the one Her Majesty's Leader of the Opposition had been preparing to swear to on oath in court.

6

John and Mary's story was told for the first time in painful detail to a tabloid reporter, who had been stalking them for some time. 'John', more properly known as Rai Thurpa, had served with the Gurkhas in Borneo in the early days, but a back injury had forced him into early retirement. On his return to Britain, he was rewarded with a fraction of the pension and benefits extended to other members of the military forces with comparable service. Without any other means to support himself and his wife, he decided to use what he had learned in his time in the camp kitchens and got work 'doing' for some retired military chiefs and their families.

Andrew and Helen had always had occasional staff, even when he was just starting out in Notting Hill. But when Gilcaster Head was acquired, they soon realised they would need someone to manage and maintain the property when they were not in residence. A chance meeting with Andrew's Uncle Gerald at a family birthday party had led to an introduction to 'Mary and John'. The Thurpas and the Landfords had got on well initially but this all changed as soon as they settled into Gilcaster Head. The reasons were now made all too clear in the Thurpas' confessional which was emblazoned on every front page in the land: 'Low pay, verbal harassment, racial abuse and unsatisfactory working conditions.' Their repayment in kind had been to eavesdrop on and record some of the more sensational conversations at Gilcaster Head using their phones. John had stood at the door and listened when Matt Dilcombe had asked us all to reveal any skeletons in our closets. Not only did he have all of that conversation on tape, but he also had Andrew confessing to the owl incident and seeking our counsel after the event. The indiscreet conversation I had had with Caroline while John was driving proved to be just that. Several noisy and drunken rows between the Landfords that I was unaware of were also alluded to, but most damaging of all, they had a recording of Helen yelling at Andrew, 'Why didn't you just take it to the vet like Charles suggested? Why do you never listen to anyone else?' Finally, there was a shaky video of our recent supper, with glimpses of Andrew pacing about with a cigar, promising me that I would be 'thanked'.

Until John and Mary had suggested otherwise, in the public view, Andrew Landford had only committed the sin of being caught up in a minor road traffic accident, the kind many people in Britain had every day. He had also been poorly advised, both at the time and since, by the kind of cynical media professionals who exerted too strong a grip on politics in general. Yet despite these unfortunate attacks on his character and good name, he had stayed strong. He had not ducked the questions in interviews, but faced them head-on. It was agreed that overall the entire saga had only highlighted the value of British wildlife and intensified public support for its protection; an outcome few could grumble at. The perseverance, strength and decisiveness he had shown were deemed to be the fundamental qualities required in a party leader and potential prime minister.

What Andrew hadn't counted on was how the public would react when the mask finally slipped.

Despite the dismay and shock rippling out from the large rock his former domestic servants had just lobbed into this pond of perfection, Andrew seemed oblivious as he once more addressed the press from the steps of Conservative Central Office. His face seemed redder and more inflamed than ever as he looked down the barrel of the lens. It was absurd, but I felt my pulse quicken, as if he were addressing me directly.

'You will be aware of the very serious allegations that have been made today against me and my wife by some former employees. Let me be very clear about one thing. I will contest their claims with every fibre of my being. I will not rest until they are defeated. However, I would like to thank the Thurpas for bringing to my attention the scandalous way in which brave Gurkhas are being treated by our country, and I will make improving their conditions a priority for any future Conservative government. But let us not allow gossip and rumour to divide us. I was recently elected to speak for a party which seeks to represent the whole nation, be you

311

Gurkha or owl. We believe Britain can do better. I believe in our future success. If you want to be part of that success, come and join the Conservative Party. I have no further comment at this time.'

And with that, Andrew pocketed his notes and withdrew behind a glossy front door into the shadows. I wasn't sure if I had misheard the line about Gurkha or owl, but in the event, it was the last thing the listening journalists would pick up on.

It would also be the final time Andrew Landford spoke in public.

That was on a Friday. After that, Andrew declined all further opportunities to put his side of the story to the public. He was like a dog racing off with a bird in its mouth, refusing to listen to a single entreaty to drop the prize. Over the weekend, soundbites began to appear in the press from former loyalists in the party, with statements such as, 'I still have total confidence in Andrew,' which meant more or less that the game was up. In the lobbies and the tea rooms of the House, the leadership struggle seemed anything but settled by the recent contest, and members' allegiances were jumping to Maldwyn faster than iron filings to a magnet.

By Sunday morning, the crescendo of dismay over Andrew's treatment of his staff, and their all too audible proof of his true feelings had quite overwhelmed any lingering resonance his oratory may have had.

By Monday, calls for his immediate resignation were being publicly made, by those in the party and outside. On Monday afternoon, the CPS indicated that it was once again looking to press charges against him, on a number of fronts, from obstructing the course of justice to defrauding the Revenue.

But Andrew didn't resign.

He disappeared.

Calls to his phone went unanswered. He had not been seen at his office, his London flat, or Westminster.

As news of his disappearance spread, speculation began to fan out like wildfire, burning sense and reason in its path. He had gone to America. He had made some kind of defection to Russia. He was at the bottom of the Thames. The police made a brief and inconclusive search of both his homes, to no avail.

Which was when Maldwyn rang me. 'I'm assuming you haven't bumped him off for setting you up,' he began.

'I'm not really in the mood for jokes . . . '

'You rarely are. My finest lines are wasted on you. I need your help all the same. Your favourite owl murderer and mine has vanished off the face of the earth. Not answering his mobile, nor any landlines, nowhere to be seen in Westminster or Westmoreland. Even his worst enemies are worried.'

'I thought you'd be thrilled. He's probably cooling off somewhere. You know how . . . exercised he can get. Can't you take over the reins while he sorts his act out?'

There was an exasperated sigh at the end of the phone. 'That's precisely what I'm worried

313

about. The last thing the party needs is the newly elected leader doing anything rash. I'm champing at the bit to take over but he does need to resign first. We have a mechanism to depose him, of course, but the worry is he'll do something reckless while he's still in office.'

'And what do you expect me to do about it?'

'He has always listened to you, Charles. I know that he must be your least favourite psychopathic former employer in the world right now, but won't you have a shot at bringing him to heel? Besides, as former members of that absurd dining club I would have thought you were sworn to help him by some Masonic oath or other. You've always been able to talk truth to power, that's why we love you so.'

'Go to hell, Maldwyn,' I said in my friendliest voice, and put down the phone.

But I knew what I had to do.

7

This time there was no Andrew to greet me at the station. I had tried several times to ring him from the train, but the house phone had rung and rung until a severe voice informed me that 'The other caller is not picking up'. His mobile voicemail was full, and his office appeared to have no idea where he was.

The last train to Carlisle was nearly deserted, and I spent most of the journey staring out at my reflection in the glass as the darkening countryside sped past. As soon as I stepped on to the platform, the cold air tore at my skin.

I shivered, and hurried out to the taxi rank.

We approached Gilcaster Head, speeding along the narrow road where this had all begun, the trees and peaks on the horizon shrouded in black. The taxi driver seemed to be in a hurry to get home, and I had to reach forward and tap him on the shoulder.

'Could you be careful along this road, please.'

The man grunted, but didn't slow down.

We didn't see any owls. In fact, we didn't see much at all, until the familiar gabled prow of Gilcaster Head rose up through the gloom like a ghost ship. There were no lights on apart from a solitary lamp above the porch. I paid the driver, and was left alone in the yard.

I knocked on the door, but no answer came.

I hammered louder.

'Andrew? It's Charles. We need to talk.'

His Range Rover was parked up behind me, so I knew he had to be nearby, even if the police hadn't had any joy finding him. Moving round the front of the house, I pressed my face against the windows. As I shone my phone through the panes, I was shocked to see what looked like the aftermath of a burglary. Bookcases were upended, their contents strewn over the floor. The expensive Mayfair curtains were half-torn off their poles, hanging in shreds at a lopsided angle. Plates and glasses lay smashed on the floor, and one of the intruders must have torn up some cushions or a pillow, because a light dusting of white feathers had settled over everything, a few still turning in the air.

A noise made me start. I turned around, but there was no one there. 'Hello?' I said again, to the empty house.

Then the noise came once more. It was carried on the wind, over the roofs and eaves of Gilcaster Head. A muffled cry, but whether human or animal, it was hard to tell. Fantasies of intruders having kidnapped Andrew for reasons yet mysterious flooded through my brain. Absurd, of course, but it felt as if the line between reality and fantasy was increasingly difficult to detect. The sound came again, a strangulated cry, from the other side of the house, towards Minniver Wood.

'Hang on, I'm coming!' I shouted.

Struggling to find my way around this unfamiliar part of Gilcaster Head, I tore my trousers on a barbed wire fence.

I kept reminding myself that I was not here to settle a score, or wreak revenge, but to try and get Andrew to see sense. As I stumbled through the rough grass and sheep mess of the field, I spotted a figure, waving his arms in the moonlight.

It was Andrew.

I approached him slowly, the torch beam sliding drunkenly as I navigated the slippery ground. He turned to face me, and I nearly dropped the phone.

How could this be the same man, the person I had first met striding out of the college chapel all those years ago? He was no longer recognisable as the enigmatic star, the College Swan. His hair stood up from his head in various different directions, his cheeks were scratched and inflamed, his beard coarse and unkempt. He was wearing a loose coat that seemed to be quite without warmth, his shirt and trousers in rags underneath.

Andrew stared at me for a moment, stretching out his arms — whether to repel me or beckon me towards him, I couldn't tell. The nails on his hands were long and encrusted with dried blood and grime.

'Charles,' he said hoarsely, shielding his eyes from the torchlight.

'I hope I'm not interrupting anything . . . it's just you hadn't returned any calls . . . People are worried . . . '

'I had to come back. They wouldn't let me sleep, you see.' He cocked his head, studying me. There was something jerky and unnerving about

317

his movements, his natural poise gone. His eyes were rimmed red with either tears or exhaustion.

I extended a hand of my own.

'Come on. You'll freeze to death out here in that get-up. Why don't you come in, I'll pour us both a stiff drink and then you can tell me all about it.'

Andrew shook his head sadly, and backed away. 'You need to see. How can you possibly understand what I've been through, if you don't see for yourself?'

I looked around obediently. In the inky blue of the night sky, Gilcaster Head seemed even more grand. The roofs and gables that yoked the old farm buildings together rose up through the darkness. Andrew snatched my phone and waved it about, casting a bright spotlight on window frames, doors, guttering and brickwork. Everywhere the light shone, I saw scratches and welts gouged out of paintwork and wood, turning them into livid raw wounds.

'And look,' he said, striding off down the field, pointing the light towards the ground. Beneath our feet, the rough pastures behind the house were covered not just with the leaves of years gone by, but with hundreds of white feathers. In some places they lay thick enough to form a kind of pelt that, away from the direct glare of the beam, looked like light snowfall.

Andrew strode through them, kicking up the soft down with his boots, as if such a sight was completely normal.

'They're everywhere. Look at this mess. No bloody escape.'

318

'How many of them are there, do you think?' I asked, staying where I was. My back still felt a glow of warmth from the heated house behind us. Meanwhile, the man who was, until only a few days ago, the bookmaker's favourite to become the next prime minister, disappeared behind a dusty cloud of owl feathers. He shouted something, but I don't think he was talking to me.

He was addressing the owls of Minniver Wood.

Standing there in the bitter cold, my breath freezing in the air, Andrew's shouts fading as he blundered into the thorny undergrowth, I too could think of nothing else. I could hear their cries, and in my mind, they swooped and pecked, their powerful wings beating in a fury.

For a moment, I paused.

This man had used me, smeared me, damaged my marriage and wrecked my career. I could simply walk away, and leave him to his fate, however grotesque that fate might be. Or perhaps I could use the phone in my hand to alert the police. Or the media. Even Andrew would struggle to spin his way out of this one.

Some instinct, perhaps long buried, told me that this was not the time to stick the knife into my old acquaintance, regardless of what he had done to me. I was the last Fryerne of Fryerne Court — a man who was by accident of birth, if not bound to believing in the truth, at least very strongly committed to it. The truth of this situation was that Andrew was in danger.

I hurried after him, my hand over my mouth, in an attempt not to inhale the trail of gritty feather dust he had kicked up. Standing on the edge of the wood, the thickets seemed to be even more wild and impenetrable than they had looked from the house. A strange cry came from within. I pushed my way past the briars.

Andrew stood a little way into the wood, in a sort of clearing, where twigs and yet more plumage lay all around, gleaming in a shaft of moonlight. His fists were clenched and he raised his head up to the sky, as if in some kind of exultation.

But, at first, there were no owls.

Then, as I stepped on a twig just behind him, he whirled round and signalled me to be quiet, a finger to his lips. Slowly, he inclined his head towards the circle of branches that enclosed us. I followed his gaze and found my stare returned by many others. A hundred or more pairs of eyes, blinking, watching us impassively. Wide discs of sulphurous yellow, each with a black and unyielding centre that seemed to follow our every breath. I stood and gazed back, to see if I could detect any message in their golden stares. And to my surprise, I found no malevolence, no animosity — only sorrow. Andrew began to mumble under his breath. At first I thought he was advising me what to do, how best to exit this owl grove we had stumbled into with minimum injury to either side. But gradually I realised that he was in fact making an appeal.

To the birds. That was when I also realised he had quite lost his mind. That he had been losing it for some time, I just hadn't understood it until now.

'Believe it or not,' he said, 'I really do think I can make a difference to this country. The party's in a state, the country's in a state, and you know that as well as I do. I may not have much in the way of Maldwyn's charm, and my contribution to the Wildlife and Countryside Bill Committee may go down in history as . . . unexpected, to say the least.'

I could have sworn that one of the watching owls gave a soft hoot at this. He then began to repeat what he had said to me the night I agreed to take the blame, followed by a condensed version of his leadership acceptance speech.

'I offer leadership, the kind that this country sorely needs. When I want to get something done, I make it happen. And I'm not going to let some wretched birds stop me.'

Now there was a distinct ruffling of feathers from the boughs around us. I didn't for a moment think they understood what Andrew was saying, but there was an unmistakeable sense of territorial transgression in the air, almost as if we had pulled back a veil on a sacred place, crossed a threshold that we should not have.

'Andrew, shall we take this conversation back indoors?'

'No. We need to leave this conversation exactly where it is, if you don't mind.'

'Why, for goodness' sake?'

'Because I need you to see these birds, to feel their power.' Suddenly, he clapped his hands. He might as well have fired both barrels of a shotgun. We ducked, covering our eyes and faces as the owls rose into the air around us with shrieks and wails, scratching and tearing where they could. For what seemed like an eternity they spun around our heads like winged Furies, before finally dissolving into the shadowy depths of the wood. I felt the hot trickle of blood on my left hand. Andrew lowered his guard, looking around.

His expression was not one of fear or relief, but wonder.

'I have never seen power like it. And I was in Russia when the oligarchs took over. Do you see now what I am up against? I see them in my dreams. I hear them scratching at the window. Even in London, I swore I could hear one clawing at the glass the other night. And that was when I realised. I don't understand how, but I realised then that they will never leave me alone. They are a waking nightmare from which I can never escape, unless I take radical action. The kind of action a leader is expected to take.' He turned to me, clasping my wounded hand in a rare show of physical intimacy. 'Help me. We can destroy them together. The party will thank me for it. The country will thank me for it.'

How could we destroy what we didn't understand? I had heard the birds calling to me, sensed their power in the night. I did not fully understand what the source of their power was, only that it was to be respected.

Caroline had seen the owls too. Whether the whole affair was a series of bizarre coincidences, some unexplained natural phenomena, or something more sinister, some long-buried elemental force reawakened, I no longer knew. Through its death, a single owl had created more devastation than it was possible to imagine. Andrew's career. My reputation. My marriage.

I felt a wave of sudden dizziness, and I wondered if I had been infected with something. It seemed unlikely. But then again, almost everything about this situation, standing in the black wood with Andrew, who clasped my hands in supplication while the icy wind nipped at our faces, seemed unlikely.

What I wished for more deeply than anything else in the world was for it all to cease. I wanted to be free of this man and his delusions of power. If I never saw Gilcaster Head again, I wouldn't regret it for a second. I wanted to be back with Caroline, in a house no longer battered by malevolent birds, our lives no longer in thrall to a tawdry tabloid drama played out on the national stage. Above all, I wanted to leave this wood before the owls returned. Maldwyn had sent me here to speak truth to power, but the real power in these woods could not be spoken to.

I tried to back out of the clearing, but Andrew gripped my hands more tightly.

'We can do something,' he said feverishly. 'Come and work for me. Come out of the cold.'

'I'm not the one who needs to get out of the cold, Andrew — ' I began, but he was no longer listening.

'There's too much disorder in the world,' he said, letting go of my hands. 'Too much chaos, too much of this . . . ' He swung his arm round at the haunted wood. 'We can sort it all out, Charles.'

Then he began to babble. Words were coming out of his mouth, but I could no longer make out what they were. He had stopped addressing me, and was talking instead to the trees, the sky, to the moon. Wrapping the remains of his coat around him, he wandered off into the shadows of the forest, mumbling as he went.

I did not follow. Instead I walked away, turning back through the trees towards the old house at the end of the field.

8

Andrew Landford would never see me again after that night. In fact, he never saw anyone.

It was Tom Gazelee who found him. He said he had been taking a walk in the field next door to the wood, although I suspect he might have been nosing around, looking for his ruins. Either way, that was when he heard the cries.

'Keening,' he said later, when I rang him up in an attempt to discover more. 'That's the only word I can use. A keening wail. I've never heard anything like it before or since. Like an animal caught in a trap, or worse. I thought . . . well, you know my views on the Landfords. We've never exactly seen eye to eye on country matters. I wondered if they'd put some totally unnecessary traps in the wood, and caught a fox or a deer.'

I winced. 'But did you see any feathers, any birds, anything at all of that nature?'

'No! I saw nothing like that. I saw a wild bit of woodland, at least, what was left of it after his parents cut it back to the stump of a thing it is today. I saw spruce and alder and hawthorn, holly bushes and drifts of leaves. The noise was getting louder and louder, and it was coming from the middle of the forest. The closer I got, the more it sounded like sobbing. And before you ask, I did see some blood. Flecks here and there on the bark of the trees, some on the ground. Similar to the kind of blood trail an animal in distress would leave, a lot of panicked and disorientated movement within a small space. And then I saw him. He was unrecognisable at first. His clothes were torn to shreds, and there were scratches all over his body . . .'

Tom's straightforward tone began to falter as he described what happened next.

'But I could see . . . it was Andrew. I mean, I recognised his hair, the shape of the body, you know. But I couldn't see his face, it was buried in his hands. What a sight. Fingers covered in blood, everything . . . it was awful. He was all huddled up in the middle of this clearing, shaking . . . making this horrific sound. 'Andrew?' I asked him. 'Is that you?' I had to be sure.

'He didn't reply at first. I had to ask him two or three times, then he just shook his head. I said 'Are you all right, do you want me to call somebody?' You know, because I thought this might just be something he did . . . some weird ritual. He shook his head, violently this time, so I took that as a no. Then the boys came in, sniffing about as they do, so I shooed them away. I put my hand on Andrew's shoulder.

"It's OK, Andrew. It's Tom. I'm here. Everything's going to be all right."

There was a silence at the end of the line.

'That was when he dropped his hands. I never saw anything as horrible in my life. Why would anyone want to do that to somebody?'

* * *

326

No one was ever charged with the blinding of Andrew Landford. After he left hospital, where he would not receive visitors, not even Helen, and he retired from public life. Not just public life, but all life. He pulled one final disappearing trick and vanished. Gilcaster Head was sold in a private sale to a local charity, who announced their intention to convert it into a bird sanctuary, after a substantial donation from an anonymous donor. He never formally resigned as leader of the Conservative Party, but was removed from the post following an extraordinary motion put forward by a group of Maldwyn's backers. Maldwyn duly became acting leader then, following a vote of confidence, leader.

Last spring he was elected Britain's first openly gay prime minister, with a slim parliamentary majority. A reporter for a Sunday newspaper claimed to have tracked Andrew down for comment, supposedly hiding out in a mountain cave in northern Greece. But Matt Dilcombe, now employed as Maldwyn's director of communications, immediately saw to it that a huge increase in military spending was announced the same day the story broke, and the world moved on.

Caroline and I are together again, in our way. It is not perfect, but we have what we have. The winter after these events happened she finally exhibited her owl sculptures. They seemed to have been — and almost certainly were — produced with a visionary intensity. There they stood, high on their plinths, looking down on the viewer. She insisted the gallery spotlight and backlight them in the most dramatic way. Every curve of each beak, every line of the feathering, blazed not just with indignation and contempt for human folly, but with a mysterious otherness that I found hard to believe came from Caroline alone.

The show met with rapturous critical acclaim, of a kind she hadn't enjoyed for years, and several of the pieces sold for large amounts of money. Yet talking by ourselves, I found it hard to get her to talk about them. I knew, of course, that they had been conceived amid the tumult of the Landford scandal, but whether they were meant to be mythical creatures, or moral judges, or something else — she would not be drawn. Not on inspiration, not on meaning.

'You were there. You saw them too. How else was I meant to respond?' was all she said.

Caroline and I don't go back to London much now. She made enough money from her owl show to semi-retire, and we sold the studio. 'Quit while you're ahead, don't you think? We both should have done that a long time ago.' She still works though, selling the odd piece from a converted barn just inland from the coast at Bamburgh. Everything is in what we call her 'Northern style'. There are no more owls or toad princes: these sculptures are abstract, with jagged lines and intersecting planes that are constantly surprising. They carry the shape of the grey waves we see from our clifftop walks, the spikes of the reeds below, the undulating dunes, the scudding clouds. I think they are her finest work, and hardly anyone knows about them.

The last time I can remember either of us being back in the south was for a small family service, when we renewed our vows at St Mary's-Without. Indeed it was so small that, apart from the vicar, we were the only people there. For the first time, Brad was unable to make it over to a Fryerne gathering. He pleaded ill health and sent an overflowing bouquet of flowers, but I suspected that much like us, his heart was no longer in the Fryerne myth. Caroline and I shook hands with the bemused-looking vicar, and standing for a moment on the church path, we saw that the housing estate which had replaced Fryerne Court was itself being demolished. Some hoardings proclaimed the forthcoming arrival of Fernlands, 'two hundred state-of-the-art investment opportunities. Penthouses available.'

Unless one felt inclined to see the allusion in Fernlands, no trace of our name remained. Not five minutes' drive away, the Fryerne Arms had also given way to a gardening centre. We exchanged some polite words with the vicar about the pace of change, got into our car, and didn't stop till we reached Newcastle.

I still have Uncle Roland's book, of course, gathering dust on a shelf somewhere. But neither of us is inclined to dwell much on the recent past.

We now find our comfort elsewhere.

Once or twice a year, if the weather is fine — on one of those crisp winter mornings, when the sky above the moors has the look of very thin air, the peaks on the horizon as sharp as a beak — we drive out towards Gilcaster Head. We try to arrive early, to avoid other visitors, rubber-neckers or tourists, and we always leave before the light starts to fade. It's never a journey on which many words are exchanged, and we coast along the narrow roads, ever vigilant for any creature that might stray into our path.

Gilcaster Head itself is encased with scaffold-ing, shrouded in tarpaulin, as it is slowly being turned into a Visitor Centre for the bird sanctuary. We park in the drive, exactly as we did when we were guests. Entrance to the sanctuary, through the wilds of the Landfords' former garden, is free — although we leave something in the honesty box each time.

We take the path that winds over the bumpy field to Minniver Wood, which is already full of young trees in plastic sheaths, as the replanting of the reserve begins. If we get there early enough, we are normally the only ones there. A path has been hacked through the thicker parts of the wood, and laid with wood chips. Bordering the trail, laminated signs at knee height invite children to guess the age of a tree or identify the species by the leaf. Shrubs and bushes are labelled, as are several kinds of moss. There are also pictures of birds nailed to trunks — woodpeckers, hooded crows, terns and owls. There is rarely any sight of the birds themselves, although the nature trail marked along the path makes suggestions about the best time of year and day to see them.

We don't stick to the path. Once we are deep

inside the wood, we step off the chippings and push aside prickly swathes of holly and gorse until we reach a small clearing, quite hidden from view. When we first came here, there were still discarded police gloves and scraps of incident tape stuck to the leaves, but all that is gone now. There is no trace of the horror that happened here.

We walk through the glade, to a wall I never noticed when I came here in the dark. A wall is not a fully accurate description; it is more the remains of a wall. Large slabs of weathered, yellowing stone, well over six feet high, trailing away to nothing on either side. This is what Tom Gazelee was campaigning about. Now the ruins have been found, he's chosen to leave them alone.

A wise decision.

For if you pull apart the strands of moss and bracken that cover the central slab, there is the faintest trace of carving, covering the entire section. It might be Roman, although no one knows how long the wall has been there. Following the shallow indentations with your finger, it is still just possible to make out the portrait of a goddess. She sits with a shield and a spear, as sharp as the claws of the owl perched on her shoulder. Some say she is Minerva, the Roman goddess of wisdom, and that Minniver Wood was a local corruption of her name. Others say that is pure speculation.

But whatever the time of year, whether there is frost hard on the ground, or there are bluebells spread out in the sun around us, when you place your hand on the stone, it is warm. The stone is still warm.

We do hope that you have enjoyed reading
this large print book.

Did you know that all of our titles
are available for purchase?

We publish a wide range of high quality
large print books including:
Romances, Mysteries, Classics
General Fiction
Non Fiction and Westerns

Special interest titles available in
large print are:
The Little Oxford Dictionary
Music Book
Song Book
Hymn Book
Service Book

Also available from us courtesy of
Oxford University Press:
Young Readers' Dictionary
(large print edition)
Young Readers' Thesaurus
(large print edition)

For further information or a free
brochure, please contact us at:
Ulverscroft Large Print Books Ltd.,
The Green, Bradgate Road, Anstey,
Leicester, LE7 7FU, England.
Tel: (00 44) 0116 236 4325
Fax: (00 44) 0116 234 0205

WHAT SHE NEVER TOLD ME

Kate McQuaile

Louise Redmond left Ireland for London before she was twenty. Now, two decades later, her heart already breaking from a failing marriage, she is summoned home. Her mother Marjorie is on her deathbed, and it is Louise's last chance to learn the whereabouts of the father she never knew. Stubborn to the end, however, Marjorie refuses to fill in the pieces of her daughter's fragmented past. Then Louise unexpectedly finds a lead: a man called David Prescott — but is he really the father she's been trying to find? And who is the mysterious little girl who appears so often in her dreams? As each new discovery leads to another question, Louise begins to suspect that the memories she most treasures could be a delicate web of lies . . .

PARADISE LODGE

Nina Stibbe

It's 1977, and fifteen-year-old Lizzie Vogel is working in an old people's home. The place is in chaos, and it's not really a suitable job for a schoolgirl — she'd only gone for the job because it seemed too exhausting to commit to being a full-time girlfriend or a punk. She's also distracted by her family's financial troubles, keeping up with schoolwork, and deciding which brand of shampoo to use. When a rival old people's home opens, offering better parking and daily 'chairobics', business at Paradise Lodge takes a turn for the worse, and everyone must chip in to save the home before it's too late — from the crazed Matron, to the assertively shy nurse who only communicates via little grunts, to the very attractive son of the Chinese takeaway manager . . .